Beyond Peleliu

About this book...

On the eve of the Second World war, two unlikely people get married: Tom McQuade, a relentlessly driven medical student, and Virginia Russell, an exotic mind-reading magician.

The McQuades move to Boston where Tom enters a prestigious surgical residency and they celebrate the birth of their son David.

The war destroys the McQuades' idyllic life together. Tom is drafted and shipped off to the South Pacific where, during the horrific Battle of Peleliu, he sustains a gunshot wound that destroys his medical ambitions and eventually drives Virginia and David from him.

Forty years later, when David is a powerful San Francisco trial lawyer and Tom is in the early stages of dementia, father and son reconnect. For the first time, David learns the liberating force and redemptive power of truth

Beyond Peleliu

Peter D. Baird

Ravenhawk™

Books

Beyond Peleliu

PETER D. BAIRD

Ravenhawk™ Books

Beyond Peleliu

Copyright © 2008 by "Peter D. Baird"

Book Design by Hans B. Shepherd, Jr.

Library of Congress Cataloguing-in-Publication Data
Baird, Peter D. -
Beyond Peleliu / Baird, Peter D.- 1st ed. p.cm.

"A Ravenhawk™ Book"

ISBN 1-893660-14-1

I. Title

2007   LCCN

Printed in the United States of America

FOR SUSANNE

Acknowledgments

Books are rarely written without help and *Beyond Peleliu* is no exception. My wife Susanne, my agent Andy Whelchel, and my late partner John Frank always believed in this story even when I didn't. Ted Reid, M.D., Carolyn Pettit, M.D., Rob Tyson, M.D., Bruce Stadwiser, M.D., Curtis Dickman, M.D., and Ron Glick, D.O., protected my characters from quackery and me from stupidity. And, without the extraordinary support of my partners, associates, and staff at the Lewis & Roca law firm, I could not have written this book.

"...as for murderers, fornicators, magicians, idolaters and all liars, their lot shall be in the lake that burns with fire and brimstone ...."

Revelations 21:8

PROLOGUE

September 6, 1996

James Douglas McQuade
Hulings Boat Yard
Box 47 Point Arena, CA 95468-0047

Julie Elizabeth McQuade
c/o Mrs. Beth McQuade
1470 Page Mill Road
Palo Alto, CA 94304-1124

Dear Jim and Julie,

Thank you for your letters and concerns but please don't worry about me. It turns out that prison isn't all that bad for a lawyer when his clients are inmates, guards and the Warden himself. Here, I'm the "Bighouse Counsel" and my perks include "Trusty" status, an office, a computer, a law library and a comfortable cell.

Best of all, I've had time to do some research into our family history and, specifically, into the World War II Battle of Peleliu that your grandfather fought. As the enclosed manuscript suggests, I've also done a great deal of writing.

You are not the only ones who have asked why I would risk losing my liberty and my license by taking a life that was, for all practical purposes, over. Even harder for everyone to understand is how I could possibly find peace in a place like this.

As with so many of life's questions, there are no answers, only stories. Partly remembered, partly reconstructed, this is mine.

Love,

Your father

David McQuade
Number 754639-T
Utah State Prison
Draper, Utah 84020

CHAPTER ONE

HOMESTEAD, PENNSYLVANIA
JULY, 1917

*I*n a cramped tenement built decades earlier by the Carnegie Steel Company for its workers and their families, LaRoux McQuade sat at a small kitchen table next to her ten-year-old son who was holding a live frog. The mill's five o'clock whistle had sounded and an industrial night of heavy soot, thick smoke and early darkness had fallen. Beneath an unshaded light bulb, mother and son considered the wax-bottomed tray, scissors, miniature forceps, needles, straight pins, and glass of milk that lay before them.

"Are you ready, Tommy?" LaRoux asked in a quiet brogue. She was tall, thin-faced, gentle in both features and bearing and wore, as she always did no matter the occasion or season, a plain ankle-length skirt, white blouse with puffy sleeves and hair done up in a soft Gibson Girl cushion.

"Oh, yes," he said, as the frog squirmed in his hands.

She reached over and stroked the top of the frog's head. "Okay then, but we must first pith Mr. Frog."

"What does 'pith' mean, Momma?"

She smiled because none of her high school biology students knew what "pith" meant either. "Well Tommy, it's a procedure that

1

will kill Mr. Frog as quickly and humanely as possible so he doesn't feel any pain during our dissection." She went on, "If we didn't do that, we would be cutting open a live animal and that would be called a 'vivisection' and would be cruel."

"But momma, you said that you were going to show me a live heart and, if we kill Mr. Frog, won't his heart die also?"

"I did say that," she said, still smiling because that too baffled her students. "It's a wee complicated but frogs' hearts keep on beating for a time even after they're dead and even after their hearts have been cut — " Suddenly, she winced and lurched forward and, after some deep breathing, she reached for the milk, took a sip and then another.

For months, LaRoux had coped with stomach ulcers by wearing her "Scottish smile" that concealed clenched teeth. Lately though, her stoicism was no match for the wrenching cramps and debilitating aches that the doctors said warranted surgery before the ulcers started to bleed dangerously. As soon as the McQuades could afford it, she would have the surgery, but it would be in Pittsburgh by a specialist rather than in Homestead by the company doctor whose ineptitude was as well-known as his alcoholism.

As Tommy always did when he saw his mother suffer, he recoiled in fear, as much for himself as for her. After her pain seemed to have subsided, he melded his concern about his mother with his curiosity about the frog into a single question and cautiously asked, "If you and Poppa die, will your hearts keep on beating?"

Avoiding the mortality issue, she took another sip of milk. "Oh my no. Poppa and you and I are mammals and our hearts need a constant flow of warm oxygenated blood to keep on beating. Frogs are amphibians and their hearts are different."

"So, how are we going to pith Mr. Frog?" Tommy asked.

"We'll use that needle," she said, pointing. "But first, we must pray that Mr. Frog won't feel any pain and that he'll go to Frog Heaven and that we'll be forgiven for taking his life."

They bowed their heads and LaRoux prayed in a thicker brogue that Tommy heard on Sundays in their Presbyterian Church, "Heavenly Father, please protect Mr. Frog from pain, accept his soul into Your Kingdom and forgive us for taking his life which we do only in the name of science. Amen."

"Amen," Tommy murmured.

LaRoux took the frog in her left hand and, with her right, stuck the needle into its spine and swiftly ran it up and down what she called "his vertebral canal." The frog went limp.

"Mr. Frog is now with God, Tommy," LaRoux said quietly as her son stared at the lifeless amphibian. After more milk, she turned the deceased frog over on its back, pinned its legs to the wax-bottomed tray and, with the scissors, cut the frog's underside open from crotch to head, exposing its entrails.

Tommy was bug-eyed.

"Do you see the pale, bean-shaped structure in the lower belly?"

Tommy nodded.

"Those are his testes and that means he was a boy frog and we were correct in addressing him as 'Mr. Frog.'" As Tommy stared at the frog, she asked, "You know what testes are, don't you?"

He thought he did but shook his head anyway.

Having anticipated his reticence, she explained, in her best biology teacher's voice, that "Mr. Frog's testes make sperm that he puts into Mrs. Frog when they mate and the sperm fertilizes her eggs so that they can then hatch into baby tadpoles." She paused and said, "In boys, 'testes' are called 'testicles'. I believe you call them 'balls.'"

Tommy turned crimson. He wasn't about to talk about "balls" with his mother.

Amused by his embarrassment, she went on. "See the round, worm-like tube that curves around the testes?"

"Uh huh."

"Those are his intestines that you would call 'guts?'"

"I guess."

"Why don't you find where Mr. Frog's heart is?"

He pointed to an area in the upper left chest that was throbbing. Yet he wasn't sure because it was nested among some red lobes and didn't look like a heart to him.

"Those red lobes are Mr. Frog's lungs and liver and a little lower is his gall bladder." Sensing his uncertainty, she said, "You can't actually see the heart itself until we've done a wee more surgery."

With that, she picked up the scissors and proceeded to slowly cut away what she told him was "the pericardial sac." Then, using the forceps, she lifted the severed, beating heart out of the frog's chest and into full view.

Tommy gasped.

"Open your right hand, Tommy." As he did, she gently placed the pulsating organ in his open palm. Then she sat back and, fighting another round of pain, beamed at her son and his happy fascination.

He was transfixed by what his eyes were seeing and what his palm was feeling. Indeed, his own heart was beating faster than the frog's.

LaRoux whispered, "I think I hear poppa in the bedroom. He must have just come back from the mill. Do you want to show him what you have?" She had heard her husband's heavy breathing that rattled and rasped on inhalation and wheezed and gurgled on exhalation.

Without taking his eyes off the heart, Tommy nodded.

LaRoux quietly stepped out of the kitchen and, moments later, returned with Thomas Douglas McQuade, Sr., who had just gotten off work as Furnace Foreman at The Homestead Steel Works. He was broad-shouldered, but stooped; wide-framed but thin; and his work shirt, overalls and boots were caked with coal dust and sparkly metal particles. His face was black with soot and he looked like a minstrel peering out through the two white circles where his goggles had been.

"Tommy, me laddie, whatya got there?" his father said in a dense highland brogue.

"Poppa, it's a frog's heart and, look, it's still beating, all by itself!"

Tom and LaRoux exchanged grins and Tom asked, "Where'd it come from?"

"I caught the frog at the Monongahela River this morning and momma pithed him and then she cut his heart right out of him."

Tom coughed up some phlegm and then joked, "Nice that

mom finally taught you how to pith." They all laughed at his play on words.

"You like this cutting out hearts kind of thing?"

"Oh, yes, poppa."

"You want to grow up to be a biology teacher like your momma?"

Tommy thought long and hard about his father's question and then turned his face down toward the floor and was silent.

"Tommy," LaRoux asked, "what's wrong?"

Still staring at the floor, Tommy shook his head and started to sob.

LaRoux knelt beside him and said, "Tell us Tommy."

Crying, he said, "I don't wanna be a teacher, I wanna . . . wanna. . . . be a doctor."

"And why would that be Tommy?," his father asked.

Choking back tears, he said, "So I could make you and momma well."

Eleven days later, LaRoux's ulcers started to bleed badly and she was rushed to the company infirmary for emergency surgery where she died on the operating table. In his autopsy report, the coroner said the surgery was technically successful but, as the company doctor was closing her up, there had been an "inadvertent overdose of chloroform anesthetic that took the patient's life." Presumably intending to exonerate the company doctor, the coroner said, "It is very difficult to maintain the proper level of chloroform during a long surgery" and then added, "everything that could have been done was done."

Seven months later, Tom McQuade's silicosis, contracted from years of inhaling coal dust and steel particles, became so acute that he couldn't work and a week later the Homestead Steel Works terminated him as well as his at-will lease on the company-owned tenement. After losing wife, job, income and home and having to fight for every gulp of air, Tom McQuade fell into a paralyzing melancholia that put him in the Pennsylvania Asylum For The Incurably Insane where he was lobotomized and numbly vegetated until he died in The Great Influenza Pandemic of 1918.

Tommy McQuade grew up as a ward of the county and was

left with nothing more than a fierce determination to be a doctor, a surgeon, a heart surgeon, no matter what. During the next two decades, there would be many "no matter whats" to overcome, including orphanages, foster homes, The Depression, Pittsburgh University at night, digging trenches and pushing wheelbarrows for the WPA, applying for scholarships and waiting, waiting, waiting, always waiting to be a doctor.

Eventually, nineteen years after Mr. Frog's dissection, the Carnegie Foundation awarded him a scholarship to The Syracuse University College of Medicine, in Syracuse, New York. He suspected that the scholarship was the result of belated corporate guilt about his father and workers like him but, nevertheless, Tom was finally on his way to becoming a doctor, a surgeon, a heart surgeon, no matter what.

Chapter Two

CROUSE IRVING HOSPITAL
SYRACUSE, NEW YORK
APRIL, 1940

*F*rom the outside, Crouse Irving Hospital didn't look like a hospital. When it was built in 1913, the doctor founders were so worried about its financial success that they had it designed to look like a hotel, just in case. However, inside the patterned brick, Greek portico and Roman pilaster exterior, Crouse Irving was all hospital, complete with antiseptic aroma, wall-to-wall whiteness, public address pages and the bustle of staffers in white and visitors in mufti.

Inside was also where fourth-year medical student Thomas Douglas McQuade, Jr., had spent his last two years of medical school, rotating through one clinical clerkship after another. The decades spent waiting had left him bald and near-sighted and the years spent digging ditches and pushing loads of wet cement had left him looking like a heavy-weight boxer, easily able to take the hospital stairs, three steps at a time, on his way to the Department of Surgery. He hadn't been this excited since the operation on Mr. Frog.

Tonight, in his last weeks of a surgical clerkship, Tom would finally operate on a living human being. All he had done so far was stand in the operating room, watch, hold retractors, watch, cut sutures, watch and get dumped on by the lords of surgery with their masks, gowns, gloves and distempers. Indeed, their badgerings and bad-mouthings had confirmed the old joke that the only difference between a medical student and fecal material is that nobody goes out of their way to step on fecal material. But tonight it would be his turn to cut, clamp, stitch and tie and, making the occasion even better, his supervisor would be Dr. Wayne Landry, the finest surgeon in the hospital and one of the few nice guys on a faculty steeped in arrogance and impatience.

Earlier in the day, Dr. Landry had called Tom to the emergency room where a 47-year-old male had come in complaining of pain in the belly. After the examination, Dr. Landry diagnosed appendicitis and, with an avuncular smile, told Tom, "Get ready. He's your patient tonight. I've got to supervise another student appendectomy at 6:00 p.m. so let's do yours at 7:30."

Tom returned the smile and, with his heart racing, said, "Don't worry, Dr. Landry, I'll be ready."

"I know you will," the senior surgeon said, patting Tom's back.

For the next four hours, Tom read, re-read and re-re-read the section in *The Atlas of Operative Technique* on appendectomies that he had memorized long ago. Whenever his nervous fidgeting got the best of him and he couldn't concentrate on the dog-eared pages any longer, he would pick up a spool of catgut and, while pacing the halls and ignoring quizzical stares, tie surgical knots on anything with the rough circumference of a human intestine.

When Tom burst into the Department of Surgery at 7:00 p.m. from the stairwell, Dr. Landry was not there. According to a scrub nurse, Dr. Landry had encountered problems while supervising the other student appendectomy. However, Dr. Landry's instructions were that Tom's patient should be anesthetized and everyone should be scrubbed and ready to go and he would be there as soon as possible. For the next ten, fifteen, and then twenty-five minutes, Tom, the nurses and the anesthesiologist made small talk in the operating room shadows while the patient's exposed midsection glowed an alabaster white.

Finally, at 8:15, the supervising surgeon arrived but it wasn't Dr. Landry; instead, it was Brewster F. Napfield, III. Because of his last name, diminutive stature and toxic personality, students called him "Dr. Napoleon" or "Dr. Nap" for short. Making his entrance in a voice much too loud for an operating room, Dr. Napfield announced that "Dr. Landry's operation should have finished a long time ago but the student pulled the stump stitch too tight, broke the stump open and contaminated the peritoneal cavity." Dr. Napfield chuckled, "It's always sepsis season around here when the kids get knives."

Tom scowled beneath his mask. He wasn't a "kid" and, in fact, he was older than Napfield. Not only that, he had seen Napfield operate before and considered him a mediocre surgeon.

"Ready?" Napfield asked in a military tone. After a muttered chorus of "uh huhs," Napfield said, "Let's see if the soon-to-be class valedictorian is as good with his hands as he is with the books." Napfield's expectation was obvious: Tom may be at the top of his class in academics but, like almost all medical students, he would jelly with nerves and bungle the operation.

"Give him a scalpel," Napfield snapped. Tom took the shiny instrument in one hand and, with rubber-gloved fingers on his other hand, drew an imaginary line across the patient's abdomen. Before cutting, Tom shot Napfield a daggered glance of class-based contempt. Napfield was Boston, society, Princeton, leisure and wealth. Tom was McKeesport, foster homes, Pitt night school, trenches and wheelbarrows.

Unfazed by the dirty look, Napfield addressed Tom for the first time with an order, "As you open him up, tell me the names of each layer of tissue you are cutting in the abdominal wall."

"O.K.," Tom mumbled and then swiftly and evenly ran the blade into and along his imaginary line without the usual beginner's jerks, jogs, stabs or hesitations. While cutting, Tom rattled off "skin . . . fat . . . fascia . . . muscle" and, finally, "peritoneum," the smooth, glistening inner lining of the abdomen.

Surprised by Tom's deft technique, Napfield held the upper

hand with a technical question. "Skin, doctor? Around here we use words like, 'epidermis and dermis.'" Before Tom could respond, Napfield said, "Start clamping." As fast as the nurse could hand him hemostats, Tom applied them to the severed vessels and, again, Napfield was impressed but still expected a blunder.

"Not bad, now let's see you tie." No matter how long and how diligent students practice tying, they almost always do something wrong in their first, real-life attempt. Fingers get greasy with fat; ligatures don't get knotted; ties slip off; and sometimes glove tips get sutured into the patient's wound. Yet, with the speed and dexterity of a black jack dealer, Tom tied off each vessel.

Napfield was taken aback but rather than issuing a compliment, asked another technical question. "You know what portion of the bowel the appendix is attached to, Dr. McQuade?"

"Yeah," Tom said, "it's the cecum."

"That's right. So go get it and pull up the appendix." Napfield recalled his own first time trying to locate the damned cecum: he couldn't see it; he had reached into the slick intestinal folds where everything felt like everything else; the first thing he pulled up was a section of the small intestine; the next thing he came out with was the sigmoid colon; and, finally, he gave up and sheepishly asked the supervising resident for help.

Tom nodded and stuck two rubber-gloved fingers through a crease between layered sections of the intestinal hose. In fewer than five seconds, he pulled up the cecum with a hot appendix flopping from it. Agape beneath his mask, Napfield dropped his Dr. Nap persona and watched in deflated silence for the rest of the operation as Tom proceeded to tie off the appendix at its base, cut it off above the tie, invert the stump, hold it in with a purse-string stitch and then close up the wound with smooth dispatch.

Afterwards in the locker room, Napfield smacked off his gloves, pulled down his mask, and said, "You've got good hands, Dr. Tom McQuade. You'll be a great surgeon someday."

"Thanks."

"By the way, as class valedictorian, what have you decided to do about The Colonic?"

"I haven't decided anything."

Napfield laughed. "Well, you'd better get moving because graduation is just around the corner and we're all waiting to see how you're going to humiliate the shrinks."

Chapter Three

MADAME FORTUNO

*A*t 8:30 the following morning, Tom McQuade dragged himself through the door to his postage-stamp sized apartment. He was too tired from surgery to stay awake but too jangled by coffee to sleep. The place smelled of mildew and kitchen grease and every surface was covered with unwashed dishes, empty cans, medical books, butt-filled ashtrays or dirty clothes. His first thought, as it always had been when he confronted the chaos of his own bachelorhood, was to do something about the stink and the mess but he was well-practiced at deferring action until there was more time, more sleep or more of anything else that happened to come to mind.

His next thought was prompted by the question from Napfield last night and it was one he could no longer put off: What was he going to do about The Colonic? As valedictorian of the medical school class of 1940, tradition required that Tom arrange for the intermission entertainment, called "The Colonic," at the upcoming graduation dinner dance. So far, he had done nothing.

The Colonic was the graduating seniors' opportunity to even the score with a faculty who believed that overloading and browbeating turned sweaty-palmed memorizers into caring physicians and who had, over the past four years, managed to drive one student to suicide, five others into nervous breakdowns and another twenty-seven to drop out altogether. In 1938, for example, the valedictorian had hired a fire-eater to spit flames at members of the ear, nose and throat department. In 1939, circus clowns freakishly costumed as doctors, dragged each surgery professor up on the stage and, using oversized butcher knives and speaking in a venomous operating room argot, "removed" saws, screwdrivers, and even a toilet plunger from the draped surgeons.

The show was called "The Colonic" because chiropractors prescribed "colonic irrigations" and, at Syracuse Medical School, chiropractors were considered charlatans and quacks. Since the medical faculty also believed that colonic irrigations were worthless and sometimes dangerous, their cruelest rebuke was to announce, in class or clinic, that "a colonic would be better" than what the floundering student had just suggested.

This year, it was the Department of Psychiatry's rotational turn for "a colonic" and Tom wanted to do as much satirical damage to them as possible. Because of the lobotomy that had turned his father into a vegetable and himself into an orphan, he bitterly denounced the psychiatrists when he discovered that, in the Syracuse Medical School Department of Psychiatry, lobotomies had not yet gone the way of leeches. Vowing never to let himself or any patient become a vegetable, he expounded publicly to anyone who would listen and many who wouldn't how superior real vegetables were to the human variety because "carrots and turnips don't drool, don't stare at the floor and don't pee in their pants."

Trying to get his mind off The Colonic, Tom switched on the lone floor lamp, flopped down on the disheveled hide-a-bed and picked up *The Syracuse Herald-American* in search of spring training baseball scores. He glanced at the front page about the war in Europe and then, thumbing his way to the sports section, caught a headline out of the corner of his eye in the society section that read, "Madame Fortuno Reads Minds of Spring Ball Goers." It seemed there was a mind reader in town and, from her photograph, she was an attractive gypsy who gave "extra-sensory perception" shows. Apparently, she told well-dressed members of Syracuse society what their futures would be, what they were thinking and what the names were of their childhood pets.

Tom sat up, grabbed a coffee-stained telephone directory, riffled through the Yellow Pages, and called each talent agent listed alphabetically until he spoke to a gravely-voiced old timer named Simon Wizanski. According to the agent, he represented Madame Fortuno and, besides that, knew her well because she was a good friend of his daughter. Madame Fortuno gave a great ESP show the agent said; however, he was concerned that she might "overdo the satirical damage" and, therefore, Tom might be happier with "Priscilla the Pretzel," a sexy contortionist who could teach the physicians a thing or two about anatomy.

Since this year's Colonic targeted minds not bodies, Tom insisted on Madame Fortuno and was pleased that she might "overdo the satirical damage." With Tom's mind made up, Wizanski explained that Tom would have to call Madame Fortuno directly because she screened all jobs that involved, as The Colonic surely would, special arrangements.

Lighting up a Lucky Strike, Tom called the number Wizanski had given him. "Good morning, Syracuse Girls' Club," a cheerful female voice said.

"Is this Central 4577?"

"Yes it is."

"Well, this may sound nuts, but I'm trying to reach someone . . . I think she's a gypsy or something . . . named Madame Fortuno."

"Oh," the receptionist laughed, "you want our director, Virginia Russell. She's Madame Fortuno. I'll connect you."

After several rings, Tom McQuade heard a female voice say, "This is Virginia Russell speaking."

"Uh . . . I'm . . . calling for . . . uh . . . a . . . Madame Fortuno."

"This is she," Virginia said in low-octave tone that Tom thought sounded sultry.

Despite having just heard the words "Syracuse Girl's Club" followed by the unaccented voice of an educated woman, Tom nevertheless imagined the person he was talking to as a bejeweled, dark-skinned foreigner who was, at that moment, hunched over a crystal ball in a heavily draped parlor filled with lighted candles, Tarot cards and luminous-eyed cats. He was accurate in only one respect: Virginia had light brown skin.

With the telephone to her ear, Virginia sat at her desk in a spacious, well-lighted office with a sweeping view of the Syracuse University campus. Books, photographs and diplomas lined the walls and uneven stacks of paper rose up from her desk. In her early thirties like Tom, Virginia wore a smart, hounds-tooth business suit that couldn't conceal a shapely figure. Her horn-rimmed reading glasses meant business and her black pearl eyes radiated intensity.

On weekends, however, Virginia Russell did resemble the image in Tom's mind. Come Friday and Saturday nights, she rouged up, donned a Gypsy costume, put her hair up in a white bandanna, slipped on heavy gold jewelry and packed two large, leather satchels with a 'nail writer,' an 'add-a-number' pad, a 'force book,' a double-flapped slate, a windowed envelope, a 'billet knife,' heavy crayons, one ping pong ball, a 12" by 18" pad, flash paper, igniters, wires, smoke pots, three small manila envelopes and a specially stacked deck of cards. Once "loaded," Madame Fortuno raised money for the Girls' Club by performing mental magic and spiritual sorcery championed by Sir Arthur Conan Doyle, debunked by Harry Houdini, studied by Dr. J. B. Rhine at Duke University and broadcast to millions each week on CBS Radio by the basso-voiced magician, Joseph Dunninger.

"This is Doctor McQuade calling," Tom said, fudging because he had not yet received his degree.

Virginia Russell looked up at the Seth Thomas wall clock and said, in a business-like but intriguing voice, "Doctor, I'm sorry but I'm in a hurry. Saturdays are very busy around here and I'm due at a budget committee meeting in five minutes. I assume you're calling about Elaine D'Angelo, the little Italian girl who broke her arm on our playground yesterday?"

"Well, no," he admitted. "Actually, I wanted to book your Madame Fortuno act and I just talked to Mr. Wizanski who told me to call you and I wondered if you'd be willing to use your 'mental powers' to lampoon the psychiatry department at the medical school graduation dinner dance on June 4. I read about you in the *Herald-*

American and I'd like you to 'read' the shrinks' minds and tell everybody what utter fools they are."

Virginia ended the conversation in a hurry. "I'll do the show if the medical school will pay the fee Simon negotiates with you and also donate $20 to the Girls' Club but it'll be my script, not yours. I don't use magic to lampoon or demean anybody, not even doctors. Never have. Never will. If those conditions are acceptable, confirm it with Simon. Thank you but I really must go."

Tom McQuade heard a click and then a dial tone. In seconds, he was back on the line with Wizanski, pumping the agent for information about Virginia Russell, aka "Madame Fortuno." Happy to get the booking but hesitant to talk about Madame Fortuno's background, the agent clammed up and tried to get off the line with three "I gotta goes" and two "I'm lates," but Tom wouldn't let him.

In an emphatic voice that implied consequences, Tom laid it on the line. "Hey, bub, there's not going to be a booking for Fortuno or a commission for you unless I get some information."

Wizanski thought for a moment and, yielding, said, "O.K. but there are a couple of things you'd be better off not knowing."

"Like what?"

"Like she's part colored for one thing," the agent blurted. Then he quickly added, "but she can pass and nobody can really tell but if this bothers you then —"

"It doesn't," Tom said. He had only one prejudice and that was an automatic hostility against comfortably born, silver-spooners like Napfield. Growing up poor and alone, Tom had a better understanding than most Caucasians about what life was like for Negroes and, until the juvenile officials decided they were "colored," Tom's favorite foster parents "passed" during the day but lived as Negroes nights and on weekends. Tom then asked, "You said, 'for one thing,' is there 'another thing?'"

"Well, there is and it's the reason I was worried that she might 'overdo the damage' at your show."

"That would be great if she did but she said she wouldn't so what is it I'd be better off not knowing?""Well . . . she's a Christian Scientist and isn't very keen on doctors."

Tom thought that was pretty funny. "Tell you what: if she

keels over on stage, we'll ignore her, call the undertaker, and go on drinking."

The agent laughed too and was relieved that he had gotten the touchy subjects of race and religion off his chest. With nothing else left that could jeopardize his commission, Wizanski rattled on at length about Virginia Russell. She was raised in a small town in north central Illinois; her father was a prominent lawyer; and her only sibling was a much older sister in Boston. In the early 1800's, the Russell family ancestors had been Abolitionists and had taken in a runaway slave named Molly Sykes whose mystical powers to reveal the past, predict the future and heal the sick were still legendary in that part of Illinois. Lost to history or hidden by discretion was the identity of the father of Molly's son whom she delivered at the Russell house and who became a member of the family, too.

The agent suspected, but didn't know, whether the Molly Sykes stories influenced succeeding generations of Russells to embrace the teachings of Mary Baker Eddy or whether the stories enhanced Virginia's interest in magic. All he knew for sure was that, in 1918 when she was ten, Virginia saw Harry Houdini perform at the Majestic Theatre in Chicago and saw him escape from "The Devil's Death Chamber." After that, she was hooked and, refusing to be a "lovely assistant," she became a ham-handed magician herself, doing the now-you-see-it-now-you-don't type of tricks for anyone who was interested and many more who weren't.

Wizanski knew when, but not how, Virginia had become an accomplished mental magician. What he knew was that, after getting her master's degree in social work from Northwestern University, her first job was in the "colored" cell block at Illinois' Dwight Prison For Women and that's where, somehow, she had learned the arcana of mental magic and the misdirections of illusion.

What the agent didn't know was that, at the prison, Virginia met Wanda "The Wizardess" Freeman, a dark, nimble-fingered bunko artist and generously curved prostitute from Jamaica. She was the daughter of a British gambler father and a mulatto cabaret singer mother. Early on, Wanda realized that her father's secrets, her mother's skills and her own body were the tickets to money, adventure and escape. Employing these talents in the casinos and first class cabins of the steamships that plied the waters of the Atlantic and Caribbean, Wanda eventually became the well-cared-for mistress of a wealthy Chicago industrialist. When he died years later and left Wanda nothing, she joined a succession of midwest carnivals and performed whatever tricks were necessary, both carnal and magical.

In prison for fraud, Wanda was intrigued by Virginia's color and, after learning about Molly Sykes, set out to teach this straight-laced young social worker "real magic." Over the course of a year, Wanda schooled her bug-eyed pupil in "center tears" and "billet switches" ("dumb bastard'll never guess you got his birthday or sweetie's name straight from him"); "nail writers" ("when the mark tells you how much he weighs, just write it down secretly with your thumb, like so, then open the window envelope and he'll think you guessed his weight by looking at his fat ass"); "cold reading" ("tell 'em stuff that would fit almost anybody, like they're too hard on themselves or they worry a lot about money"); "forces" ("you can get anybody to take any card or to think of certain things if you do it right"); "smoke pots" ("You can vanish an elephant with them"); and "flash fires" ("they'll illuminate anything"). As a determined teacher, Wanda didn't just show and tell, she drilled and critiqued her student until, the night before Virginia left for Syracuse, she appeared as "Madame Fortuno" and gave a full length show for the entire prison population, confirming earlier predictions, revealing unspoken secrets, setting off dense curtains of smoke and igniting brilliant cones of fire. She was a hit.

The next morning, Virginia and Wanda hugged and wept their respective goodbyes to each other. Dabbing her eyes with one hand, Wanda handed Virginia a farewell gift with the other. "Here's a book I've used for a long time, Ginny. It's got instructions, diagrams, moves, wirings, patter, descriptions, and everything you'll ever need to do your magic and make money for you or for anything or anybody." Before Virginia could thank her, Wanda shook her head and said, "There's one thing I am sorry about and that is I never answered your questions about men; but, if I had and if the warden had heard that a hooker had corrupted an innocent do-gooder like you, he would have thrown my black ass in the hole for a month."

"That's alright, Wanda," Virginia said with a chuckle. "I really am ignorant of . . . well . . . ."

It's O.K. to say 'sex' Ginny girl."

Virginia blushed and mumbled, "sex."

"One more time."

"Sex," Virginia said it loud and clear.

"Much better."

"The problem is that nobody ever talked to me about 'sex' and, if I get married, I'm not sure what I'll do."

"You'll do fine, honey," Wanda said. "Just remember two rules about men." Slipping into a Jamaican patois, she said, "Don't give 'em lovin' if they don't give you somethin'." And, "Cut 'em off if they piss you off."

Tom McQuade booked Madame Fortuno for Saturday night, June 8, 1940 at The Hotel Onondaga but he didn't know why he had done it. She believed in Christian Science and the audience would be doctors. She was part Negro and there wasn't a single person of color on the faculty or in the student body. She was a woman, there wasn't a female on the faculty and there were only two woman students in the entire medical school. She wouldn't use his script. She refused to embarrass anybody. She would deprive The Colonic of its retaliatory purpose. Yet, he booked her.

Maybe it was because of her alluring picture in the newspaper or her sultry voice on the telephone. Maybe she was just another challenge, like the foster homes, the streets of Pittsburgh, the wheelbarrows of cement, night school, organic chemistry and anatomy. Whatever the reason, he wanted to find out what it was.

Chapter Four

THE COLONIC

*I*n the early evening of June 8, 1940, newly degreed physicians, medical school professors and university administrators escorted their women onto the chandeliered expanse of the main ballroom of the Hotel Onondaga. The Hotel occupied an entire city block in downtown Syracuse and, though it had fewer rooms, "The On" was an imitative contemporary of New York City's Waldorf Astoria Hotel. Like the Waldorf, it ran to art deco excess with chevrons, bronzes, marbles, matched woods and long, straight, silver lines.

On a bandstand festooned with crepe paper, balloons and a banner reading "Congratulations Doctors," the sixteen-piece "Twilight Serenaders" played current favorites, like Glenn Miller's "Moonlight Serenade" for slow-dancing and Count Basie's "One O'Clock Jump" for jitterbugging. Overhead, in the center of the sprawling dance floor, a mirrored ball slowly rotated, throwing off hundreds of lighted dots onto the ceiling, walls, tables and milling dancers.

Just past 9:30, Tom McQuade mounted the stage, dismissed

the band and bade everyone to be seated. He was older, balder, taller and heavier than his classmates. His 240 pounds were wood-hard from physical labor and they fit tightly to his big-boned, six-foot two-inch frame. Yet, on stage that night, it was hard to think of this man as formidable. For the occasion, he had stuffed himself into a second-hand tuxedo that was two sizes too small and was held together by chains of partially-visible safety pins added after the seams had been cut open to accommodate his bulk. Making him look even less imposing were his wire-rimmed glasses that reflected the ballroom spotlights and looked like the highbeams on a small truck.

In his upraised right hand, Tom held a giant enema bulb he had purchased from a veterinary supply store. With his left hand, he pulled the microphone against his lips and, into an already over-amplified sound system, shouted, "For this year's Colonic, we've selected an entertainer who will prove to you that, when it comes to knowledge of the human mind, Professors Thompson, Glick and Rosenberg are barely in kindergarten." As he started to say something else he considered funny, an electronic screech rattled the ballroom and Tom jerked his head back as if the microphone had punched him in the nose.

Flustered, he abandoned the rest of his planned remarks and, from a safer distance, went straight to the introduction: "Please put your hands together and welcome our Colonic entertainer for graduation 1940. . . The amazing . . . the incredible . . . MADAME FORTUNO THE REVELATIONIST!"

The ballroom turned pitch black. After several seconds, a spotlight flashed on and illuminated a darkly attractive woman. She bore more than a faint resemblance to Lena Horne and stood behind the microphone wearing a white bandanna, a flowered blouse and a billowing black and orange skirt and angled her arms, hands and fingers toward the ceiling. Suddenly, fireballs blazed into the air from her fingers and puffs of smoke blew skyward from a row of pots in front of the stage.

All eyes were on this woman who seemed to make eye contact with everyone in the room at the same time. Her soft, purring voice over the sound system rose and fell with the fluid undulations of her jeweled hands. Madame Fortuno pointed to Dr. Landry's wife and said, "your name is Sylvia; you grew up in Duluth, Minnesota; your maiden name was Underwood; and, when you were a little girl, you had a white cat named Snowball." After a stunned pause, the woman nodded.

Next, Madame Fortuno tossed a ping pong ball out into the crowd and instructed the man who caught it to think of a "two digit number between one and fifty" and "visualize one geometric design inside another." After a pause, she asked if he "had thought of the number 35" and if he had "visualized a triangle inside a circle?" He shouted "yes" and the audience gasped.

Then she did a "cold reading" of six randomly chosen members of the audience and told the men about scars on their knees, women about too many loose shoes in their closets, and all of them about their anxieties over money. Then, she picked out a table and, as if she were Sherlock Holmes, told each guest their aversions, weaknesses and medical specialties.

For her finale, Virginia displayed that day's *Herald-American* with its grim headline that, in the lengthy journalistic style of the times, read: "200 Planes Drop 1,100 Bombs on Paris, Kill 45; Swift Reprisals Forecast in Allied Capitals; Nazis Prepare Army for New Drive in France." After that, she called up on stage the President of Syracuse University, Dr. Robert R. Hornaday, a dour academic who brought with him a sealed envelope he had received from Madame Fortuno two weeks earlier. Under her prodding, he read off the postmark and swore that the envelope had been in his exclusive custody at all times and it had not been opened or tampered with.

In an air of nervous solemnity, Dr. Hornaday held the envelope as Madame Fortuno slit it open with a wide-bladed, jeweled-handle knife. Dr. Hornaday slowly removed a letter from the envelope and, in a voice that quavered when he reached the second paragraph, read Madame Fortuno's message to the stilled audience.

Dear Dr. Hornaday:
I understand you will be attending the annual medical school dinner dance on June 8, 1940. Consequently, I am sending

this to you with the accompanying instructions not to open this letter, but to notice the postmark and note the date you receive it and to bring it with you, fully sealed, to the graduation gala at The Hotel Onondaga.

I am writing this letter on June 3, 1940 and will mail it tomorrow. Keeping that in mind, let me now predict that the headlines of the Syracuse Herald-American for June 8, 1940. They will be disquieting and will read as follows: "200 Planes Drop 1,100 Bombs on Paris, Kill 45; Swift Reprisals Forecast in Allied Capitals; Nazis Prepare Army for New Drive in France."

Mystically yours,

/s/ Madame Fortuno

When the slack-jawed University President finished reading Madame Fortuno's prediction, the audience momentarily gaped in silence and then exploded with bravos, spoons against glasses, foot stamping and, eventually, a standing ovation. Beaming and bowing, Madame Fortuno blew kisses to the crowd with both hands and, during another round of smoke, fire and darkness, disappeared from stage.

Immediately, the Twilight Serenaders broke into "I'll Never Smile Again" but nobody danced. Instead, they buzzed among themselves how she "did it." "My cat's name *was* Snowball." "Are you really from Duluth?" "I'll be damned — there is a scar on my right knee." "My closet is filled with shoes I never wear." *The Herald* is such a rag they must've tipped her off." "Do I look like a urologist?" "Were you thinking of the number 35, too?" "What about the triangle inside a circle?" Meanwhile, at the psychiatrists' table, there were smiles of relief that they had not been "Coloniced."

Fifteen minutes later, Tom McQuade spotted Virginia Russell as she crossed The Hotel Onondaga's tapestried lobby carrying her satchels. Over chairs, sofas, potted plants and sleepy guests, he shouted, "Hey, Fortuno, wait up!" Sprinting, he caught up with her at the main entrance beneath a mural of sleek-lined Indian princesses and stammered, "You were . . . well . . . I don't know . . . just . . .fabulous!"

"Thank you, doctor." Then needling him for the way he had introduced himself on the telephone when first they spoke, she said, "I guess since you graduated today, you can truthfully call yourself a doctor now." She pushed her way through the hotel's heavy revolving door and walked out into the cool air of an early June night.

"Fortuno . . . Madame . . . Virginia." As if deaf, she said nothing, turned and started walking toward the streetcar stop some 50 yards away at the nearest intersection. "Join me for a beer? A cup of coffee? Reveal my past? My future?"

Late-night socializers, a passing policeman and a down-and-outer stared at the sight of a Gypsy being trailed by a big man in a shabby tux. Smiling and visibly pleased with herself, Virginia continued to walk and peer down Erie Boulevard for distant sparks or the headlight of an approaching streetcar.

"Well, how's about it?" No answer. "Hey, I got you this job. It's only right that you make a few predictions about my future with you."

"You already have a date. I saw you dance with her before the show."

"Oh, Gloria?" He went on to explain how he had only taken her out on those few occasions when he wasn't studying or working and had extra money. Then he asked, "What about you? Do you have a fellow?"

"You're a nosey doctor."

"I just told you about Gloria. Fair's fair."

She sighed. "There's a man I grew up with across the street in Illinois. Name's Jeff." They reached the streetcar stop and Virginia stopped beneath a sodium vapor street lamp that soaked the corner in a deep yellow light. She squinted at the streetcar schedule on the lamp pole and then at her watch.

"What's he to you?"

"A lot of things."

"What's that mean?"

They waved off a taxi in search of a fare as she relented with a few facts. "He graduated from Annapolis. He's in the Navy. A

24

lieutenant commander and an electrical engineer. He teaches at The Great Lakes Naval Training Station north of Chicago. That's about 100 miles from where he and I grew up. Town called Ottawa."

"Fortuno, your hearing's bad. I asked, 'what's he to you?'"

"Your manners are as bad as my hearing, doctor." She kept watch for the streetcar and went on. "If you must know, we were brother-and-sister for a long time and later became boyfriend-and-girlfriend. Now we're engaged to be married next year when he'll be out of the Navy and I've finished my contract with the girls' club."

Tom frowned at the word "engaged" and switched subjects. "Look, Fortuno, if you really are a revelationist, tell me about my past and future before a streetcar gets here."

She smiled.

"Please? Pretty please?" He begged in mock supplication and he dropped one knee to the sidewalk and, in a loud rip, split open the pants seat of his tuxedo. Then, in the thickest, most charming Scottish brogue he could muster, Tom said, "M'lady, th Heather won't grow without thy voice."

"O.K.," she said in a tone that implied "you asked for it." Then, using information from a friend of a friend who had once dated Tom McQuade's freshman year roommate, Virginia looked straight at him and let loose: "Your mother's name was LaRoux. She was from Scotland. She died in 1917 from an overdose of chloroform administered by an idiot doctor during stomach surgery. After that, your father, who was also Scottish, contracted silicosis from inhaling steel dust at the Homestead Steel Works near Pittsburgh where he worked. He was bitter, destitute, unemployed and unable to take care of you. He fell into a deep melancholy, and, eventually, was locked away in a state insane asylum where another idiot doctor gave him a lobotomy, turned him into a vegetable and left you hating psychiatrists and dreading becoming a vegetable yourself someday. After your father's silicosis, you lived in foster homes and fought for everything you ever got, working construction during the day and going to school at night. All you cared about was becoming a heart surgeon and you eventually got to medical school on a scholarship from the Carnegie Foundation which probably had the guilts about what the Carnegie Steel Company had done to workers like your father."

"Holy Cow, how'd you do that?"

Three blocks away a streetcar turned onto Erie Boulevard and, with its lone headlight flickering, rumbled toward them. "I did it very well," she said, using a stock magician's retort and rummaging in her purse for a token.

"Well, if I ask nicely, will you see me tomorrow night?"

"No, I don't think so, Doctor McQuade." She pulled out a token and snapped her purse shut. "I've already told you that I'm engaged and it doesn't take a mind-reader to know that you and I are opposites in every respect. Besides, I only partially trust doctors."

"Yeah? Your agent mentioned something about that," Tom said, trying to keep the conversation going. "Do you really believe that crap?"

"It isn't 'crap,' doctor," she snapped. "Mary Baker Eddy makes a lot of sense in a lot of ways."

"Mary Baker Eddy? The lady who started the Christian Science Church?

"Yes."

Tom tried to sound respectful and asked a question Virginia had heard many times before. "How does she make sense?"

"She understood the relationship between mind and body. She took seriously what the Bible said about God's healing power. And she taught that men and women were equal, inside and outside the church."

He ignored the gender and Biblical issues and went straight to the medical. "You mean, if you get an appendicitis or a broken arm, you would rather pray and read the Bible than go to a hospital?"

"I didn't say that," she said, waiting for the nearly empty streetcar to come to a stop. "If I ever needed surgery or a bone set, I'll probably see a physician. But, there's a healing power that comes from God's love and the patient's mind and I'll always seek out that power. Christian Science principles saved my mother who almost died from lupus."

"I suppose that your friend, this Jeff guy, is a Christian

Scientist?"

"Yes," she said crisply. "He's a Certified Christian Science Practitioner. He helps heal naval personnel who belong to the Church." Streetcar number 35, marked "Syracuse U. Campus," stopped and flapped open its doors.

"I'll leave you with a prediction, Dr. McQuade," Madame Fortuno hoisted up her satchels, stepped aboard the streetcar and dropped in the token, letting it tinkle into the coin box. While the accordion doors were still open, she turned and looked down at Tom on the sidewalk below and said, "I predict that you and I will never see each oth——." The doors slammed shut in her mid-sentence and, with an electronic groan, the streetcar rolled away in a shower of orange, crackling sparks. That was one of the few predictions Virginia ever made that turned out to be wrong.

Confounded by her magic, enchanted by her beauty and challenged by her religion, Tom McQuade walked back to the Hotel Onondaga, oblivious to the toasts he should have given as valedictorian or to the furious date whom he had left unattended. "Virginia Russell *is* magic," he said to himself. "She may be nuts, but she *is* magic."

In the four-week lull between graduation and the start of his internship at Crouse-Irving Hospital in Syracuse, Tom spent days wheelbarrowing wet cement and nights pursuing Virginia wherever she happened to be — board meetings, fund raisers, girls' swim meets, dance recitals, magic shows. Once, he even attended services at the Second Church of Christ, Scientist, cowering in the back pew and later pretending that he had found it to have been "interesting."

On July 26, 1940, Virginia sent a "Dearest Jeff" letter to her naval commander fiancé. With girl-across-the-street-I'll-always-love-you anguish, she said how sorry she was that she hadn't written or called and how awful she felt about that and how she felt even worse about what she was going to say and hoped, somehow and someway, that he would forgive her.

Two days earlier, in the Hendricks Chapel on the Syracuse Campus, Virginia Edith Russell married an overpowering doctor whom she had met only weeks earlier and who never took "no" for an answer from anybody about anything, not from her and not even from himself. At the couple's request, the pastor spoke about "opposites attracting each other" and how "hot and cold," "alpha and omega," and "yin and yang" were "inseparable" and how "one always needs the other."

At the reception in the Syracuse Girls Club cafeteria, the toast that provoked the greatest reaction came from Dr. Landry, who raised his glass and said, "Let's drink to Tom and Virginia and wish them every happiness and hope that, over the course of a long marriage, they'll eventually figure out which one is cold, alpha, and yin and which one is hot, omega, and yang." Everyone laughed, especially Tom and Virginia.

Chapter Five

*T*om loved Boston. That's where Massachusetts General Hospital was; that's where his surgical residency was; and that's where his promised fellowship in cardiac surgery was going to be. Tom's only problem with Mass General was its "Ether Dome."

Built in 1821, Mass General's most striking architectural feature is the majestic portico surmounted by the graceful "Ether Dome," so named because beneath its convex curvature is the surgical suite where ether was first used successfully in a major surgery and where Dr. Oliver Wendell Holmes, Sr. coined the terms "anaesthetic" and "anaesthesia." Although most of the time it was nothing more than a building to Tom, there were moments when the Ether Dome sent his thoughts back to his mother, LaRoux, and how she had died from a chloroform anesthetic and how she might have lived with an ether anesthetic and how she would have read to him, cooked for him, tucked him in, kissed him and taken care of him and how she would have nursed and saved Tom Sr. from the lobotomy so he could have taken his son to Pittsburgh Pirate baseball games and told him more stories about hunting stags on Ben Nevis as a boy.

Virginia also loved Boston because the Mother Church of Christ, Scientist was there, set back from Huntington Avenue by a spacious plaza of stone and sculpture. Besides that, her sister Tess lived in Boston where she was an assistant editor of *The Christian Science Monitor* and she represented another opposite in Virginia's life. Unlike Virginia who was darker, freer, shaplier and 13 years younger, Tess had fair skin, a stocky build, short-cropped blonde hair and was as humorless as she was judgmental.

For both Tom and Virginia, the best thing about Boston was that, on July 16, 1941, David Douglas McQuade was born there. Laughing about their different expectations for their son, Virginia wanted him to be a lawyer like her father and a magician like herself while Tom wanted him to be a physician like himself and a baseball player like Ted Williams who, that summer, was batting .406 for the Red Sox. Tess didn't laugh about her expectation and knew that David would be a Christian Science Practitioner because he was born on Mary Baker Eddy's birthday.

Except for the minor flap in Syracuse on Erie Boulevard after The Colonic, Tom and Virginia had never quarreled about their medical-religious differences. There had never been any reason for such a talk until Thanksgiving Day, 1941 when the plan was for Tom to finish up at the hospital by five p.m. and join Virginia, Tess and the baby for a traditional turkey dinner at six that evening.

At Mass General that afternoon, things were slow and Tom busied himself updating patient records, smoking and having arguments in his head with Tess whom he had told his wife was "the patron saint of know-it-alls." At 3:30 p.m., Tom got a call from a colleague who was tied up with a polio case getting desperate. Would Tom do the admission workup on a new coronary case that had just been wheeled up from the emergency room? The patient was stable and had already been seen by his own physician.

Pleased to leave the blank charts and imaginary arguments with his sister-in-law behind, Tom briskly made his way to room 474, where he met a well-fed, full-bodied 58-year-old Irish insurance salesman named Sean Flynn who, after drinking and eating his way through a five-course Thanksgiving feast, had experienced what he described as the "worst case of indigestion in the State of

Massachusetts." It turned out, as the electrocardiogram in the emergency room showed, that he had suffered an infarction and there was damage to a small area on the heart wall.

Even in the hospital following a heart attack, Flynn was the effervescent insurance salesman. Beaming at the sight of an up and coming young physician, he propped himself up against two pillows and, with twinkling-eyed Irish charm, asked about Tom's family and what provisions Tom had made for them in case he had an infarction of his own. Although initially put off by the talk of whole life policies and cash value build-ups, Tom quickly warmed to this sociable patient and soon they were talking Red Sox baseball, Jack Benny, Roosevelt, the War in Europe and, with Tom barely aware of it, back to whole life policies and cash value build-ups.

Time passed and, suddenly, Tom saw it was five-thirty. There were charts yet to finish. The subway was on a holiday schedule. He wouldn't get home until seven, maybe seven-thirty. If he knew his implacable sister-in-law, a missed Thanksgiving dinner would generate more ammunition for her war against the medical profession in general and him in particular.

Quickly, Tom stood up and reached out to give the patient a good-bye handshake. Just as Flynn leaned forward, his head, neck, arms and upper body slammed backwards into the pillows. As if jolted by a powerful electric shock, his eyes bulged out of their sockets like a cartoon character; his face and neck turned a swollen purple; and he fell sideways on the bed with a long, gurgling breath.

Tom yelled "Mr. Flynn," and felt the man's pulseless carotid artery. While shouting at the hallway for help, he grabbed the muslin-wrapped thoracotomy kit that, in those days, was standard issue for any hospital room with a coronary patient. He tore it open and pulled out a scalpel. Then, hesitating momentarily to gather his wits and remember how to do something he had seen but had never done, Tom cut the man's pajama top down the middle and quickly located the left nipple. With his fingers, he counted down to the fifth rib and then swiftly ran the scalpel just below it on a line from the breastbone toward the backbone. If Tom needed confirmation of death by cardiac arrest, he had it when only a dark ooze leaked out of the blood vessels he had just severed. After another long cut

31

through the bloodless muscle, Tom slipped a retractor between the man's ribs and, turning the ratchet, spread the ribs far enough apart for his hands to get inside the chest cavity.

Grasping Flynn's heart in his hands, Tom could feel it wiggle and flutter in the death throes of ventricular fibrillation. With both hands, he gently squeezed it while breathing out and then released it while breathing in. Oblivious to the passage of time or to the nurses and doctors who had gathered around the bed, Tom went on breathing, squeezing and releasing for five, ten, fifteen, twenty minutes until, eventually, gentle arms and soothing voices guided him away from the lifeless body and into the nearest chair. Defeated, Tom buried his face in palms sticky with blood and pericardial membrane.

At six o'clock, Tess and Virginia ate warmed-over turkey and put David down for the night. By seven, the dishes were done, the refrigerator was loaded with leftovers and, for the next two hours, Virginia fretted about her husband while Tess criticized doctors and raved about their old neighbor, Jeff Fry, whom Virginia had jilted.

Finally, at 9:45, a shaken Tom McQuade slowly walked through the front door. "I'm sorry I'm late." His voice was weak.

Virginia embraced him with a kiss. "Don't worry about the time, honey, I'll get you a drink and warm up some dinner." Heading for the kitchen, she said over her shoulder, "I hope everything's all right."

"You're not just late. You're almost four hours late," Tess said from the living room with an edge in her voice.

"I'm aware of the time, Tess," Tom responded with an edge of his own. He hung up his overcoat and took a bourbon and soda from Virginia. Cautiously, he sat down across from his sister-in-law whose Radcliffe education always seemed to give her license to talk down to him and whose favorite pastime was steering conversations to subjects he knew nothing about. Last week, it was Etruscan art.

"So, what's the excuse this time?" Tess asked.

"Tess," Virginia called from the kitchen, "why don't you let Tom unlax and enjoy his drink? Besides, it's late. Now that he's here you can toodle-loo on home."

32

"My 'excuse,' if you want to call it that," Tom said, "was a 58-year-old man I lost to cardiac arrest. I did a thoracotomy but couldn't bring him back."

Virginia overheard her husband and cried, "Oh, Tom, I'm so sorry."

"I'm sorry, too," Tess added. "I'm sorry for the man who died."

Tom took a long swallow of bourbon. "For once, I agree with you."

"So, what's a thoracotomy?"

"There are various kinds and they all involve getting inside the chest cavity to repair a wound or recharge the heart. With this poor guy, I reached in and massaged his heart and tried to get an electric charge going."

"You did that?"

"Yes, I did that. I did everything possible for the man."

"I'm sure you did everything medically possible but did you pray for him?"

"Did I do what?" Tom was incredulous.

"I asked . . . did you pray for him? You said you 'did everything possible' and I want to know if you asked God to help save this man's life?"

Virginia rushed out from the kitchen. "That's enough, Tess! We live and let live around here."

"Oh," she mocked, "Did Tom 'let live' today?"

Tom jumped to his feet and shouted, "Let me tell you something, you superstitious-know-it-all bitch! Nobody in the whole goddamn world feels worse than I do about this man's death! I did everything, absolutely everything, to keep that man alive." Virginia stepped between her standing husband and her seated sister as Tom added in a trembling voice, "I looked around for God but He wasn't there to do the thoracotomy!"

With her jaw locked and eyes fixed, Tess slowly stood up and, in a steely voice, spoke to Tom through Virginia between them, "You weren't *looking* for God, doctor, you were *playing* God. And, *if* you were looking for God at the hospital, *then* you were looking for Him in the *wrong place!*" With that, she detoured stiffly around

Virginia and Tom, put on her coat, and left without a good-bye.

Virginia wrapped her arms around Tom and hugged him tightly. "Tess behaved poorly tonight and I apologize for her. She's spent too much time at war, fighting for women's rights, battling men in the newspaper business and defending her faith against a skeptical world. She didn't mean that you did the wrong thing. She only wondered whether, well, maybe, there had been time for a little prayer?"

"Prayer?" Tom barked into his wife's face from close range.

"Just try for once, Tom, to understand us, please," she said, standing her ground

"Understand? What the hell does prayer have to do with a thoracotomy? Would you tell me that before I try to 'understand' your goddamned mumbo jumbo?"

"Goddamned . . . mumbo . . .jumbo," she repeated his words slowly with long silences in between each one. Then she spitfired straight at him, "It's *not* mumbo jumbo and I wish you would respect me as much as I respect you!"

"Well, I'll tell you something, Mary Baker McQuade. If you really respected me, then you'd keep your dyke sister and her wacko religion the hell away from me and my son." Virginia's face froze and her eyes narrowed.

In successive weeks, each spouse retaliated in his and her own way and in his and her own time. During the first week after Thanksgiving, Tom slept on the sofa, left for the hospital before Virginia woke up and got home after she was asleep. Virginia's turn for a pay-back came a week later when Tom had returned to their bed and expected sex in the mistaken belief that he had made his point and that Virginia had learned her lesson. Practicing Wanda's Rules, Virginia pretended to be as unwakable as a hibernating bear or, if forced into copulation, as stiff as a frozen zombie.

Chapter Six

WAR

*A*fter two weeks of reciprocated spite, Tom and Virginia abruptly forgot about their Thanksgiving clash because, on December 7, 1941, The Empire of Japan bombed Pearl Harbor. America attacked meant America at war and, like the rest of the country, the McQuades were caught up in the indignation, fervor and patriotism of the day that President Roosevelt told the nation "will live in infamy." That night, the McQuades shared cocktails, dinner and the dishes, and, after jointly putting David to bed, made love to the limits of their sexual nerve and knowledge. The next morning, they were joking about "Dr. Yin" and "The Rev. Mrs. Yang," and speculated about what lay ahead. They didn't have to wait long to find out.

In January, 1942, Tom was drafted into the Army Medical Corps as a Captain and was assigned to the 81st "Fighting Wildcat" Division. Leaving Boston was easier than he had thought because Mass General had promised him a fellowship in heart surgery after the war and, as an added bonus, Tess Russell would be left behind in Boston. Leaving wasn't as hard as Virginia thought either because she and David could live with Tom at any stateside base and, admittedly, Tess had been hard on their marriage.

Traveling on sooty trains and dusty buses and living in toiletless quonset huts and cramped apartments, Virginia and baby David followed Tom and the 81st from one base to another as the Army kept changing its institutional mind about what the 81st should be trained to do, which depended on where the 81st would fight. When North Africa was raging in 1942, the 81st was stationed at Camp Horn in the middle of the Arizona desert between Phoenix and the California border. There, the McQuades coped with the relentless heat as well as with the local assumption that, with her dark hair and tan skin, Virginia must be a Mexican domestic.

When the war moved to Europe, the 81st was shipped to Camp Rucker, Alabama, which someone in the War Department, who had never have been to Europe, thought resembled the French countryside. There, Virginia was tolerated as the "Captain's Nigra" on the base and as a segregated "colored" or a denigrated "nigger" off the base. Yet, on the positive side, Alabama was where the McQuades met the skinny, bespectacled Sydney E. Silverman, M.D., a Johns Hopkins Professor of Medicine who was busted from captain to first lieutenant for having ordered a driver off a segregated Army bus and for having driven it back to the base, lurching and stalling, with Virginia in the front row and who, in addition to filing one appeal after another about his demotion, became the McQuades' closest army friend.

Eventually, when the battles in the Pacific started to be fought on land and not just in the air or on water, three troop trains hauled the 81st across country to Camp San Luis Obispo, California which was one of the jumping off points for the Pacific Theater and was located near Morro Bay, a small fishing village with the rugged cliffs of the Big Sur to the north and the gentle beaches of Southern California to the south. After withstanding Arizona heat and Alabama hostility, Tom and Virginia luxuriated in the cool breezes from the sea, the relaxed acceptance by the locals and the cozy warmth of their white stuccoed bungalow that overlooked the harbor and its massive guardian, Morro Rock.

Except when Tom was on maneuvers or was tied up at the hospital, he was home every night to watch David wallow in his father's size 13 combat boots and to wear his dad's army cap that fit like a pup tent over David's head. To Tom's delight, David loved playing doctor and listening through a stethoscope to the heartbeats of every child, dog, cat and good-natured adult in the neighborhood. To Virginia's delight, David also loved playing magician and his favorite effect was "the disappearing boy trick," which meant he "disappeared" when he closed his eyes and then "re-appeared" when he opened them and which, for reasons that stumped him, worked with his parents and Dr. Silverman but never with neighborhood kids or uninitiated adults.

On the bright, gusty morning of December 1, 1943, Virginia was washing the breakfast dishes and, out the kitchen window, spotted a large naval vessel getting pushed into the harbor by a tugboat. There were so many fishing boats always coming and going that she almost didn't pay any attention. This ship was too large to be a trawler and it needed a tug; yet, it was too lightly armed to be one of the warships that sometimes called on Morro Bay. No, this ship must be . . . a . . . troopship! That realization iced every sensory nerve in her body and, unaware, she let a coffee cup slip from her hands and fall to the floor, sending shards in every direction.

Her next thought was, "I haven't heard from Wanda yet." Untying her apron and brushing back her hair at the same time, she left the unnoticed broken glass behind and marched straight to the telephone and called the Dwight Prison for Women in Illinois long distance. Yes, they had received Virginia's letters. Yes, they had traced Wanda. Yes, they had sent on Virginia's letters to Wanda at the Rockford, Illinois City Jail where she was being held on charges of prostitution and where, curiously, there was pressure from the Mayor's Office to release her. And, yes, in light of Virginia's service with the Illinois Department of Corrections, they would arrange a short, five-minute telephone call with Wanda on a state-leased telephone line two days later, between 8:45 and 8:50 in the morning.

"Hello."

"Wanda?"

"Ginny girl?"

"How *are* you?"

"'Bout the same," Wanda said with a Jamaican echo in her voice.

"Are you still . . . well . . ."

Wanda laughed at Ginny's puritanical reticence. "Yep, honey, Ol' Wanda's still readin' minds and poundin' puds. And you, girl?"

"I'm good, really good, actually. I've got a wonderful son and I'm married to a wonderful doctor and —"

"Doctor? Aren't you one of those scientific Christians?"

It was Virginia's turn to laugh. "You've got a good memory, Wanda. As I tell everybody including myself, it's a case of opposites attracting each other." Then, remembering how little time they had, she said, "I don't mean to be in such a rush but we've only got a few minutes and my husband is the reason I wrote to you and he's why I'm calling and I love him so much but I feel so inadequate in bed and he's going to be shipped out any day and I asked you about this stuff at the prison and you couldn't talk about it then and I may never see him ag —"

"Hold on, honey. I read your letters. First, tell me a couple of things about your man. He a big guy or little?"

"Big."

"Tough?"

"Very tough."

"He have sisters?"

"No."

"What about his momma? He close to her?"

"She died when he was a little boy and, a year later, his father also died. Since then, he's been on his own."

"In bed, who's in charge? You or him?"

"Geez, Wanda . . . ."

"Ginny, we're losing time here. Who's in charge? You or him?"

"Well, him, of course."

"You gotta be in charge." Wanda heard a self-conscious gulp on the line. "Forget how tough this big doctor of yours is. This is the kind of man who needs you to take care of him between the sheets and that means you can take care of yourself at the same time."

"But, I don't know what to do."

"Listen up, Ginny. We don't have time for details but here are some tips."

With that, Wanda rattled off carnal generalities while Virginia took cryptic notes. "Men are toasters and women are ovens . . . Go low and slow and then go lower and slower still. Go soft and light and then go softer and lighter still. Use everything you got from tits to tongue on everything he's got from scalp to soles. . . Start on his back and gradually work your way down into the grand canyon where Mr. Johnson lives . . . Don't have Mr. and Mrs. Johnson get together until you're both panting like dogs . . . And just let yourself go —" Suddenly, the line went dead.

Virginia wasn't supposed to know it but, like everybody else in Morro Bay, she did: On the morning of December 4, 1943, her husband, Syd Silverman and the entire 81st would board troopships and the tugs would come and push them past Morro Rock and usher them out to the open ocean and off to war. There was talk about the Aleutians to "protect Alaska" or Hawaii to be "held in reserve" but few believed it. The only destination that made sense was the South Pacific where, as everyone put it, there were "Japs and jungles."

Earlier, Tom and Virginia had agreed that their farewell dinner with David would not be a "last supper" of sadness but a joyful celebration of their marriage and their son. Yet, try as she might, Virginia couldn't keep her word and, more than once, had to jump up from the dinner table and dash to the bathroom for a cry while Tom and David chattered on about the rabbits in the backyard and Tom's carbine, helmet and battle gear stacked next to the front door.

Once dinner was over and the dishes were done and David was asleep on the living room couch, Tom and Virginia turned off the lights and slid into bed next to each other. Immediately, Tom pressed himself, naked and already stiff, against Virginia and hurriedly began to nuzzle and kiss her and pull at her nightie.

"Tom, please stop for a minute." Either he didn't hear her or he didn't want to hear because he kept on fumbling at her nightclothes.

"Tom, honey," she took both his hands in hers and kissed

Peter D. Baird

each one gently and then said, "slow down, just for a moment, please."

"SLOW DOWN? For Christ's sake, Ginny, in a few hours I'll be gone and who knows when I'll get back and be with you like this again. What in the hell are you talking about?"

She put her finger to her lips and whispered, "shhhhhh . . . just turn over on your stomach and relax and listen to me." With a reluctant grunt, he rolled over and she began, ever-so-lightly, stroking his arms, head, back and later the sensitive crevices between his parted legs while occasionally enhancing the effect with her tongue and hot breath. To allay any suspicions he might have about why they weren't in their well-practiced, one-on-top-of-the-other position that Tom called the "missionary sandwich," Virginia told Tom in a whispered voice about Wanda and who she was and how they had met and what Wanda did for a living and of their recent telephone call and of Virginia's sense of sexual inade-quacy and how she wanted Tom to feel how much he meant to her and how badly she would miss him and, for almost five minutes, she kept on talking and justifying herself until Tom held his finger against his lips and whispered, "shhhhhh."

During their hours of serial love-making, a thick fog rolled in from the Pacific that darkened the night and delayed the dawn. By 4:30 in the morning, the bungalow was pitch black and the only light was the burning, moving tip of Tom's lighted cigarette. He was sitting up, leaning against the headboard while Virginia had her face buried in a pillow, sobbing.

"I don't know what Davey and I are going to do without you," she whimpered.

"You'll do exactly as we planned," he said between long drags on the cigarette. "You'll go back to Ottawa and live with your folks. You and Davey will stay in one place for a change. You won't have to work. If you want, you can do your Madame Fortuno show at the Chicago USO Club down in the Loop, but," he tried to sound unconcerned, "you'll have to stay away from all those handsome young guys in uniform who'll want to have their way with you." He paused and then asked, "By the way, is that guy you were engaged to, what's his name?"

40

"Jeff."

"Is he still stationed near Chicago?"

"Yes, although my mom wrote and said that he's expecting orders that'll either send him to Connecticut or to Annapolis."

"So I don't have to worry about him?"

"No, absolutely not." With that subject out of the way, she coiled her body around his and said, "I'm scared, Tom."

"Honey, I'm a *doctor* for God's sake. I won't be shooting or getting shot at. Syd and I'll be operating in a tent *behind* the front lines or, more likely, we'll be *floating* in one of those white hospital ships with huge red crosses on the sides."

"I don't want you to go," she moaned, sniffling.

"Ginny, there's something really important I need to ask you to do." When he heard a wet "okay," he said, "It's about you and Davey."

"What about us?"

"I mean it's about your religion." He felt her pull back as he extinguished his cigarette.

"What about it?"

"Except for that godawful Thanksgiving with Tess back in Boston, there's never been a problem between my medicine and your religion but . . . ."

"But what?"

"But I need you to promise me something."

"Anything, just ask."

"If Davey ever gets hurt or is sick — and I mean ever as in whether I get hurt, killed or come back in one piece as I certainly expect— you've got to promise me that you'll always have him treated by a medical doctor right away." Tom added, "It's all right with me if, afterwards, you want to pray or go to church or read from that Mary Baker Eddy book. But I want a doctor, a medical doctor, to treat Davey at the first sign of anything wrong. Understand?"

"I will, Tom, that's the least I can do for . . . for . . . you." On the word "you," her tears didn't stop until Tom's troopship had disappeared into the Pacific horizon.

Chapter Seven

PELELIU

Peleliu is six miles long, two miles wide and 4,000 miles south and west of Honolulu. Japan had appropriated Peleliu since it belatedly entered World War One on the side of the Allies and had stolen all of Germany's South Pacific possessions. Except for a phosphate plant, Peleliu had little worth owning, let alone fighting for. Its closest neighbor, the smaller Island of Angaur, did not even have as much as a phosphate plant.

From a distance, Peleliu looked like a "Japless paradise" to the American reconnaissance pilots in September, 1944. But up close, it had craggy ridges, wide swamps and sheer limestone walls that were covered with choking jungle. It stayed wet from 140 inches of rain a year and crawled with millions of mosquitos, "no-see-um" gnats and semi-poisonous centipedes. Upon unacclimated outsiders, Peleliu could inflict coral wounds that didn't heal, fungus that rotted feet, dysentery that wouldn't quit and heat prostration that quickly turned into delirium.

To the U.S. military, Peleliu had no strategic importance. It was too small to be an Allied staging area. American aircraft had already mined the harbor and cratered the airfield. However, because General MacArthur wanted his "right flank protected" when he returned to the Philippines and because American intelligence had determined that Peleliu was "lightly defended," U.S. strategists decided to invade the island. There would be few casualties, they reasoned, and an easy conquest would boost morale after Guadalcanal. The invasion, planned for the early hours of September 15, 1944, was named "Operation Stalemate," a title that would later haunt invasion planners. According to Marine Corps Major General William Rupertus, "Peleliu will take three or four days."

In fact, Peleliu was a death trap. Its narrow shoreline, jungled valleys and 750-foot-high ridges had been mined, booby-trapped, and covered with triangulated crossfire angles and pre-positioned targets. Hidden in the island's tunnels and caves were 13,000 unseen Japanese soldiers sworn to fight to the death. Rather than three or four days, the battle raged for two months of point-blank firing, hand-to-hand combat, dysentery, fevers, delirium and carnage. It ended only after the Japanese had been annihilated and the Americans had sustained over 9,000 casualties.

At 11:30 on the morning of the invasion, Captain Tom McQuade and First Lieutenant Syd Silverman climbed down rope ladders on the side of the hospital ship, *The Mercy,* and boarded a landing craft filled with corpsmen, tents, operating tables and medical supplies. Two days earlier, McQuade and Silverman had received orders that they were being temporarily attached to the First Marine Division which had been victorious at Guadacanal but was short on medical support from the Navy. After the Marines had established a beachhead, the two doctors were ordered to go ashore at "Orange Beach 3" and set up an aid station in a clearing, spotted by reconnaissance flights, some 200 yards inland on a road leading to the bombed out airfield.

Although the Marines who had landed on the beaches to the north had taken heavy casualties, the resistance at "Orange Beach 3" had been scattered. By the time Doctors McQuade and Silverman had jumped off the landing craft into waist-high water, the invading Marines had already secured the aid station site and reached the airfield and were in sight of the steep, jagged outcropping later dubbed, "Bloody Nose Ridge," that held, within its camouflaged tunnels, thousands of Japanese soldiers poised for a well-rehearsed, surprise counterattack.

"I thought I might get shot but never thought I'd puke to death," Tom McQuade told the soft-spoken Syd Silverman who was as green-gilled from sea sickness as his superior officer but too stoic to complain and too refined to curse. Followed by their supplies and medics, the two doctors sloshed ashore as the beach in front of them teemed with jeeps, artillery and half-tracks; throngs of Sea-Bees assembling prefabricated docks; SPs directing traffic; and, everywhere, Marines in battle gear double-timing it into the jungle.

"Keep your eye out for anyone resembling a Paul Gaugan descendant," Syd said.

"I'll be sure to do that right after I spot our promised escort if there is one."

The doctors stood on the beach, dripping wet, and scanned the beachfront chaos for their escort. Finally after what seemed like a chaotic eternity, an unshaven Marine corporal approached and, with a Mississippi accent, asked, "Cap'n McQuade?"

"Yes."

"Corporal Hodson, suh. Me and ma' squad is gonna git ya up to th' clearin' and hep ya all git them tents 'n stuff set up."

"Japs give you any trouble?"

"Hardly none here, suh."

Through the confusion on the beach and the tangle of the jungle, the Marines led the medical entourage to the designated clearing. It was just off the road to the airfield. On the beach side of the clearing, there was a deep, irregularly-shaped bomb crater from the pre-invasion bombardment and it was as good a place as any for stowing supplies. To everyone's surprise, there weren't that many casualties coming from the front and most of them could be ferried directly to the hospital ship without surgical intervention. Meanwhile, the Marines drove tent poles into the crumbling coral, hung canvas and helped set up a makeshift operating theater. From a distance came the crump crump of heavy artillery.

Late in the afternoon, Tom and Syd were standing next to the bomb crater, looking for a missing box of instruments. Nearby, Corporal Hodson was barking out wrap-up instructions to his men.

"Oh, my god." Tom reached inside his shirt and pulled out a wriggling centipede whose legs were moving in sequential waves and whose mandibular pinchers were covered with blood. "I'm glad we're not being shot at. But this place is still the shi—"

Suddenly, the jungle became a deafening, metallic inferno. From dozens of camouflaged caves, Japanese mortar and artillery erupted and thousands of Japanese soldiers poured out of their tunnels and into the fading daylight for the ambush. As the Americans learned later, the Japanese expected to decimate the first waves of Marines by an enveloping counteroffensive and then drive the stragglers back into the sea.

Corporal Hodson lunged at Silverman and McQuade and knocked them backwards into the bomb crater. "Git your weapons out!" Hodson yelled at the two doctors tangled up with each other amid plasma bottles, kits, boxes and coral.

In seconds, McQuade straightened his glasses, grabbed a nearby carbine and, in the dusky light, started firing blindly at the jungle, barely missing Corporal Hodson's left ear. Silverman fumbled with the .45 revolver strapped to his side, threw his right hand over the edge, pulled the trigger three times but felt nothing more than a series of unrecoiling clicks.

"Jeesus Keyrist," Hodson said, looking away from the doctors' sorry combat performance and slamming another clip into his automatic rifle. Just then, Hodson swung his weapon over the side of the crater and, in two short bursts, dropped a Japanese infantryman whom neither doctor had seen in the jungle alongside the road.

Moments later, Marines came running, diving and rolling in from the beach that was now under Japanese bombardment. They dug in at the edge of the clearing and, off to the doctors' left side, set up a machine gun placement just in time to cut down a screaming wave of bayonet-wielding attackers.

The firing, wounding, killing and dying went on through the night without either side gaining or losing ground. By 03:30 hours the next morning, the intensity of the battle had shifted away from the field hospital and seemed to be concentrated about a thousand yards to the north.

Hodson leaned over to the doctors and whispered, "We got

45

damn near no ammo left. If th' Japs rush us agin, we cain't kill 'em with fuckin' plasma bottles."

"What do you suggest?" Lt. Silverman asked, sounding more as if he were in a hospital staff meeting than in a bomb crater under fire.

"I'll git us some more ammo. Ya gonna be cover'd by the macheen gun boys over yonder," he pointed. "By mornin', the Shermans oughtta be here 'n run over 'em fuckin' Japs. You docs be O.K.?"

Neither one felt okay but nodded anyway. McQuade said, "We can't do much for anyone who's wounded. But if you see any medics, tell them we're here."

The Marine peered over the edge and said. "It's as dark as the inside of a cow tonight. So, if ya hear anyone comin', shoot 'em unless ya hear 'em say, 'Lulu.'"

"Lulu?"

"'Lulu.' It's the password," he said. "Nips cain't say 'L's. But they're goddamn good night fighters. Great with knives. One of ya stay up." Neither doctor could imagine falling asleep. With hardly a sound, Hodson was gone.

The doctors huddled in the bomb crater and listened to the sounds of night combat. McQuade clutched his carbine. Silverman held onto the butt of his now-loaded .45, fretting that he was going to shoot Tom. A mortar round exploded behind them and the near-by American machine gun unit chattered away in short bursts. In the midst of the firing, Tom leaned over to his colleague's helmeted ear and said, "I thought we were doctors, not sitting ducks."

"That's for damn sure," Syd said, breaking his no-curse rule.

Tom muttered, "'Lightly defended,' my ass. General Rupertus is probably on *The Tennessee* right now, drinking Manhattans and listening to "In The Mood" while we're in this crater and I'm in the shittiest mood of my life."

"Lulu." Startled, both doctors quickly realized what was happening as a medic lowered a Marine sergeant into the crater who had nothing left of both legs except bloody strings of flesh and splinters of bone. Syd groped for a first aid kit and, after rummaging in it, gave the moaning Marine a shot of morphine. Tom crawled over to the other side of the crater where, just above the edge, there was a box of clamps and compresses. When Tom grabbed what he needed, an orange flare rocketed overhead, illuminating the entire field hospital site. Out of the corner of his left eye, McQuade saw movement a few yards away on the other side of Syd, the medic and the legless sergeant.

It was a member of the Japanese Army's elite, close-quarter, night combat unit. He wore tropical khaki shorts, carried only a bayonet, and was crawling toward the American machine gun when, unexpectedly, he came upon the crater.

Immediately, the invader sank his bayonet into the medic's chest. With his other hand, he landed a powerful blow to the side of Syd's neck, knocking the doctor unconscious. Then he did a shoulder roll and started to come back up on his haunches with the bayonet in his upraised left hand. When the Japanese soldier was about to spring, his right foot slipped on a loose plasma bottle. Off balance, he swung the bayonet, missed Tom and fell onto his back just as a burst of tracer bullets streaked across the night sky.

In that moment, the advantage shifted from the 5 foot 4 inch 128 pound Oriental to the 6 foot 2 inch 240 pound Caucasian. Before the Japanese soldier could get up off his back and strike again, the doctor rolled over on top of his assailant and slammed the attacker's bayonet hand into the gravel. The Japanese fighter kicked his bare foot into Tom's lower abdomen, narrowly missing his groin. Tom gasped and then, not from training but from wild improvisation, tried to choke the attacker by thrusting his left hand at the Japanese soldier's exposed throat. The night fighter knew how to deal with a frontal strangulation attempt and immediately pushed his chin down against his chest to cut off access to his throat which meant that Tom's incoming hand overshot his assailant's chin and the base of Tom's left palm rammed the enemy's nose back up into his head and two of Tom's left fingers penetrated the Japanese soldier's eye sockets. Momentarily, Tom felt the little man's body go limp.

Hyperventilating, Tom slowly withdrew his left fingers from the moist suction of the night fighter's orbital cavities. He rolled face up, fought for air and crawled through the debris to the knifed medic who had no pulse. Tom turned to the Marine sergeant and felt only a feeble pulse and then tried to revive the crumpled Silverman.

"Syd, you Okay?"

Syd put his hand on his neck. "Oh, God."

"Drink." Still panting, Tom opened a canteen and put it to Silverman's lips. McQuade fumbled in one of the kits. "Take this." He handed Silverman a pill. "I hope it's codeine."

"What happened?"

Between gasps for air, Tom said, "Jap killed the medic . . . Nailed you . . . Damn near got me . . . The sergeant's almost dead."

"Holy cow."

"Look, Syd . . . Keep the sergeant snowed with morphine and I'll grab my carbine and stand guard."

Tom clutched his carbine, crawled up the side of the bomb crater, peered over the edge and tried to slow his pounding heart. It was then that he felt the stickiness on his left fingers from the dead soldier's membranes. It was then that he felt what it was like to have killed another human being.

As a kid on the streets of Pittsburgh, Tom had been in some two-fisted brawls, but they had ended in nothing more serious than black eyes, missing teeth, bloody noses and split lips. In his twenties, he had cold-cocked a union steward who, threatening Tom with a crowbar, had demanded a percentage of his construction wages. But never had Tom taken a life or had even thought of such a thing.

He was a <u>doctor</u> for God's sake! And, now, he had killed a man with the same left hand that he used to operate and save lives. Of course it was war. Of course the man had killed the medic. Of course he would have finished Syd off. Of course he would have killed Tom. Of course he would have crawled over and tried to kill the American machine gunners too. Yet, all the "of courses" in the world could not keep Tom from leaking tears, aching with self-revulsion, tasting the bitter up-flow of stomach acid and grinding his sticky left hand into the loose coral until the dead man's membranes had been scraped off and Tom's left hand was bloody with abrasions and sharp splinters.

For the next three hours, Tom felt insects burrow and bite;

listened to the sergeant die; wet his pants; squinted into the muggy blackness; and trembled at the satanic sound and lights show. Tracers. Grenades. Off-shore guns. Radio crackles. Flares. Screams from combatants in close-quarter combat. Machine gun fire. Smells of smoke, decomposing flesh and human feces. Men crying for their mothers in two languages.

When the streaks of first light seeped into the jungle, a train of Sherman tanks roared into the clearing from the beach and headed, firing as they went, into the dense foliage and down the road to the airfield while carrier-launched Gruuman Hellcats flew just above the tree-tops, carpeting the jungle with blankets of bullets. Faced with armored reinforcements and air power, the Japanese fell back into their caves and tunnels and dug in for a fierce defense.

When it was safe, the two doctors crawled out of their crater and ate canned Australian mutton and drank cold coffee. Then, as quickly as possible, they put the field hospital into rudimentary order, scrubbed, donned gloves, gowns and masks and started their surgical marathon.

Tom was in awe of Syd whose skills were better than anyone at Crouse-Irving or Mass General. Even in the sweltering tent without x-ray, adequate light or decent suction and surrounded by blood, mosquitoes and severed body parts, Syd was fast and deft and always knew where he was and what had to be done inside and outside the wounded, mangled, and sometimes unrecognizable Marines. Years later, Tom was not surprised when Syd became Surgeon General of the United States and then Dean of the University of Michigan College of Medicine.

Seventeen hours had passed by the time they were performing an anterolateral thoracotomy on a Marine major who had taken a bullet in his upper left chest and whose left anterior descending coronary artery had been grazed and needed closure. Looking across the patient, Tom told Syd about another type of thoracotomy he had unsuccessfully tried to do on an insurance salesman at Mass General. "I've never botched a thoracotomy since, Syd. Hope this won't be my second."

"It won't be, you're doing a wonderful job," Syd said. "But I should tell you something else. Besides being one of the best surgeons I ever saw, you're the best friend I've ever had. You saved my life today or was it yesterday or the day before? No matter when it was, I don't know how I'll ever repay you."

"There's nothing to repay, Syd. But if there is, I still owe you for standing up for Ginny and stealing the bus in Alabama."

"And for getting busted to first lieutenant," Syd laughed.

Tom was inside the major's chest cavity affixing clamps to staunch the bleeding as his voice dropped to a solemn octave. "I never thought I'd kill a man; I never thought I'd use my hands to take a life."

Over the sound of the diesel generator outside the tent, Syd said, "Tom, this is war! You *had* to do it."

"I know it's war, Syd," Tom said through a mask wet with sweat and flecks of blood. "Maybe I'd feel differently if I'd shot him. But . . . " He stopped and glanced down at his rubber-gloved left hand.

Because Syd's neck throbbed and head hurt and reminded him of his body, he drank water constantly, ate quick meals, swallowed a whole packet of salt tablets, and got several hour stretches of sleep. But Tom, ever the iron-man, just stood there, operating, sweating, feeling what the coral splinters had done to his left hand and scalding his soul for what his left hand had done to another human being.

The official report about what happened later said that Captain McQuade had been operating for approximately seventy-two hours before the incident occurred and he had consumed only occasional cups of water, ate little food, took only a couple of cat naps, was dehydrated, took one salt tablet, exhausted and, most likely, delirious. Tom himself never knew how many hours or days he had been in surgery, only that he couldn't remember anything except waking up on the operating table with Syd hovering over him.

Chapter Eight

ILLINOIS

$\mathcal{A}$t 11:40 on a Friday night in January, 1945, Chicago's LaSalle Street Station was still busy. Redcaps, servicemen with duffels, conductors, late night commuters, Pullman car porters, an occasional nun in full habit and families with groggy children milled beneath the vaulted ceiling and a massive, hanging, four-faced clock. From scattered kiosks, paper boys barked out late edition headlines and lost their voices in the cavernous rumble and echoed announcements about the arrivals, departures and destinations of Rock Island, New York Central and Nickel Plate passenger trains.

The 24-hour coffee shop was located beyond the line of ornately-grated ticket windows. It was within sight of Track 37, the subterranean port where the Rock Island's "Nighthawk" waited to leave at midnight for its run downstate. At a wooden table in the far corner of the coffee shop, a lanky naval officer talked to a rouged woman whose winter coat covered a Gypsy costume.

"Ginny, I'm sorry I missed your USO show tonight," the lieutenant commander said. "But, by the time you called, it was too late to get off duty. I took the first train I could." He waved across the coffee shop, caught the eye of a waitress and motioned for a refill on coffee.

Despite the uniform that hung on his tall, lanky frame and the Annapolis education that his father had insisted on, Jeff Fry was not the hard-charging, take-command sort of naval officer. Quiet and reflective, he had a mind for electronics and a disposition for theology which he fused into an abiding embrace of Christian Science. In mufti, he had often been mistaken for an ascetic clergyman, once as a professor of medieval literature on the campus of the University of Chicago. Tilting his thin, Lincoln-shaped face downward, he glanced at Virginia's wedding ring, winced to himself and pushed his wire-rim glasses back up the bridge of his long, sharply tented nose. "How's Tess?"

"She's fine. We had a big blow-up in Boston several years ago and didn't talk for a long time, but last summer she spent some time with me, Davey and the folks in Ottawa. We cleared the air, at least between us."

Commander Fry and Mrs. McQuade fell silent as a gum-chewing waitress filled up both mugs and, spotting a generous tip, gushed out a "thanks sailor."

Jeff Fry ended the lull. "I'm expecting a transfer soon."

"Where'll you go?"

"I want Groton, where the subs are. My expertise is in underwater electronics and, if I'm ever going to be a combatant, it'll be in a submarine. I've been trying to get on a sub ever since I left Annapolis."

"Why've they kept you at Great Lakes, floating around Lake Michigan?"

"They say it's my height but I don't believe it."

"Why then?"

"Can't prove it but it's probably because of my religion." Fry took the mug in both hands and raised it to eye level, looking across the table at the woman he had once been engaged to for over two years. "*Our* faith," he added.

"Before you went to the Academy, didn't you tell me that the military had formally recognized Christian Science Practitioners?"

"On paper, yeah. But, in reality, they think we're batty. Off the record, I was told that a sub is the last place the Navy wants someone like me."

"But, you graduated near the top of your class from Annapolis."

"If I hadn't, they'd probably have me at Point Barrow, counting walruses. If I don't get to the subs, then I'll ask for a teaching position at the Naval Academy. Either way, I'm pretty sure that, after the war, I'll resign my commission and work for the church full time."

Virginia glanced at her watch to make sure she didn't miss the "Nighthawk." It would leave in 15 minutes for Ottawa and points south. "Jeepers, I've got to get going."

"Ginny, stay a little longer, please. I didn't come down here in the middle of the night to talk about subs or walruses."

"Jeff —"

"I need to talk to you." He pushed at his glasses that hadn't slipped.

"Okay, I suppose I've got it coming."

Commander Fry hunched his bony shoulders. "I thought *we* were going to get married. Isn't that what *we* agreed? Isn't that what *you* promised?" He put down his mug and waited for an answer.

She dropped her eyes. "Yes . . .we . . . I . . . I did . . .and I can't tell you how guilty I feel."

Jeff pressed his case. "I spent all that summer writing and calling. Didn't hear a word from you. The next thing I know is my mom calls from Ottawa and says you married a doctor you met at one of your magic shows, someone you barely knew. Then, I got your 'Dearest Jeff' letter but it didn't contain a syllable about us or what had gone wrong and, after that, all I got from you was an occasional post card with chatty news about your son and that just made me feel worse."

She nodded.

"How could you do that to *me*, of all people?"

Her voice dropped to a near whisper. "I didn't have an explanation that you would understand. Besides, it all happened so fast."

"I'm not just some guy you met at a magic show."

Her voice got weaker with each nod. "I know."

"How many years, vacations, Christmases, family gatherings, Fourth of July's, church services, and prayers have we shared?" He didn't give her a chance to do anything except to keep on nodding. "Without the Practitioner from our church, your mom would've died when the doctors had given up. Didn't any of that *mean* something to you?"

"Of course it did and I feel dreadful," she said, gathering strength. "At first, I thought my feelings for Tom would pass and, since my feelings for you never changed, that I would marry you as we planned. Then, before I knew it, I was married and it was all I could do to send you that one letter. I knew I'd have to face you someday, just like this." She looked down. "You deserved better from me."

He kept pressing. "But what were we?"

She thought for a moment. "Kids across the street, playmates, brother-sister, steadies, fiancés but. . . . "She started to say something more but stopped.

"But what?"

"I've got to go," she said with a sudden burst of energy, grabbing her satchels. "Thanks for coming down to see me, Jeff. You're a wonderful man, I'll always care for you."

"There's something more, isn't there?" He rose, towering over her.

"Oh, I don't know." She turned and made for the door.

"You don't ever don't know, Ginny Russell-or-whatever-your-last-name-is-these-days." He followed on her heels. "Come on, truth time, dog-gone it, I'm *entitled* to know."

"You were just too like me in some ways and too different in others."

"I don't get it."

"I didn't think you would." She shook her head and walked out of the coffee shop toward Track 37. He matched her stride for stride and the scene briefly reminded her of her walk with Tom on Erie Boulevard after The Colonic.

"Spell it out, would you please?"

Just then, the gates to Track 35 opened up and they found themselves fording a stream of passengers from the New York

Central's "Twentieth Century Limited" which had been delayed by a blizzard in Ohio.

Once free of the throng, Virginia stopped, turned to him and said, "Growing up, we were mirror-images of each other. Everybody thought so. You thought so. I thought so. Our families did too."

"Still are, as far as I'm concerned."

Virginia nodded and said, "But you were always so serious, contemplative, looking inside yourself for spiritual strength and to God for eternal principles."

"So did you."

"Sometimes. But between God up there and us down here there's a huge thing called life with excitement, risk and fun and I guess I chose life."

"I'm not alive enough?"

She ducked the question. "Let me try to put it this way. Remember Molly Sykes, the runaway slave and her son?"

"Sure."

"Remember how excited I was to learn about her escape as a young woman and how they tried to recapture her and how my family had taken her in and how she had mystical powers to see and know and heal?"

"I remember the healing part."

"And how that got me fascinated with magic and I did all those dumb shows and looked like a dope?"

"I never said you were a dope."

"Of course you didn't because you were too nice but, eventually, when I kept at it, you said that you were 'embarrassed' for me."

"Yeah, but what I meant —"

"You were right, I should have been embarrassed. My stupid magic shows flopped so many times I couldn't count them. Plus, only boys were supposed to be magicians anyway and I looked like a fool and that bothered you, didn't it?"

"A little, I guess."

"And you were embarrassed for me, weren't you?"

"Maybe . . . ."

55

"Jeff, I'd rather take risks and look foolish than play it safe and be dignified. You never understood that, did you?"

He shrugged.

She went on. "You didn't think it was 'dignified' to be a social worker in the colored section of a woman's prison either, did you?"

"Ginny, I didn't object to you helping coloreds in prison. What bothered me was your friendship with that Wanda person whom you said had been a prostitute and who was teaching you things that you wouldn't tell me and I was afraid to ask."

"Jeff, that's my point."

"What point? I don't get it."

"The point, my dearest Jeff whom I adore and always will, is that we *are* different and, besides that, I'd better get on that train." With that, she broke into a speed step with him at her side. When they reached the gate for Track 37, they stopped in front of a grandfatherly conductor holding a ticket punch.

"This Tom of yours, does he have religion, a faith?"

"Not any more. He was raised as a Scottish Presbyterian. Says all he learned in church was to feel guilty and hate Catholics."

"Does he know about me?"

"Yes."

"Does he know you're a Christian Scientist?"

"Of course, I've — "She was drowned out by a reverberating public address announcement about the imminent departure of "The Nighthawk."

Fry raised his voice over the amplified recitation of outbound stops — "Joliet, Rockdale, Marseilles, Ottawa, LaSalle, Peru" — and asked, "what's going to happen when you and this medical doctor cross swords over healing and faith?"

The announcement ended and Virginia said, "Tom and I fought through that in Boston but we respect each other too much to ever do it again. There really is something to opposites attracting each other."

"I'm even more confused now. Didn't you just say that you didn't marry me because I was different from you? Then you go off and marry somebody who is as different as apples are to . . . well,

56

kangaroos."

Virginia didn't try to explain away the contradictions and handed her ticket to the conductor who, lifting his brow and looking over his glasses, said, "Lady, you'd better get a move on. It's 'all aboard' in less than two minutes."

From behind her, Jeff said, "Well, Ginny, I guess it's goodbye."

Suddenly, she pivoted about and, throwing her arms tightly around his neck, put her lips into his right ear, kissed it and said, "It'll never-be-goodbye-for-us-because-I'll-always-love-you-Jeff-Fry." Then, pushing away from him before he could get off a responsive embrace, she dashed down the ramp, satchels swinging, toward a string of dirty brown coaches and a locomotive hissing steam and smelling of coal.

To her disappearing back, he cupped his hands to his mouth and yelled, "ONE WAY OR ANOTHER I'LL ALWAYS BE CLOSE, GINNY!"

The next morning, Virginia woke up in bed in the house on the street in the town where she had grown up. Population 11,900, Ottawa, Illinois was on the other side of the planet from Peleliu and had been built where the muddy Fox River merged with the even muddier Illinois River. People there made glass for car windshields, raised corn, painted radium on watch dials, and picnicked at nearby Starved Rock State Park.

Virginia's bedroom was her time capsule. It had aging dolls and frayed teddy bears in the closet; prom cards and a picture of Jeff Fry on her dresser top; a vanity upholstered in lace and valentine pink fabric; and a glassed-in wall cabinet containing playing cards, wands, and a spirit trumpet. The wallpaper was a light blue, fleur-de-lis pattern on which hung a Phi Beta Kappa certificate and a theatrical poster, billing "The Devil's Death Chamber" at Chicago's Majestic Theater and showing a grim-faced Harry Houdini handcuffed in the path of an approaching buzzsaw.

Smelling coffee, she turned over and glanced at the brass alarm clock. Just then, the door burst open and David bounded into the bedroom followed by his grandmother.

"Mom, let's do the diss-pearing boy trick!"

Virginia smiled, leaned over the side of the bed and gave her son a tight hug. "O.K., Davey, we'll do the disappearing boy trick. Ready? Close your eyes real tight."

He slammed them shut, contorting.

"Grandma, where <u>did</u> that boy go?," Virginia said in a sing-songy voice.

"I don't know, Ginny." Edith Russell sing-songed in reply. "Davey was just here until he closed his eyes and then he vanished."

"Grandma, I hope he reappears soon because I brought him a present from Chicago."

At the word "present," David's eyes flew open, prompting his mother and grandmother to clap their hands and laugh, "There he is! He's reappeared!"

After David ripped open the present and put on a pin-striped Rock Island engineer's hat, Grandma Russell shooed him out of the bedroom and, with an unsteady hand, tendered a tissue-thin War Department envelope. Mother and daughter exchanged grave looks.

Virginia took a deep breath, carefully opened the envelope and read a letter Lt. Sydney Silverman had written more than twelve weeks earlier.

Dear Ginny:

I am terribly sorry to tell you that Tom was wounded in the left hand during hostilities on the Island of Peleliu. Reconstructive surgery will occur next week on our hospital ship, The Mercy.

Tom is very down emotionally but is in good, overall physical condition. He says he'll write to you as soon as he is able.

You should know that Tom saved my life. I thank God that he is right-handed. As you know, Tom is a gifted surgeon, probably the best I've ever seen.

Also, Tom is a mensch (good guy) who adores Davey and loves you. I'm proud to be his subordinate, colleague and friend. I'm also proud of you for helping me steal that bus in Alabama.

With all good wishes,

1st Lt. Sydney E. Silverman, M.D.
81st Division
United States Army Medical Corps

Spring came early that year. The Illinois River melted into a dirty soup and carried barges and warships in increasing numbers south to the Mississippi River and the Gulf. Robins returned to take advantage of the still-soft ground. Corn farmers were already in their fields. The long garden that swept down to the river from the Russell residence had started to green up. The news from the Pacific was good and, from Europe, it was even better.

After Syd's letter, Virginia canceled the rest of her USO shows, stayed home and waited for more letters. During the day, she took in the mail; did magic with David; and helped her parents with cleaning, shopping, rationing and aging. At night, they ate supper in the heavily draped Victorian dining room that overlooked the Illinois River while they listened to "Fibber McGee and Molly" from a brown RCA radio shaped like a chapel window.

After the 7:00 p.m. radio show was over, Virginia and David followed the same bedtime routine. After a bath and once in his pajamas, David would get into bed and ask Virginia when his daddy was coming home so they could "play doctor" again and she would say "someday soon." Then she and David prayed for their daddy and for America to win the war and, one last time, David would insist upon doing the disappearing boy trick. After it was over for the umpteenth time that day, he would ask, "How'd we do that, mom?" "It's magic, Davey," she'd say, knowing the script and smiling. Then she would kiss his forehead, tuck him in and turn off the light. "It's real magic, Davey. Don't *ever* forget there's *real magic* in this world."

The second War Department letter arrived on March 25, 1945; this one was addressed in a familiar hand. With her heart racing, Virginia dropped into a glider on her parents' screened-in front porch and, oblivious to the traffic that rattled by on the red-bricked

street, read and re-read what her husband had written many weeks
earlier:

> *Dearest Ginny:*
> *First of all, I'm all right. By the time you read this,*
> *I'll be somewhere in the Pacific headed to San Francisco.*
> *So much has happened, I hardly know where to start. But I*
> *guess it began with the invasion of Peleliu last September*
> *when Syd and I went ashore with the 1st Marines. Hell could-*
> *n't have been worse. What we lived through was indes-*
> *cribable. What I did was even worse.*
>
> *After landing, we found ourselves in the middle of*
> *the fiercest battle that even the Marines from Guadalcanal had*
> *seen. It was almost 24 hours before we could get a field hospi-*
> *tal up and running.*
>
> *From that point, Syd and I stood in the heat and*
> *operated for, what seemed like, forever. The carnage was awful*
> *and there didn't seem to be an end to the poor guys the medics*
> *brought to us. Those who were horibly blown apart and were*
> *either dying or would spend the rest of their lives as vegetables*
> *I put out of their misery with blasts of morphine (you remember*
> *my anti-vegetable pledge in Syracuse?).*
>
> *For those who had a chance to live in a meaningful*
> *way or keep a limb, we did everything we could with what little*
> *we had. I lost track of time, sleep, salt pills and I guess my own*
> *sanity and don't remember what happened next. Syd said I*
> *became delirious with heat prostration and he found me outside*
> *the field hospital on the ground. The next thing I remember is*
> *that I was on the operating table and Syd had finished up trying*
> *to put my left hand back together. It was a mess.*
>
> *Last month, I had more surgery on the The Mercy*
> *and the specialist said that, if Syd hadn't been so skilled, he*
> *would have had to amputate. If Syd was great in Alabama for*
> *you, he was even better on Peleliu for me.*
>
> *As it is, my left thumb and index finger are pretty*
> *much okay now. The problem is that my last three left fingers*
> *are immobilized by metal splints but I hear there's a great hand*

surgeon at the University of California Medical School in San Francisco and I'm sure he'll be able to get the sensations and functions back in those three fingers and then I'll be "good as new."

Syd says I'm "depressed." He even suggested that I see a psychiatrist. Can you believe that? Remember what I wanted you to do at The Colonic? However, the shrinks at Syracuse may have been right about one thing: if I can't get my hand back 100%, then I might want a lobotomy.

There's going to be some kind of ship-board inquiry into what happened on Peleliu. I don't know what the hell will happen but Syd assures me that he'll be there and it'll be all right.

I'm sure you and your folks are taking good care of Davey. Are you and he still doing the disappearing boy trick yet? Does he still play doctor?

Before you know it, we'll be back in Boston and I'll be back at Mass General. When we get back to Boston, would you please quarantine Tess from me? In the meantime, don't forget to take Davey to a doctor at the first sign of a health problem.

All my love,
/s/ Tom

Chapter Nine

Syd sat in the back seat of a taxicab headed toward Oakland on the Bay Bridge and, ignoring the distant lights that rim the East Bay at night, debated definitions with himself. What was the right word to describe his euphoria? "Happy" wouldn't do; it described an emotion that was entirely too ordinary. "Giddy" was out; too frivolous. Maybe "joy" was what he felt and, if so, would the adjective be "joyous" or "joyful?" Or would they be adverbs because they modified an emotion? Whatever the word, he now knew how the ancient Israelites felt when, in the wilderness, God suddenly gave them manna.

That morning, he had received a telegram from the Judge Advocate General of the Army, advising him that he had won his appeal; that the demotion to first lieutenant in Alabama had been "ill-considered," and that he was a captain again, entitled to back pay. Maybe all the angry letters he had written to everybody who was anybody in Washington, D.C. had paid off. Maybe the Army was getting more sensitive to civil rights, at least Syd hoped so.

Right after lunch, there was more manna. Orders had come through that assigned him to the elite Walter Reed Army Hospital in

Washington, D.C. Since he had taught at Johns Hopkins University Medical School just down the road in Baltimore, Syd knew the medical brass at Walter Reed and, with those connections and some political luck, maybe he could do some medical policy-making someday.

Just as he was imagining himself testifying before a Senate Committee, Syd yanked himself back into the present when a lighted road sign appeared that announced, "NEXT EXIT: YERBA BUENA ISLAND AND TREASURE ISLAND NAVAL STATION." "Take this exit, driver," Syd instructed, "and then follow the signs for Treasure Island and, after we cross the causeway and get past the guard gate at the Naval Station, I'll show you how to find the Officer's Club."

Miffed to be told how to find the most popular Officers' Club in the Bay Area, the driver, an older man with an Italian accent, said, "You thinka I'm just offa the boat, Mack?" Sheepishly, Syd apologized as the cab glided down the off ramp and into the descending curves of rocky Yerba Buena Island which intersects the Bay Bridge in the middle of San Francisco Bay. Once at sea level, the cab turned north toward the Naval Station which sat on a 440-acre land-fill called Treasure Island and which was where, on the west side, the Officer's Club overlooked the water and faced San Francisco in the distance.

At the guard gate, Syd forgot about his manna and buried himself beneath an avalanche of guilt. How could he be so joyful or joyous or whatever the right word was when his best friend, the man who had saved his life, was bound to be so miserable? Today was the day Tom was supposed to see the hand specialist at the University of California Medical School and Syd had known all along what Tom would be told. Today was also the day that Tom was going to hear from Mass General about his promised fellowship and Syd had known all along what that message would be. Ever since Peleliu, Syd had said nothing about Tom's left hand and, at the club door, he braced himself for a difficult night.

In the smoky, half-light of the Officer's Club, Tom was not hard to spot. He was sitting, hunched over and alone, at the bar with a row of "depth charges" — jiggers of straight bourbon paired up with cans of beer chasers — set out before him. There was no telling how many he had consumed before Syd said "hi" and mounted a bar stool to Tom's right.

Silently, Tom stared straight ahead, across the bar and at the city in the distance. His only acknowledgment of Syd's arrival was to slide a diagnostic report from the University of California and a telegram from Mass General along the bar and in front of his colleague.

Syd knew what they would say without reading them but, after ordering a glass of white wine, he studied them carefully while, at the far end of the club, a chubby, cheery woman played the piano and sang, an old George Gershwin standard, "There's a somebody I'm longing to see: I hope that he, turns out to be, someone who'll watch over me."

When he had finished, Syd looked up from the papers and stared across the bar, the tables and the diners at the distant lights of San Francisco that blurred in the humid air and shimmered on the rippled water. "I'm a little lamb who's lost in the wood," the woman crooned.

"What do you think," Tom asked in a hard voice.

Not sure of what to say, Syd mindlessly replied, "about what?"

Whereupon Tom exploded, "YOU KNOW GODDAMNED GOOD AND WELL ABOUT WHAT."

"You're right, I do."

"Well?"

"Okay," Syd said and began his confessional. "I haven't wanted to say this and it's very difficult for me to do it but I agree with the hand guy — your left fingers are as good as they're going to get BUT I also agree with him that you'll *still* be a competent surgeon and you'll *still* have a good career and . . ."

"And?"

"And . . . what Mass General told you today is also what I expected. To be blunt about it, there's no advanced surgical fellowship program in cardiac surgery I know of that would take you with your left hand in that shape. BUT, AGAIN, TOM, you'll still be a fine general surgeon."

"Why the hell didn't you tell me what you thought while we were floating back to San Francisco?"

"Because I'm not a hand specialist and because I'm not Mass General and, more than anything, because I didn't want to dampen your hopes for the hand or the fellowship." Syd paused to sip his wine and went on. "But again, *you* aren't hopeless, and *neither* is your ability to practice medicine."

Tom threw back a jigger of bourbon and then chug-a-lugged half a can of beer. "Jesus, how could I have been so stupid?"

"You weren't stupid, Tom. If anything, you were a hero, for me and for dozens, maybe hundreds of guys whose lives you saved."

Tom polished off the rest of his beer and put his left hand on the bar so he could glower at it while Syd continued. "There's nothing to feel foolish or bad about and there's nothing to forgive yourself for. Granted, the Army thought that it had no choice but to bust you just as the Army thought it had no choice but to bust me in Alabama. But the Army's findings of facts are forgiving, even laudatory, and you'll get an honorable discharge and, if my appeal was a winner, your's should be too if you'll file one."

The two men fell silent while the singer launched into Cole Porter's "'Night and Day' . . . *you are the one,"* when she got to *"beneath the moon and under the sun...,"* an unsteady naval officer, who had been sitting by himself at the other end of the bar, moved toward the doctors and, without giving them a chance to say no to his "you mind?" question, sat down on the empty bar stool on Tom's left. He loudly ordered "another double gin martini straight up" and told the uninterested physicians his name was "Ben."

Tom threw back another jigger of bourbon with his bad left hand and, before reaching for a beer with his right, told Syd, "at least I can still drink bourbon with this goddamned claw."

"So, how're you guys tonight?" Ben asked.

"All right," Syd mumbled.

Ben studied their uniforms and noticed their caduceuses. "You guys doctors?"

"Yes," Syd answered for both of them.

"What kind?"

"Surgeons."

"Seen action?"

"Yes," Syd said.

"Where?"

"Peleliu."

"Peleliu, that was supposed to be the shits. Was it?"

"Uh, huh" was Syd's uninviting response

"Christ, look at that hand," Ben said, slurring slightly and pointing at Tom's left hand. "Holy Christ, you get that in Peleliu?"

"He did," Syd said with irritation. "Look, buddy, we're in a pretty deep conversation here and —"

The naval officer cut Syd off and asked Tom, "How'd it happen?"

Syd tried to cut Ben off, "I don't mean to be rude, but please take your drink and your curiosity somewhere else."

The drunk ignored Syd and asked Tom point-blank, "How in the hell can you operate with that goddamned thing?"

As he was looking down at Tom's left hand, he didn't see the right one coming. Even though Tom was seated and didn't have the full strength of his legs and back, the bar stool had a rotary seat that allowed Tom to push off with his right leg and spin around and swing his right fist into Ben's open face, knocking the startled naval officer off his stool and sprawling back onto the floor. Tom stood up and loomed over his victim, who slowly rose up and, screaming "ARMY ASSHOLE," lunged at Tom but again collided with the same right fist which, this time, was powered by all of Tom's firmly planted 240 pounds.

It was early morning in Ottawa when the telephone rang at the Russell residence. Virginia was awake and had the phone at her ear after three rings. She could tell from the crackling sounds it was long distance.

"Hello."

"Ginny?"

"Yes!"

"It's Syd."

"Syd?," she gulped, "is Tom okay?"

"He's okay."

"Where are you?"

"I'm at the Treasure Island Officer's Club in the middle of San Francisco Bay."

"Is Tom there?"

"He was." Syd paused. "Tom was drunk and got into a fight. The M.P.'s or S.P.'s or whatever they're called hauled him off a little while ago."

"What?"

"He punched out a naval officer."

"I don't believe it. Why would he do such a thing?"

"The guy was hounding Tom about his left hand and Tom cold-cocked him."

"This is incredible, Syd. The last thing I got from Tom was a letter saying that you guys were going to San Francisco where the nerves, muscles, bones and what not in his hand were going to be surgically restored by some famous doctor at the University of California and then we'd go back to Boston."

"He was lying to you and fooling himself."

"Syd, this is my husband you're talking about."

"I know and Tom's the best friend I ever had but he conned you just like he conned himself. After his surgery on the hospital ship, he knew, I knew, we all knew that his left hand would never get any better."

"What was the stuff about the University of California?"

"Oh, this morning he saw a renowned hand surgeon at the University of California Medical School who told Tom, personally and in writing, what everybody else knew but didn't have the heart or guts to tell him: that the left hand is as good as it'll ever be *and* Tom can still have a career as general surgeon if he's careful."

"He didn't tell me about this."

"I know. He was hoping that, despite the hand, Mass General would take him back. He didn't want to call you until he had heard from Mass General so he could say that you guys were going back to Boston."

"Did he hear from Mass General?"

Syd sighed. "Yes. To make everything even worse, that happened today too. The telegram had been waiting for him when we disembarked but he didn't actually pick it up until today of all days."

"What did Mass General say?"

"They said what I knew they would say after they read the report from the orthopedist on *The Mercy*. No dice on the fellowship."

"How could they do that? They promised."

"I know, but they only want the best in their cardiac program and, with his left hand, Tom isn't the best anymore."

Ginny's voice trembled. "What's left for him as a doctor?"

"A lot, but he doesn't believe it."

"Well, what *is* left?"

"Tom has about 90% use and maybe a little less than 75% sensation in his left thumb and left index finger. His left middle, ring and little fingers are permanently steel-splinted. They're frozen into a 45-degree, claw-like arc by three, implanted steel splints. They're useless and numb."

"Can he still do surgery?"

"Yes, but not at the level of his remarkable skills or in any fellowship program I know of. Certainly not at Mass General." He slowed down and chose his words carefully. "His suturing will be slower. Tactile exploration won't be as reliable. If he holds a scalpel in his left hand, for example, and if he has an unfelt spasm, there is the remote chance he could inadvertently cut something and not even know it." Then Syd brightened up, "but he's *right-handed*. His left thumb and left first finger are normal enough and they're the digits that count the most. Ginny, he's a brilliant surgeon who's probably better with what he's got left than 99% of the docs I've ever scrubbed with. Yet . . . ."

"Yet?"

"Yet, psychologically, he's a mess. He drinks. He rages. He lies about the wound. Sometimes he says it was from a Jap sniper. Other times says it was from shrapnel or from a slammed Jeep door. *Never* ask him about Peleliu or the hand, okay?"

"What did happen to it?"

"I can't get into that. I gave Tom my word and I've got to keep it, even with you. Tom's not just my best friend, he saved my life."

"Then when will I hear from him?"

"I'll get him out of the brig tomorrow morning and try to have him call you before his first depth charge."

"Depth charge?"

"It's what he drinks these days: jiggers of straight bourbon followed by beer chasers. It's potent."

"Oh, Syd."

"Believe me: if he can come home, find a position, cut out the booze and accept his limitations, then there's no reason why he can't have a rewarding medical career and be the same man he was in Syracuse, Boston, Arizona, Alabama, and Morro Bay." Syd stopped for emphasis. "But right now, he's a long way from all of that."

"When will I see him?"

"Hard to say but probably soon. The Army may need him in some capacity. I'll put in a good word with some influential army docs in D.C. and maybe they'll be able to have him temporarily assigned to do something in Ottawa until you guys get settled. If I can pull that off, then he'll be able to resign at any time with a monthly disability check for the rest of his life for the injury to his left hand."

"There's more that you aren't telling me, isn't there, Syd?"

"What'd you mean?"

"Tom wrote to me about an 'inquiry' on *The Mercy*."

"Oh, that?"

"Did it happen?"

"Yes."

"Well, what kind of an 'inquiry' was it?"

"All I can tell you is that Tom was demoted to first lieutenant which is automatic in situations like this."

"What kind of a situation was it?"

"Ginny, please don't ask me to say anything more."

"What do I have to do, Syd, hire a lawyer to find out what has happened to my husband?" Virginia snapped.

"No," came the feeble answer. "But I can't tell you anything more . . ."

"Why, because I can't be trusted?"

"Of course you can be trusted. I'm just honoring Tom's

wishes." He took a deep breath. "There is one thing more I will say: despite the demotion, Tom was exonerated and he will get an honorable discharge."

"You've got to tell me the rest of what happened to my husband."

"I can't, Ginny. Please understand."

Chapter Ten

HOMECOMING

*I*t was ten o'clock in the morning in Washington, D.C. at historic Union Station when the Pennsylvania Railroad's "Liberty Limited" steamed to a jerky stop on Track Number 4. Moments later, a rested, breakfasted and smartly uniformed Captain Silverman alighted from a Pullman car and hailed a Red Cap. With his bags following on behind him, Syd fell into the flow of passengers streaming alongside the train and into the marbled depot din. Syd made his way to the cab stand outside and, after the bags were in the trunk and he was in the backseat, he told the driver, "Walter Reed Army Hospital." The words had a nice rhythm to them; maybe eight beats to the bar or was it seven?

Nine hours later and over six hundred miles away, The Rock Island Line's "Downstate Rocket" came to a stop, just long enough for an unslept, bourbon-smelling First Lieutenant Tom McQuade to stumble off the club car vestibule and onto an empty platform in Ottawa, Illinois where he had been temporarily assigned to conduct physicals at the LaSalle County Induction Center. As the red and white streamliner glided away and left Tom standing there alone, he squinted through the dusk at the one-room depot for signs of life and didn't see any, not even a ticket agent.

Suddenly, the station disappeared behind a Madame Fortuno curtain of fire and when the smoke cleared, a giant "WELCOME HOME TOM" banner appeared as did David, Virginia, her parents, friends and relatives who quick-stepped toward Tom. Ginny led the charge with David on her heels. Just before she slammed herself against her husband, she saw that Tom's eyes were sunken crypts and his posture was a defeated slump and everything that Syd had told her on the telephone was true.

She threw herself at him nonetheless and gave him a long kiss on his mouth that tasted of sour mash. "Welcome home, Tom" she said.

He put his right arm around her while leaving his left hanging at his side. "Good to see you, Ginny," he said in a weary voice.

David yelled up at his father, "Where's my present, daddy?" Unable to get Tom's attention because of Virginia's embrace, David jerked on Tom's left hand for an answer.

"GODDAMMIT, DON'T EVER TOUCH THAT HAND, DO YOU UNDERSTAND?" Tom bellowed, quieting the crowd and sending David running back to his grandparents at the station, crying.

"TOM, you frightened him!," Virginia yelled. "He's been so excited ever since we heard you were coming that he hasn't stopped talking about playing doctor with you and counting the rabbits with you and he's been waking up nights asking me if it was 'time for Daddy's train?'"

Tom sighed and said "I'm sorry but nobody can touch or talk about my left hand. Not him, not you, not anybody."

"His name is DAVID, not '*him*,'" she barked, "and he is your adoring son and you scared the daylights out of him and I expect you to make it up to him, me and everybody else who came to welcome you home."

After a silent, sullen ride from the depot to the Russell residence with Virginia at the wheel and with David in a separate car driven by his unsettled grandparents, Tom marched into the Russell house, dropped his bags inside the front door and dropped onto the first sofa he came to and started snoring. When he woke up, it was well after midnight and the house was dark and his mouth was alum dry and his head throbbed horizontally from ear-to-ear, and the aftertaste of bad bourbon persisted even after he had found the downstairs bathroom and had downed four glasses of water. Remembering that Virginia's room was upstairs, he felt his way in the dark to the stairs and, no matter how lightly he stepped, each wooden floor board announced his approach with a high-pitched squeak or a low-pitched creak.

Tom climbed into bed carefully so as not to disturb Virginia but she was wide awake. "I couldn't believe that you could be so cruel to your own son."

"I'm sorry. I've been out of sorts lately. I'll make it up to him. We'll go to a dime store tomorrow and I'll buy him a squirt gun or something."

"He's terrified of you now."

"He'll get over it."

"He won't unless you get over whatever's bothering you," she said as they both lay on their backs, staring and speaking to the dark ceiling.

"If you're referring to my left hand, it's a subject that's off limits."

"How'll I know what's eating you or what's changed you?"

"You won't. Just don't worry about it."

"Syd said - -"

"Syd? What the *hell* did he tell you? He promised to keep his goddammed mouth shut?"

"Calm down, Tom," Virginia ordered, "You were the one who wrote to me about an 'inquiry' and you're the one who got shot and you're the one who's no longer a captain and you're the one who got into a fight at an officers' club." She paused and said, "Syd had every right to call me and I had every right to ask him questions about my husband."

"That sonofabitch, Syd."

"Tom, if it makes you feel any better, he didn't tell me what happened on Peleliu or what the inquiry was about except that it resulted in an odd combination of automatic demotion and honorable discharge."

Tom seemed relieved by that information, and, in a softer

tone, said, "Let's not talk about this stuff now. I don't want to alienate Davey or fight with you."

"Mmmm," was her disbelieving response

He slowly rolled over and put his right hand suggestively close to her breasts. "I've missed you and this and all I thought about when there was time to think was about our last night together in Morro Bay."

Wanda's rules flashed into Virginia's mind as she said, "I'm too upset, too tired, too everything elsed to re-enact Morro Bay tonight, Tom."

He persisted, she gave in and they reverted to their "missionary sandwich." As Tom churned away above her, Virginia remembered the famous advice Victorian mothers gave to their daughters on their wedding night: "Hang onto the sides of the bed and think of England." Virginia thought of Jeff Fry.

All it took was one week at the LaSalle County Induction Center "looking at the assholes of bent over adolescents" and Tom was ready to leave the Army and Ottawa. Besides, his son avoided him and his wife and her family would barely speak to him.

On the morning of April 12, 1946, Tom woke up after a night of too many depth charges and too little sleep. Unshaven and shaky, Tom sat down at the breakfast table, sipped black coffee and paged through the most recent issue of *The Journal of the American Medical Association*. Slowly, his optic nerve squeezed this classified ad into his brain:

> DESPERATE FOR DOCTOR!
> Physician urgently needed for small hospital in Loah, Utah serving southern Moab County. Partnership with County's other physician. Write Stanley Joseph Smith Roberts, M.D., Box 27, Meridian, Utah, or call 647, Meridian, Utah.

In less than a minute, Tom was on the telephone listening to a succession of long-distance operators switch his call from one exchange to another until he heard a gravely voice bark, "This's

Stan."

"Dr. Roberts, please," Tom asked.

"I said, 'this's Stan.' What can I do for you?" Despite its gruffness, the voice was friendly.

"Dr. Roberts, this is Dr. Tom McQuade and I'm calling about your ad in the *Journal of the American Medical Association*."

"That thing's been running for months and you're only the third son-of-a-bitch who's called," Dr. Roberts laughed. "When I told each of them how podunk we are and asked 'em how they'd feel about being the only non-Mormon as far as the eye can see, every damn one of 'em hung up in a helluva hurry."

Immediately, Tom liked this man who, he would soon discover, looked almost exactly as Tom imagined over the telephone: jovial and squat, with a face that was as full as his body was wide and with Coke bottle trifocals that magnified the world for his bulging eyes and magnified his bulging eyes for the world. If Dr. Roberts had to dress up for work, it was always in the same rumpled, green corduroy sport coat, wide blue suspenders and yellow bow tie. If he didn't have to dress for work, he was invariably clad in a white doctor's smock over fishing clothes so he could, at a moment's notice, dash off to Fish Lake or to the Nephi River to cast for trout.

Over the phone, Stan liked Tom too. Both had been in the war. Stan's bad eyes had kept him from being "boarded." Stan's wife, Lu, was a Catholic nurse from Philadelphia who needed the company of "Gentiles" as non-Mormons were called in Utah. Himself an apostate "Jack Mormon" who ignored almost every LDS precept, Stan wanted an educated drinking companion almost as much as he needed a medical partner.

Tom wasn't daunted by anything Stan told him on the telephone. About the rigid Mormons who ran the hospital in Meridian where Stan lived and also the smaller hospital in Loah where Stan needed help, Tom said that they couldn't be worse than the "Catholics who run Ottawa's St. Mary's Hospital." About the Utah beet farmers, Tom told Stan they couldn't be worse than the Illinois corn farmers. About Loah's rural isolation, Tom said he liked the idea, though he didn't tell Stan that it was because he doubted there would be any Christian Science Churches nearby.

In two days, Tom, Virginia and David were driving west.

Chapter Eleven

LOAH

*I*n the 1940's, Loah, Utah was a town of 2,753 descendants from the early Mormon polygamist families who, after driving off the Paiute Indians in the 1850's, diverted irrigation water from the Nephi River and transformed the red clay, tumbleweed and sage-brush of southern Moab County into a fertile checkerboard of sugar beet farms. The county seat, Mormon Temple and principal trading center were thirty-five miles to the north in Meridian, which was connected to Loah by State Route 51 and a spur of the Denver & Rio Grande railroad.

People in Loah irrigated crops wearing side arms to protect their water allotments from upstream poachers and treated their seasonal Navajo field hands with indifference. They worshipped at two Mormon churches called "Wards," and cranked their telephones to gossip about Maxine Benson — the town's vamp — and to be overheard by Ruby Nelson — the town's busy-body telephone operator. Suspicious of outsiders, they hardly knew what to make of the new family in town from Illinois or, as they put it, "from the east."

The McQuades were the only Gentiles who had ever lived in Loah. Tom drank and good Mormons didn't. His wife was a social worker and some people thought social workers promoted socialism.   She was, stranger still, a magician who called herself "Madame Fortuno," and who purported to read minds, palms and people. Her skin, hair and eyes were dark and that prompted suspicions about her racial ancestry since, in those days, Negroes were not allowed into the priesthood of the Mormon Church and, thus, were second-class spiritual citizens. When Loahites read about the McQuade family in the town's weekly newspaper, *The Prophet*, they were abuzz.

Tongues wagged even more when, in his first week, Dr. McQuade clashed with the Mayor and the City Council over the "pitiful state of the Loah Municipal Hospital." In forceful terms dismissed by the city fathers as "eastern," Tom demanded an anesthetist, an updated operating room, new x-ray equipment and a "current, complete, constant blood supply." Put off by the new doctor's drinking, weird wife, curious war wound and blunt talk, Loahites continued to drive to Meridian to see Dr. Roberts for their medical care and left Tom with time on his hands to treat an occasional Navajo, operate on county welfare patients, argue with Virginia about "comingtothisprimitivegodforsakenplace," throw back depth charges and call David a "mamma's boy."

The McQuade family's standing in the community started to change at 11:45 p.m. on August 23, 1946, when 17-year-old Levi Smith and a friend were driving back to Loah from Fish Lake in a clangy 1939 pickup. With a mess of trout on ice in the back, the boys were drinking beer in violation of state law, church doctrine and an edict from Levi's father, the influential President of the local Mormon "Stake" or synod. Just before reaching the "U and I" sugar beet refinery on Route 51, Levi Smith rolled down the driver's side window, grabbed an empty beer bottle in his left hand and, aiming at a triangular "DANGEROUS CURVE AND TRUCK CROSSING" sign, tossed it over the top of the pickup and missed. Then, feeling dizzy from the third beer he had ever consumed in his life, Levi turned up the radio and joined Frank Sinatra in singing "Five Minutes More."

Matching Frank Sinatra word for word at 62 miles an hour, the Smith boy negotiated the "DANGEROUS CURVE" mentioned in a triangular road sign but then his headlights illuminated the other hazard that another sign had warned of — "TRUCK CROSS-ING." At that moment, a southbound GMC truck, filled with harvested sugar beets, was turning across the center line and groaning slowly toward the refinery gate, blocking the path of the speeding pickup. Levi hit the brakes, felt the pickup fishtail and heard the screeching sounds of rubber against pavement.

When they crashed head-on into the broadside of the sugar beet truck, Levi's friend flew forward, shattered the windshield and broke his neck against the GMC's side panels. On impact, Levi's sternum slammed into the steering wheel and his head smashed through the windshield.

In minutes, a state trooper arrived and was quickly joined by a Moab County Deputy Sheriff. At the scene, officers found a frantic Navajo truck driver; a helpless gate guard; a '39 Chevrolet pickup crushed like a metallic accordion; thousands of beets strewn across the road; the aroma of gasoline mixed with beer; a young man in a broken clump; and an unconscious, bleeding Levi Smith whose upper torso was jammed against the steering column and whose head was sticking through the front windshield.

The two policemen did not wait for an ambulance. Together, they loaded each victim into their respective patrol cars and raced, with sirens wailing and red lights flashing, to the Loah Municipal Hospital. It was 12:30 a.m. when Tom McQuade got there. Minutes later, the policemen stretchered the two boys into a fluorescently lighted emergency room with its sparse white fixtures and the smell of sterilizing alcohol.

Quickly, Tom McQuade saw that one boy was dead and that the other was bleeding, unconscious, puffy and discolored. With compression, he stopped the bleeding and looked closely at the boy's yellow face and swollen chest. Out in the waiting room, a woman was crying.

On sight, Tom could see that Levi Smith had sustained a pneumothorax but, to confirm the diagnosis, he put on a stethoscope, listened to the boy's chest and heard the sucking sound of air escaping from puncture holes in the lungs, accumulating in the pleural cavity and equalizing the pressure inside and outside the lungs. Knowing that the boy's lungs had collapsed and that little oxygen was reaching his blood stream, Tom inserted an endotracheal tube down the mouth and into the lungs to keep the comatose boy's airway open. Then he grabbed a scalpel, bored holes in each side of the chest and put tubes into the holes for the drainage of blood and the release of air from the pleural cavity.

After coping with the pneumothorax, Dr. McQuade temporarily ignored the boy's concussion and dealt next with the life-threatening fact that the boy was in shock. He had lost blood and his pressure had fallen precipitously. The young man needed a transfusion.

Dr. McQuade turned to a nurse's aide named Stella Benson. "Type the kid's blood immediately."

"But Doctor . . . I . . . I don't know how to type blood. Jean Wells, our R.N., does that and she's up at Fish Lake."

"Well, then, who does know how to type blood around here?," the doctor demanded of all five people in the emergency room. Nobody answered.

Tom ran the implanted chest tubes into bottles of sterile water to prevent air from being sucked back up the tubes. "Don't everyone speak at once." Intimidated, the policemen backed out of the emergency room. "Well?" McQuade asked, looking at two other women in white nylon. Silence.

Finally, Stella murmured, "we don't know how to do that, doctor, but it doesn't make any difference."

"WHAT DO YOU MEAN IT DOESN'T MAKE ANY DIF-FERENCE?," Dr. McQuade exploded. "This kid is going to die if we don't get some blood into him!"

She whispered, "Doctor, our blood supply is down."

"Down? Didn't I explicitly order a complete, fresh blood supply last week?"

"Yes, you did," she looked down at the floor. "But there wasn't any money for the order. I didn't tell you because I didn't want to make you mad."

"Do we have any type 'O'?" he shot back.

"Not really."

"Well, what do we 'really' have, Stella?"

"A few pints of dated AB and A positive. Probably spoiled.

That's all." She was in tears.

At 1:30 in the morning, the telephone rang and Virginia McQuade groped in the dark for the phone. It was her husband in a simmering rage.

"Ginny, I've got one teenager dead and another dying after a car wreck. Right now, the survivor's unconscious and needs blood but this goddamn place is O-U-T."

She tried to say something but he fumed. "This kid can't wait for the bus from Salt Lake to bring some type O down and so I went ahead and typed him myself and he's A negative."

"I'll be there in 10 minutes." Virginia was A negative. "But what about his unconsciousness?"

"It could be bad. The kid's head went through a windshield at high speed. I can't tell if it's a simple concussion or a subdural hematoma."

"Even with my blood, can you save him?"

"With the lousy x-ray machine in this dump, we don't stand a chance of finding out and he's in no shape to be ambulanced up to Salt Lake."

"This is your first big case here, Tom. What are you going to do?"

"The boy's father is a church big-wig," he said. "Maybe the Angel Moroni will descend from Mormon heaven and save him."

Twenty minutes later, Virginia stood in the emergency room with her husband, Stella Benson and Levi Smith's parents. All of them silently listened to a florescent light tube buzz and watched Virginia's blood flow down a plastic tube into the boy's arm.

Quietly, she addressed Levi Smith's parents. "I think we can help him through this." Before Tom could ask what she meant, Virginia turned to the Smiths and said, "My husband is a wonderful doctor. He has done everything he can for your son." She paused. "It's now time for us to do something."

Tom wondered where the hell she was going with this kind of talk. It was past 2:00 in the morning. The boy was grave but stable. What was she saying?

Virginia went on softly. "Through faith, we might be able to help him." Oblivious to anything except the parents and the unconscious young man, Virginia said, "We must pray, touch, bring God's healing grace to your son."

Tom exited the emergency room, strode down the hallway, entered his closet-sized office and flipped on a goose-necked desk lamp. There, he scribbled instructions and filled out another order for blood. "Is Madame Fortuno out of her goddamned mind?" he asked himself out loud.

Moments later, he checked the private room where the boy had been moved and saw that Virginia had already started her "Mary Baker Eddy crap." He huffed out of the hospital and drove home through a moonless night and flailed around in bed and made speeches to himself about Madame Fortuno's quackery.

Meanwhile, Virginia turned off the overhead light, left one floor lamp on and pulled up three chairs beside the boy's bed. In low tones, she told Levi's mother and father, "Prayer is powerful, so please pray. But the problem with prayer," she explained, "is that the intensity of prayer usually lasts only so long as the words are in your mouths and in your heads. Sometimes, words can even obstruct a true communion of healers. But, please, pray and then I have some suggestions."

The three of them prayed together for almost an hour as Brother Monroe Smith repeated every scriptural phrase he could recall from the Book of Mormon, the Doctrine, the Covenants and the New Testament. Finally, after all three had said "amen," Virginia whispered to both parents, "Please hold your son's hands, concentrate on God's healing strength and imagine your son regaining consciousness."

The Smiths looked at each other, puzzled.

Virginia continued: "Don't worry if other thoughts come into your minds. When that happens, just be patient and they'll pass. In the meantime, feel God restoring Levi's consciousness."

Nodding approval, the Smiths followed her lead. For the next four and a half hours, they closed their eyes, bowed their heads and held the boy's hands until streaks of dawn came shafting through the thinly curtained window.

By 6:30 in the morning, Virginia and the Smiths let go of Levi's hands. Quietly, they pushed back from the bed and stood up in silent agreement that their work was finished. When they were about to step into the hallway, they heard a stirring from the bed. They turned and looked. Levi's eyes were open and blinking.

Three days later, *The Prophet* carried a front page article under the headline, "Husband and Wife Team Save Levi Smith," which read:

At 11:30 p.m. on the night of Thursday, August 11, 1946, an accident occurred on the Fish Lake highway in front of the gate at the "U and I" sugar beet refinery. Killed instantly was Gary Alred, 18, of Loah. Seriously injured was Levi Smith, 17, of Loah.

The driver of the sugar beet truck, Ernest Begay, 28, of Tuba City, Arizona, was not hurt. First on the scene was State Patrol Officer Ed Felix who said, "At first, I was sure both boys were dead. Their pickup obviously had run head-on into the side of the loaded sugar beet truck at a high rate of speed with only a few yards of braking." Deputy Sheriff Jordan Green, who arrived minutes later, said, "Levi and Gary both looked like goners to me."

The officers rushed both boys to the Loah Municipal Hospital where Dr. McQuade pronounced Gary Alred dead on arrival and then, as Levi's parents Bishop Monroe and Diane Smith told *The Prophet* later, "Dr. McQuade worked so hard and did everything he could to save our son, including emergency surgery, and we could not have asked anything more from any doctor." The Smiths also said, "Loah is truly blessed to have Dr. McQuade here for our medical needs."

However, Bishop and Mrs. Smith went on to single out Mrs. McQuade for special praise. "Levi would have died had it not been for the donation of blood and miraculous efforts of Mrs. McQuade." As *The Prophet* has learned, Mrs. McQuade gave her own type A negative blood to young Smith. After that, she led the Smiths in prayer and 'spiritual healing.' After four and a half hours of prayer, Levi Smith returned to consciousness and survived.

Brother Smith told our reporter, "Mrs. McQuade is

truly a miracle worker. She doesn't try to override our Mormon faith. Instead, she assists in the most amazing way by bringing the power of God and prayer to heal."

Mrs. McQuade declined to be interviewed for this story but *The Prophet* did speak with Dr. McQuade who explained in detail what happened medically that night. Dr. Mc-Quade emphasized the "crying need" for the mayor and town council to "bring Loah's Municipal Hospital out of the 1920's and into the 1940's."

When asked about the role his wife had played in Levi Smith's recovery, Dr. McQuade acknowledged the critical importance of her A negative blood. As for what happened later when Mrs. McQuade and the parents prayed at Levi's bedside, all Dr. McQuade would say was, "I wasn't there. I had gone home to bed. Patients come spontaneously out of concussions all the time."

Throughout Loah — at the Tip Top Cafe, both LDS Wards, the Moab Merc, Henry's Market, Rexall Drug and Tuesday's Relief Society Meeting — there was talk about Mrs. McQuade and what she and the Smiths had done "with prayer and God's healing power." According to the testimony that Bishop Smith gave the following Sunday at the Second Ward services, "We've had a miracle happen right here. We're thrilled to have Mrs. McQuade in Loah with her husband. Everybody in Moab County should thank God for these two wonderful people."

Overnight, Virginia and Tom McQuade became celebrities. After that, Virginia was in demand not only to help patients whom neither Tom McQuade nor Stan Roberts could cure but also to give benefit magic shows for churches, schools and service clubs. Tom's practice boomed; he had waiting lists of patients; he worked days, nights, weekends and holidays. Nobody seemed to care anymore about his left hand, cocktails, religion and hard-edged, "eastern" personality.

Chapter Twelve

MAXINE BENSON

*B*y the early 1950's, the McQuade family had a new house, two cars, a cottage at Fish Lake, a gardener, a maid, layers of life insurance and accumulating investments. Yet, prosperity didn't stop the depth charges, restore Tom's left hand, or reprise the last night in Morro Bay. To the extent there was intimacy between Tom and Virginia, it was an occasional "missionary sandwich" in which Tom banged away on top and Virginia thought about Jeff Fry on the bottom.

Professionally, Tom chafed at sending complex cases to Salt Lake and seethed whenever Virginia appeared at the hospital to hold patients' hands, get in his way and make it look like he lost lives and she saved them. In his mind, her Madame Fortuno shows reinforced the popular mis-perceptions about her psychic capabilities because, no matter how many disclaimers she made that her ESP act consisted of magic tricks, audiences watched her perform "the impossible" and saw her "commune with spirits" and, not surprisingly, ascribed "powers" to her that she denied at her shows but didn't when she "healed" patients Tom couldn't.

In the fullness of her early thirties, Maxine Benson had the blonde hair, fair skin, soft curves, deep-set cleavage and shapely legs of a pin-up girl and a ribald audacity that, in rural Utah at least, was unheard of in 1954. She was a devoted mother for her twelve-year-old daughter and a fastidious housekeeper for her husband, Del. Yet, she smoked, drank wine, painted nudes, wore skimpy get-ups and slept with every married man she fancied. Last year, a Mormon Bishop's Court had "disfellowshipped" her for "blatant immorality," leaving her unrepentant and amused.

Maxine had grown up as the only girl and the youngest of six children on a vast, prosperous cattle ranch outside Kanab in the southwestern corner of Utah. Her father ran cattle; owned the town's only bank; held a controlling interest in the feed store, general mercantile and power company; was simultaneously the Mayor of Kanab, a County Supervisor and State Senator; and dominated almost everything within 100 miles except for his own headstrong daughter. When he refused to let her attend art school in New York City or enroll at BYU in Provo, she ran off in a retaliatory fury at age eighteen and married Del Benson, a distant relation and Loah sugar beet farmer whom she chose because he was an older, handsome Jack Mormon but mainly because her father considered Del "unsuitable" and, after too many drinks, "unstable."

Del Benson was a rangy, sunbrowned outdoorsman as shy when sober as he was dangerous when drunk. He was something like Maxine's fifth cousin removed by a number of family degrees that LDS genealogists had once determined but that he had never bothered to remember. He bred horses, raised sugar beets and spent time on his ranch fifteen miles outside Loah — "The Lazy M" — with Eva Lighthorse, the 22-year-old, moon-faced daughter of Charles Lighthorse, Del's long-time Navajo foreman who had died three years earlier. During the summer irrigation season when water was diverted from the Nephi River and aqueducted to the thirsty fields of southern Moab County and canalled and culverted to farms and ranches like "The Lazy M," Del and Eva would, during their scheduled irrigation times, slosh together in hip boots, unclog furrows, open and close ditch gates and measure flow rates to check whether any upstream farmers were poaching and whether Del needed to use the Colt .38 pistol he always wore when irrigating.

Del and Maxine lived with their daughter, Judy, just outside

Loah in a red brick house designed by Del and decorated with Maxine's garish nudes and incomprehensible abstracts. Just over two hundred feet of lawns, gardens and a low fence away were the Bensons' only neighbors — Tom, Virginia and David McQuade.

The McQuade home had been built with Nephi River flagstones, Vermont pegwood floors and California redwood and it had been featured in a *Sunset Magazine* article about "hinterland sophistication." For hosting medical meetings, entertaining civic groups and giving Madame Fortuno shows, the McQuade house had, as one of its most prominent features, an expansive family room with curved, floor-to-ceiling windows that overlooked the Benson residence to the east, the outstretched sugar beet fields to the north and the Moab Peaks in the far distance.

After Del left to irrigate in the early evening of June 17, Maxine dropped her daughter off at a friend's house for the night and then, instead of going home, she drove slowly down Main Street under the town's lone, blinking traffic light and into the parking lot of the Loah Hospital next to Dr. McQuade's Chrysler. She knew from Stella Benson, a first cousin of Del's and a talkative nurse's aide, that Dr. McQuade would probably be in his office, alone and exhausted. As Maxine emerged from her blue and white, bullet-nosed Studebaker, she noticed narrow slits of horizontal light coming out from between the venetian blind slattings in Dr. McQuade's office window and she smiled.

During the time that the Bensons and the McQuades had been neighbors and had seen each other pulling in and out of parallel driveways or working outside in the lawns and flowerbeds that separated their houses, there were perfunctory, over-the-fence waves between Tom and Maxine when Del and Virginia were present but extended small talk, double entendres and intriguing eye contact when they weren't. With Maxine's reputation as a tart and Del's reputation as a violent drunk, Virginia insisted that the McQuades keep their social distance from the Bensons and so Tom was always "Doctor McQuade" and Maxine was always "Mrs. Benson." That formality held until the night she crunched her way across the graveled parking lot and headed for the front entrance beneath a humming neon sign that said, in red capital letters, "HOSPITAL."

In dark lipstick, shorts, sandals and a knotted, red polka-dot halter, Maxine pushed open the front door, made her way past an empty waiting room and, after tip-toeing down the main corridor, peeked through the open door and into Dr. McQuade's office. The only illumination was the weak glow from a single-bulb, goose-necked lamp that left the desk enshrouded in shadow and made the cramped office look even smaller than it was.

When her eyes adjusted, Maxine could see the venetian blinds, an Eli Lilly wall calendar, a human skeleton hanging in the corner and an extra chair mounded with medical journals. Slumped over on the desk was a big man, snoring, and on top of the loose papers were a shot glass, a bottle of bourbon, a can of beer and a pack of cigarettes.

"Knock, knock," she said.

Tom McQuade bolted upright, threw his eyes open, turned toward the voice and fumbled to put on his glasses. Once he recognized her, the doctor wobbled to his feet. "Mrs. Benson, I didn't hear you come in."

"I sneaked," she said in a girlish giggle. "Did I wake you?"

"Oh . . . no," he lied, trying to sound alert. "I was just catching up on some paperwork."

"May I come in?"

"Come in? Well, I guess, sure, come in," Dr. McQuade stammered at the sight of a woman who was not exactly dressed for a professional appointment. He stood up, cleared off the other chair, dropped the journals on the floor and squinted at his watch. "My office hours are over . . . unless of course it's an emergency. . . Mrs. Benson."

"Maxine."

"Maxine," he repeated in a weak voice. At a loss for words, Tom sat back down, stared at his visitor and mentally matched the rumors he had heard with the smooth-skinned woman only a few feet away.

She smiled, nestled herself into the empty chair, crossed her well tanned legs and took out a Lucky Strike from Tom's pack lying open on his desk. Saying nothing, Maxine looked to Tom McQuade for a light. On cue, he dug into his right pocket, pulled out a silver

Zippo lighter and reached forward with his right hand, striking the flint wheel with his thumb and igniting a low, wide flame. Maxine touched his right hand lightly, drew deeply on the cigarette and looked straight at the broad-shouldered, slightly drunk doctor.

Exhaling, she broke the brief silence. "We've been neighbors, but we hardly know each other, do we?"

"Maybe . . . well . . . probably not."

"Let me guess," she smiled, "Virginia doesn't want the McQuades and Bensons to get 'too friendly?'"

"I . . . I don't know . . ."

"Tom, your wife reads minds. I read bodies." Maxine paused. "I've been reading your body ever since you came to town."

"Please, Mrs. Benson . . . Maxine . . . I'm a doctor . . . I'm married . . . . So are you . . . to Del."

"Del and I have an arrangement," she said in a business-like voice. "We have Judy and we both love her very much. Del has Eva and the Lazy M. I have my art. And, to put it bluntly, I'd like to have you, too."

Dr. McQuade gulped. "Del has always been so good natured about . . . you and your. . . ?"

"No," came her clipped answer before Tom could find a polite synonym for the word "affairs." Maxine explained, "Before Eva came to live at The Lazy M to take care of her father, Del would sometimes get drunk and go crazy with jealousy." She took a long drag on her cigarette. "One time when he was really soused — this is before you moved here — he threatened to use his .38 on a man who was in my life at the time."

The mention of a ".38" jarred Dr. McQuade. "He was going to *shoot* somebody?"

"He was drunk and that was years ago. Now he has Eva. And the arrangement has worked well for both of us."

Tom swiveled the wooden chair away from her and, for several seconds, gazed at the human skeleton in the shadows. "That 'arrangement' may be fine for you and Del, but I don't think that Virginia would be, how should I put it, a very good sport." He turned back and unclinically studied her body again.

Maxine noticed his sightline. "Let me ask you something,

Tom. When was the last time you and Virginia made real love?" Even though the desk lamp barely illuminated his face, she saw it go flush.

He shifted his weight, glanced at the venetian blinds and, rambling, talked in the abstract about Virginia's religion and about Mary Baker Eddy's well-known aversion to sexual intimacy. Taking those verbal convolutions as proof of virtual celibacy, she whispered, "That's what I thought."

"But —"

She cut him off. "Neither one of us should be living in this God-forsaken town. You aren't Mormon and they've kicked me out. According to Stan Roberts, you're one hell of a surgeon. You ought to be in a big city specialty, not in a two-bit place like this." Tom nodded appreciatively as she went on. "I married Del straight out of high school. He was older, good-looking, on the wild side but loved me. My father, a tough son-of-a-bitch if there ever was one, wouldn't let me go to the Art Students League in New York or to BYU or any place else until I, as he put it, 'calmed down.'"

Tom kept staring and wondering how far all of this would go.

"Maybe I would've been a designer, a model, a real artist," she mused. "For sure, I wouldn't be here with the Bensons, the Mormons, the nothing days and the empty nights.

Tom's experience in matters sexual was surprisingly limited. There had been a few, fast, clumsy encounters in high school, college and medical school but, until Virginia, he never seemed to have enough time, nerve or knowledge to start, let alone maintain, a relationship that would have involved practiced, repetitive love-making. Although Virginia had sent him into sexual outer space in Morro Bay, that turned out to be a one-time event and, ever since the war, she would occasionally let him get it over with and then go straight to sleep. He got her non-verbal, not-so-subtle message and he seethed in a non-verbal, not-so-subtle way about it.

After Tom was married, he had been faithful to Virginia, happily so before getting shipped out and grudgingly so after returning home. Of course there had been opportunities with nurses, lonely wives and even aggressive patients. However, every time he seriously considered an affair, his Scottish Presbyterian guilt kept his zipper in place and his morals intact.

Now, with Maxine at close range, Tom's moral discipline started to dissolve in the potent mixture of bourbon, beer, hormones, fatigue, spousal anger and sexual desolation. "Well, Virginia probably has supper on the table," he said with a preemptory gust.

"No she doesn't." Maxine contradicted him. "Virginia's at her bridge club tonight in Meridian with Lu Roberts and David is at Mike Eastman's birthday party at Fish Lake."

Tom McQuade felt a racing in his chest and a bulging in his groin. Again, he swung away from Maxine and toward the hanging skeleton whose days of moral dilemma were long gone.

"On the other hand," she purred, "I happen to have a steak dinner for two almost ready at my house. In fact, the burgundy is already poured."

Anticipating his next question, she blocked the doctor's escape. "Judy is at a slumber party and this is Del's night for irrigating at the ranch. He's with Eva and won't be home until tomorrow morning."

Maxine twisted out her cigarette and slinked up to her feet. "What could be wrong with two neighbors having dinner together?" She moved fluidly through the doorway using the same girlish giggle for her exit as she had for her entrance. "See you in a minute."

Tom heard the front hospital door bang shut and then her Studebaker start up and back out. His moral strength didn't stand a chance against the glandular secretions coursing through his body that turned his member to steel and that drove him to Maxine's that night.

What Maxine did in Loah was even more spectacular than what Virginia had done in Morro Bay. In their frequent encounters, Maxine was producer, director and star in a carnal production that exceeded his wildest mind movie. Her mandated location was the Bensons' guest room and she was in charge of every position, sequence and detail. The overhead light had to be off. A red night light had to be on. The curtains had to be open. The hi-fi had to be playing Louie Armstrong's renditions of "I Get Ideas" and "A Kiss

91

To Build A Dream On."

Tom's job was to lie back; calm his urgencies; watch her move, kiss, stroke and caress. Most importantly, he had to maintain a running commentary on how alluring and sexy she was with an occasional update on how close he was to coming. Between trysts, Tom wondered about himself and why sex was best when a woman — first Virginia and now Maxine — was in charge and speculated that maybe it was because of LaRoux's early death but then junked the idea as being too psychiatric.

At first, Tom's biggest concern was about being spotted from the sweeping windows of the McQuade family room which were only two hundred feet away. However, as Maxine explained, the night light had no more candle power than a Christmas tree bulb and the sense of danger would enhance their ecstasy. She had done this sort of thing in her guest room for years and no member of the McQuade family, Tom included, had ever spotted her in the act.

As the summer days passed and their assignations multiplied, Tom forgot all about the night light, open curtains and risk of discovery and started worrying about Maxine's demands that he keep his commentary about her "fresh," "new" and "exciting." "You've said that before," she'd complain. "Can't you talk as good as I can make love,?" she'd ask with growing impatience.

The truth was that he had run out of synonyms for goddess and enchantress. He had exhausted his knowledge of movie stars like Marilyn Monroe and Jane Russell. His supply of historical temptresses had never exceeded Cleopatra and Delilah. Besides, he was a doctor, not a poet who could invent new ways of describing sexual intercourse beyond the biological "copulating," the metaphorical "screwing," or the vulgar "fucking."

By early August, Maxine was bored with Tom's repetitious banalities and started talking about a "back-to-school-break" so they could each "see" other people. Tom didn't want to "see" anybody else and, as the days grew shorter, he began spending lunch hours at the Southern Moab County Library, poring over encyclopedias, movie reviews and dictionaries in search of names, descriptives and superlatives that would satisfy her narcissistic cravings and keep their rendezvous going.

Chapter Thirteen

THE MAGIC SHOW

*I*n conservative, overwhelmingly white Salt Lake City, Black people stood out as did anyone whose attire was flashy or suggestive. Consequently, it wasn't surprising that the center of attention at the Salt Lake Trailways Bus Terminal was a middle-aged Negro woman wearing a tight, Zebra-skin outfit that exposed almost enough to get arrested in Utah. Lifted here and hidden there, Wanda advertised a body that at one time wouldn't quit but now, though still voluptuous, was on the verge of going out of business.

Ignoring the gawkers, Wanda had her arm around a sobbing Virginia McQuade. "Honey," she said in a soothing voice. "When we said goodbye at the prison, I should have told you the rest of Wanda's Rules. Do you want to hear them now?"

Virginia nodded, crying.

"Here goes," said Wanda. "Leave 'em if they're cheatin'. How's that sound?"

Virginia shook her head in the negative and Wanda started to argue with her but stopped and delivered another rule. "If ya' can't leave 'em, then get 'em."

Virginia wiped her eyes and looked at Wanda. "What does that mean?"

"Anything that hurts the bastard bad."

"How?"

"One way is to take after him with a frying pan. Another is to screw another man." Wanda thought for a second and said, "With this big-shot-big-shit doctor of yours, I think public humiliation would hurt the worst."

"How could I do that?"

"You still have the book I gave you as a going away present at the prison?"

Virginia thought out loud. "I used it all the time in Syracuse and the last time I read it was when Tom got back from the war and I needed wiring instructions to vanish a small railroad station and illuminate a huge welcome home sign. But I haven't seen it in ages and it may be in Illinois but I don't know where. Why do you ask?"

Wanda smiled. "As soon as I get settled in Las Vegas, I'll dig out a copy and mail it to you with some suggestions of my own. You'll see."

"Wanda, don't send it to me at my home in Loah. Sent it to me in care of this address." She gave Wanda a card with the address of the only Christian Science Church in Salt Lake City on it. She added, "make it to the attention of Jeff Fry."

Wanda looked at her watch. "It's almost three o'clock and that's when you're supposed to get your son at, what'd ya' call it?"

"ZCMI. It's a church-owned department store and David's there casing out some magic tricks they advertised in the paper last week. But I can't just leave you here alone."

Wanda hooted. "My bus for Vegas doesn't leave for two hours. Who knows, maybe I can turn a trick here. Never had a Mormon John before."

They stood, looked straight into each others' eyes and then embraced, holding each other tightly. As Virginia was walking out the door, she looked back and saw Wanda sidling up to the well-dressed man who had had his eyes glued on her the whole time the two women had been talking.

In Loah, people still speak of that summer of heat, drought, wind, tumbleweeds, and stillborn sugar beets. In June and July, records were broken for consecutive days without rain and for scorching temperatures without relief. When the earth hardened, cracked and dusted, *The Prophet* announced that, "Every LDS ward in Moab County will, on August 5, conduct prayer meetings for rain." When the prayers failed, *The Prophet* carried another front-page story about the Moab County Extension Service having hired a barnstormer to seed the clouds with dry ice. The seeding didn't work any better than the prayers; the Nephi River was now a mossy, meandering creek; and the talk was about foreclosure, bankruptcy and ruin.

Two days after the unsuccessful barnstormer flew off and left Loah's hopes lower than the dry ground, Virginia sent out elegantly printed invitations to a select group of townspeople and their wives for a "Las Vegas Magic Show" that she would present in the McQuade's family room. Among the invited were both LDS Bishops, the editor of *The Prophet,* the high school principal, mayor, city councilmen, druggist, Lu and Stan Roberts and several leading ranchers who would not be irrigating their trickled allotments that August night.

She did not tell Tom about the event. If true to form, Tom would work late, drink and fall asleep at the hospital. Also, the Bensons weren't invited because Virginia despised Maxine and because Del was scheduled to join Eva that night to irrigate what little water there might be available.

In her invitations, Virginia asked what normally would have been the impossible: "This show is a secret. You are *not* to tell anyone else anything about it and you are also instructed to *walk in silence, not drive*, to the McQuade residence." In return for their compliance, she offered this powerful incentive: "Madame Fortuno will make a prediction whether rains will come to Moab County; however, if anyone breaches the instructions specified in this invitation, then there will be *no chance* for a favorable prediction." With their crops, farms and livelihoods at risk, the guests miraculously maintained silence and walked as instructed to the McQuade residence after dark on August 13. Even Ruby, the town's eavesdropping telephone operator, did not know about the event.

The guests assembled and sat in concentric semi-circles, facing the heavy, black-out curtains that hid the curved, floor-to-ceiling windows and that constituted the theatrical backdrop for Madame Fortuno's floor show. Chatty country women wore cotton print dresses, white high-heeled shoes and orlon sweaters over blouses with Peter Pan collars. Their well-scrubbed men came in dress-up cowboy boots, tan jackets, bolo ties and western shirts with mother-of-pearl buttons. Despite the waterless summer, the atmosphere was convivial.

The first half of the program was a Houdini Seance in which Virginia, wearing her Gypsy costume, invoked the "spirits" to write on slates, move furniture, float tables and illuminate a crystal ball that answered "yes" or "no" to questions from the audience. Eventually, Bishop Smith asked the question they had all come to hear the spirits' answer: would the drought end soon?" Everyone held their breaths until, after a long wait, the "spirits" lighted the crystal ball once, signifying that the answer was "yes." The crowd cheered and clapped at the prophecy.

After intermission, Dave put on a 78 rpm record of Jimmy Dorsey's "So Rare" and Virginia started the second half of the show, not as a Gypsy this time, but as a "mental magician" in top hat and a black, sequined, full-length gown. Using oversized pads of paper and colored pens, Virginia duplicated designs spectators had thought of, revealed a prediction she had written down and mailed to the mayor two weeks earlier about the headlines for that day's *Prophet* and she even projected her own thoughts — a triangle within a circle and the number 35 — into the minds of the audience.

While most of the audience had their hands up to acknowledge that the number 35 had come into the minds, she glanced toward the kitchen doorway where David stood with a small book in his hand, nodding in the affirmative to his mother. Immediately, Virginia launched into her peroration: "As some of you know, I performed last April at The American Medical Association Convention in Las Vegas and learned something there about Sodom and Gomorrah." The audience laughed. They knew what went on in Las Vegas and it wasn't anything the Mormon Church approved of.

Virginia's voice rose in a slow crescendo. Her long, red fingernails and jeweled fingers flowed with the words and her gown sparkled randomly from the spotlight at the back of the family room. "Tonight, I've performed the same feats that I did in Las Vegas. However, in my presentations there and here so far, I have left out two sizzling elements that are necessary before any show can truly qualify as 'Las Vegas Style Entertainment.'" Guests exchanged puzzled glances.

"Ladies and gentlemen," her voice trembled. "I now give you those two elements and when I pull back the curtains, watch for ...SEX AND NUDITY!" Virginia swept back the drapes as Dave pushed down a set of levers that switched off the lights in the McQuade family room and sent electronic signals through multiple wires running out the kitchen window, into the back yard, under the fence, across the lawns and into and along the side of the Benson house.

When the McQuade family room went dark, ten sulphur flares exploded outside in the night sky and 32 firepots burned brilliantly in parallel rows running from the McQuade house to the Benson house. Simultaneously, a recently installed 400 watt overhead light bulb flashed on in the Benson's guest room and the audience gasped when they saw, on a brilliantly illuminated bed, a naked Maxine Benson astride an equally naked Tom McQuade.

Just past midnight when the people of Loah were still jabbering on their party lines about what had gone on at the McQuade and Benson houses, the first of many thunderstorms hit southern Moab County. For the next four days, the rain pounded the parched earth; the Nephi River swelled; the irrigation ditches ran bank-to-bank; and the shriveled sugar beets sprang to life. On Friday, *The Prophet's* headline read:

"MADAME FORTUNO'S MAGIC RAIN."

Chapter Fourteen

THE TRIAL CHRISTMAS

*B*y the time David McQuade was thirteen, he already had it made. At least that was the perception in Moab County. His father was a doctor and his mother was a healer, a seer and, best of all, a rainmaker. The McQuade family had a big house in Loah, a cottage at Fish Lake, two cars and lots of money. David was a member of every honor roll, the best athlete on every team, an accomplished magician like his mother and the envy of his peers. Yet, he had no buddies, no pals, no girlfriends. He declined every nomination for class office and avoided every party. For months at a time, he lived in dark isolation where there was no time for fun, no margin for error and no license to goof off.

Tom had assured Virginia that their son's melancholia was "just a phase." Not content with that horseback diagnosis, Virginia ignored Tom's objections and overcame her own religious principles and took David to see a child psychiatrist in Salt Lake. As the psychiatrist described it, different teenagers handle puberty differently and David's way — shutting down emotionally while relentlessly pursuing perfection — was unusual but there was no immediate cause for alarm "unless he becomes suicidal." "Does that mean," she asked, "that my son has to kill himself or come dangerously close before I get alarmed?" The psychiatrist answered her question with a shrug, leaving her to do what she had always done when

David buried himself in himself — take him to see the slapstick movies of The Three Stooges, Abbott and Costello and Martin and Lewis playing anywhere in Moab County.

In those days, nobody would have thought him "depressed" because, to the extent that term was used at all, it applied to motionless shut-ins, and David was always in motion. From the moment he woke up in the morning until the moment he fell asleep at night, David worked non-stop to follow his father's rules to "never back down," "win," "don't cry," "get A's," and the all-purpose "be a man." In pursuit of those impossibilities, David's energy was radioactive.

In addition, David had three rules of his own. The first was to avoid Dr. McQuade as much as possible. The second was avoid him for sure after a patient's death, a depth charge, a Madame Fortuno show or one of his mother's faith healing sessions. The third rule was, if Dr. McQuade absolutely couldn't be avoided, then at least never eat dinner with him because that's when he conducted quizzes and punished wrong answers.

To David's relief, the magic show had revolutionized his world because, in a rage, Tom had moved out of the Loah house and into the family's cottage at Fish Lake and, in the process, lost Maxine's affections to the new high school English teacher. With his father gone, David was liberated from rules, pressures, quizzes, perfection, winning and not losing. In time, he didn't mind getting "Bs" and "Cs" or missing the winning basket; he could sleep through the night without sweats; and, on weekends when his mother regularly went to Salt Lake for worship and study at Utah's only Christian Science Church, David would go fishing with Stan Roberts.

However, on the evening of December 21, 1954, David's paradise was in jeopardy. Two days earlier, Stan had summoned Tom and Virginia to Meridian for what he called the "Moab County Panmunjom Peace Conference," so named for the village where the Korean War had recently ended in a fragile truce. At the Moab County Peace Conference, two McQuades agreed that Tom would move back into the Loah house on the evening of December 21; they would share a "Trial Christmas;" the family would dine together for the first time since the August magic show; Tom wouldn't drink any depth charges; Virginia wouldn't mention Maxine, and Tom would not bring up the August magic show. The third McQuade wasn't asked for his opinion.

When Tom, Virginia and David sat down for dinner on the night of December 21, the air in the dining room was heavy with what had happened in the past and even heavier with what might happen at any moment. Tom sat at the head of the long, ironwood table. Virginia stationed herself at the other end where she passed out dishes of potatoes, peas, roast beef and home-made bread. David sat to his father's right and to his mother's left and stared, wordless and frozen-faced, into a row of red centerpiece candles that gave the dining room its only light.

At first, the talk was small and came out in safe questions. How was Virginia's mother doing now that her father had been dead for years? Had Stan gotten his deer yet? Heard anything from Syd? How's school been? Will Loah reach the state tournament? Ever get the heater fixed at the lake place? Is the roast beef done right? Hasn't Eisenhower been a good President? Cautiously, Tom and Virginia tiptoed their way through dinner as David sat there, eating, staring into the small flames and looking forward to dessert and an early exit.

Although depth charges had been banned by agreement for the "Trial Christmas," wine with dinner had been accepted as a compromise. No limits had been set on the wine, however, and, by his fourth glass, Tom's dikes of self-control started to leak. "I don't want to get into a discussion of the magic show last August," Tom said frowning, "because we agreed that we wouldn't talk about it." Virginia and David both stiffened. Tom went on. "But I do have a question, not about that show or that night mind you, but about your entertainment policies, Ginny." Tom poured himself more wine. "I thought that you told me the very first time we ever talked — back in Syracuse when I hired you for The Colonic — that you *never* used your Madame Fortuno shows to hurt or embarrass anybody. Isn't that what you said?"

"Tom, your 'question' directly relates to the show last August. You and I and Stan all agreed, explicitly, that *you* wouldn't talk about that show and I wouldn't talk about that whore."

101

Tom knotted his napkin, dropped the subject but then turned to a topic that had not been discussed at the Moab Panmunjom negotiations. "Well, Dave, it's been a long time since we've had one of our suppertime quizzes hasn't it?" Dave's mouth turned to cotton.

"So, Dave, who is the Secretary of Agriculture? I'll give you two hints, he's a Mormon and he's from Utah."

Ripping his dry tongue from the roof of his even drier mouth, David whispered, "Ezra Taft Benson."

"Right you are," Tom said, smiling at Virginia as if this were a game they all enjoyed. "Smart son we've got, huh mom?" Virginia glowered.

Tom reached out and picked up a bottle of his favorite steak sauce. "How do you spell Worcestershire, Dave?"

Self-conscious about the sticking sounds coming from his arid mouth, David slowly spelled, "W-O-R-C-E-S-T-E-R-S-H-I-R-E."

"That's right! What's the capital of South Dakota?"

"Pierre."

"Damn, you're good. Now, how about a little arithmetic?"

Virginia interrupted, trying to sound conciliatory. "Tom, please, I think we've had enough quiz fun for tonight. Why don't you and I have dessert and let Dave go do his homework. Tomorrow's his last day of school before the Christmas holidays." She rose and, picking up the dishes with a loud clatter, asked David to help her clear the table.

Just as David started to stand up, Tom reached out and held his son's right arm on the table and thus the boy's body in the chair. "Just one more question, all right, Dave?" David looked straight into the flames. "Multiply 838 by 7."

"Dad, can I use a pencil and paper?"

"No, son, let's do it the way I do it and the way it ought to be done — in your head and under a minute." Tom lapsed into a refrain David had heard many times before: "If I ran the schools, I'd teach kids to use their heads and I'd also ban all erasures because mistakes wouldn't be allowed." Back into his role as quizmaster, Tom looked down at his wristwatch and started counting off the seconds.

Unable to do multi-digit multiplication in his head or hold a full supper in his stomach, David felt his mouth flood with saliva, his throat tighten and his stomach cramp. Then, turning toward his father for the first time all night, David suddenly retched and heaved a wide stream of warm, lumpy vomitus all over his father.

"Jesus H. Christ!" Tom McQuade leaped to his feet; shook off chunks of undigested roast beef, peas, salad and potatoes; curled his lips; and unbuckled his belt. "That was intentional wasn't it?"

Knowing what was next, Dave bolted from the table; sprinted outside into the December night; ran down the snow-packed streets and ducked into a farmer's storage shed two blocks away. For over an hour, David hid there, shivering, until he heard his mother calling from the road. "It's all right, now, Dave . . . We've called Stan . . . Your father's asleep . . . Come back . . . Please . . . Get inside . . . You'll freeze to death!"

Chapter Fifteen

THE RIGHT LEG

*A*t 7:00 a.m. the next morning, the alarm went off in David's bedroom and he awoke to an unheated darkness and the sounds of his parents arguing in the kitchen. He was hot, sweaty, washed out, his neck was rigidly stiff and his head felt as if a hatpin had been driven through his forehead and into the center of his brain. Slowly, he sat up and swung his legs over the side of the bed and, hesitating for a moment because of sudden dizziness, dropped into his customary free fall. When his feet hit the cold, green-patterned linoleum, a burst of high voltage pain shot through the entire length of his right leg which buckled and sent him crashing face-first against the night stand and into a tangled heap next to his dresser.

When he hit the floor, he cried out but, remembering his father's "no cry" rule, swallowed back the tears. His nose was bleeding from having collided with the night stand but, at first, he didn't notice. All he could think about was getting off to the last day of school before Christmas break while Tom was preoccupied arguing with Virginia.

In a hurry to avoid his father, David pulled his legs underneath him, pushed up but, again, his right leg exploded with fire and he fell back onto the linoleum. Instead of moving as he conscious-ly directed, his right leg had become an immobilized dead-weight, one with live nerves that, against the slightest pressure, ignited bolts of shooting excruciation. Something was wrong, very wrong and, as much as he wanted to avoid his father, David gritted his teeth and, dragging his right leg and dripping blood from his nose at the same time, crawled on his hands and one knee out of his bedroom, through a half bathroom and into the den where Tom always parked his black doctor's bag and where his father would pass on his way to the garage and then to the hospital. On the den floor, David pinched his nose to stop the flow of blood and heard his father's clomping approach.

When Tom McQuade entered the den, he stopped, looked at his son and barked, "What in the hell are you doing down there?"

"I can't walk, dad. My right leg's on fire whenever I put any weight on it." David lost his composure and started sputtering blood and tears down the front of his pajamas.

Tom McQuade shook his head at the sight of his thirteen-year-old son lying on the floor with a simple nosebleed, crying and acting like a helpless baby. With a jerk, Tom grabbed his doctor's bag. "How in the hell am I ever going to make a man out of you? Stop the damn tears, plug the damn nose, quit the damn malinger-ing, get on your damn feet and get off to the damn school!" Tom stormed out the door.

Four and a half hours later, Stan Roberts was at Dave's bed-side, taking his temperature, listening through a stethoscope, testing leg reflexes with a rubber mallet and trying to take a history from a boy who, by this time, could barely talk or keep his eyes open. "It's polio," he told a grim-faced Virginia.

"Oh, no."

"Dave's got the classic symptoms: a severe headache; stiff neck; drenching perspiration; fever of over 102°; elevated pulse, extreme drowsiness, and one limb that's paralyzed."

"But it's winter. Polio's a summer disease."

"It comes mostly in the summer, you're right. But infantile paralysis can strike at any time."

Stan eased himself off the bed and stepped out into the hallway, his left hand carrying his doctor's bag and his right hand guiding Virginia toward the living room. "Only his right leg is paralyzed so Dave's probably got spinal polio, which is asymmetrical and attacks just one side of the body at a time."

"That's not the worst kind, then?"

"No, he's not having any trouble breathing and there doesn't appear to be any respiratory dysfunction. Consequently, he probably doesn't have either the bulbar or the encephalitic forms that attack not just the spinal cord but also the brain. In extreme cases, bulbar can kill a kid in a day or two. If it doesn't kill the patient, the bulbar and encephalitic forms can put victims into iron lungs and leave them on crutches or in wheelchairs for life."

"Oh, Stan." She started to cry.

"I don't think Dave's got either the bulbar or encephalitic. *Please* hear me."

"Will he ever walk again?"

"Probably. We'll know in about three months, at most. The odds are in Dave's favor."

She broke down, leaning into his shoulder and wept. He embraced her and, in a soothing tone, started to lay out the treatment. "The first thing we do is to get some antibiotics into him because, even if the polio doesn't get him, pneumonia might. Right now, he's extremely vulnerable to secondary infections. There's a new drug out called Aureomycin. We'll use it."

"What about the paralysis?" she sniffled.

"We used to immobilize kids' limbs in casts and splints but we don't do that anymore. Instead, we use the Sister Kenny method, named for an Australian nurse you probably read about last month in *Life Magazine*. Boston Children's Hospital has done the most with her technique and it's probably the best place in the country for kids like Dave and the assistant chief of surgery was in my army medical unit and I'll call him right away."

Virginia backed out of his arms and wiped her eyes with a tissue. "I've heard of Sister Kenny, but I don't know her treatment."

"It's painful as hell." Stan Roberts turned her in the direction of an easy chair. "It consists of heat, manipulation and physical therapy but the toughest part is the heat. The hotter the better:

hot baths, hot packs, hot pads, hot water bottles. It seems to work. During the heat phase, patients get salt tablets, aspirin, skin balms, fluids, foot support and sometimes manipulation but you need to know that there's a lot of burning and pain."

When they reached the chair, she resisted and remained standing. "I can't let Davey burn."

"There isn't any other way."

She held a handkerchief to her mouth, thought for a time and said with conviction, "You're wrong, Stan."

Dr. Roberts glanced down at the floor and then up at her. "If you're thinking what I think you're thinking, then *please* don't think any more about it. Dave's damned sick. He could be crippled for life or even die. This is no time for risks."

"Stan, there *is* another way."

"Go ahead and pray all you want but, in the name of God, don't do it as a substitute for medical treatment. David's sick as hell!"

"Thank you for coming," she said in a confident tone, abruptly pulling herself together. "You're wonderful to have driven down here. I think we can do something for Davey, as you say, 'in the name of God.'"

Stan Roberts frowned, put on his overcoat and opened the front door. Before stepping out into the cold, he turned and said, "We'll take care of your son, Ginny. We'll get him the best treatment in the world, first here in quarantine and then at Boston Childrens. In the meantime, I'll go down to the Loah Hospital and inform that son-of-a-bitch husband of yours what he walked out on this morning."

Less than thirty minutes later, Tom McQuade burst into the house with Jean Wells, the town's registered nurse following on his heels. An ambulance waited out front. Mute and stone-faced, Virginia stood at Dave's bedside while Tom performed the same examination that Stan had done earlier. In the end, Tom muttered, "Stan's right, it's spinal polio."

"As far as I'm concerned, you've forfeited your moral and medical right to treat Dave." Her words came out like hot bullets.

"I know you're angry and you've got a right to be; but we've got to come together and get Dave through this."

Her face froze.

"Look, I'm sorry about this morning," Tom shrugged. "I thought all he had was a nosebleed and that he was trying to parlay it into an extra day of Christmas vacation. I was wrong, wrong, wrong and I feel terrible about it." Then, as if in atonement, he quickly added, "I've made arrangements at the hospital for a private room and I've asked the best infectious disease man in the state to come down from Salt Lake and examine Dave tomorrow. Stan has already called Boston Children's and they have room for him. Stan'll make the arrangements to fly him there following the quarantine."

"After the way you drove Dave out in the freezing cold without a coat and in fear of his life last night, it's no wonder he's sick!"

"What are you saying?"

"What I am saying, Doctor McQuade, is simply this: leave my son alone! I'll take care of him myself." There was steel in her voice.

"If you're thinking about praying for Dave instead of treating him, you're nuts! Besides, you gave me your word, ages ago in Morro Bay, that you'd get him medical treatment, not gospel gobbledegook if he ever got sick." Jean Wells retreated from the battle scene.

"The deal's off, Doctor McQuade. I've already called an old friend to come down from Salt Lake to heal Dave."

"Who's the 'old friend'?" Tom put his stethoscope into his bag.

"Well, if you *must* know, his name's Jeff Fry."

"Fry? Fry? Wait a minute . . . well . . . I'll be goddamned." Tom's neck bulged. "Is that your old boyfriend? The Naval Academy guy?"

"He's a dear friend."

Tom's face darkened. "Oh, he's 'dear,' is he? And he's in Salt Lake? Well, that explains what the hell you've been doing up there every weekend since August."

"After sleeping with that whore, Maxine, you've got no right to criticize me about anything! The fact is Jeff loves me and he always has!"

Beneath his parents' verbal assaults, Dave lay in bed, half asleep, burning up. "Wanna Coke or something." His parents didn't hear him.

"Well, how's this Fry guy gonna make Dave well?"

"He's a certified Christian Science Practitioner, the best."

"He's a goddamned what?" Tom's face turned crimson.

"You heard me. In fact, I told you that in Syracuse before we were married. Now, go, leave us be."

"Wait a minute, Fortuno. It's bad enough that you've humiliated me by praying with my patients and putting on that goddamned magic show in front of the whole town. But you and this Fry character aren't going to kill my son."

"We have no intention of 'killing' your son, Dr. McQuade. Stan told me about the Sister Kenny treatment and about the burning that Dave will suffer if you put him in the hospital." She stared straight at him. "Christian Science cured my mom. Jeff's done miracles. He and I are going to take care of Dave our way."

A voice from the bed came again. "Wanna Coke." This time, she heard him.

"I'll get you one, Davey." She strode out of the bedroom, into the hall and toward the kitchen.

Tom followed her down the pegwood corridor. "You're going to kill our boy, Ginny." When she ignored him and silently went about getting a Coke from the refrigerator, he marched out of the house and slammed the front door, leaving the entryway chandelier swaying and tinkling in his wake.

Ten hours later, at 12:30 in the morning, Tom pulled up in front of the McQuade residence. There was a glow coming through the drapes in his son's bedroom. He turned off the ignition and saw, through the rear view mirror, two cars as well as an ambulance come to a stop behind his. In seconds, their headlights went dark and four figures stepped out into the cold night. Following Tom, they crunched their way through the snow to the front door.

Quietly, Tom unlocked the front door and, as the four of them made their way down the hall toward David's bedroom, Virginia called out, "Is someone there?"

"It's me," Tom said as he, Stan, Lu, Jean Wells, and a paunchy Moab County Deputy Sheriff walked into his son's bedroom. Virginia was seated on the bed, holding the hand of her son who now had a 104° fever. Five feet away, beneath a poster of Harry Houdini and "The Devil's Death Chamber" sat a tall, ascetic, white-haired man who had the Bible in his lap opened to Matthew 9:1-5.

The deputy sheriff bellied his way to the front of the group. "You Mrs. McQuade?"

Virginia nodded.

"You Jeff Fry?"

"Yes, sir, I am."

"I'm serving you both with this restraining order signed a few hours ago by Judge Moeller in Meridian." He handed each of them a sheaf of papers. "I'm here for the boy and an ambulance's outside." He pointed to her son, lying asleep.

Virginia glanced down at the legal-sized papers. "Officer, I want to know what's going on."

"Ma'am, the Judge appointed the doc here to be the boy's guardian. It orders you and Mr. Fry not to interfere and it also instructs me to have the boy ambulanced over to the Loah Hospital for quarantine and for the treatment of infantile paralysis. Nurse Wells'll do the driving."

Jeff Fry stood up, straightening himself into a Naval Academy posture. "Ginny, let me handle this. We face this kind of thing all the time."

Tom jumped out in front of the deputy and, with even more heft and determination than he had used at the Treasure Island Officers' Club, threw a roundhouse right fist against Fry's lower jaw and sent the Christian Science Practitioner backpeddling and falling into a cabinet filled with model airplanes and magic tricks and then onto the floor. Immediately, the deputy bear-hugged Tom. Virginia dropped down to Jeff Fry.

Lu cried out, "May the saints preserve us."

Stan pushed his way through the confusion to David's bedside. In addition to polio, the boy now had pneumonia.

Chapter Sixteen

TREATMENT

*D*avid's court-appointed guardian was, as the deputy sheriff had put it, "the doc." But "the doc" in this case wasn't Doctor McQuade, it was Doctor Roberts. When Stan, Tom, two lawyers and a sheriff's deputy had approached Moab Superior Court Judge Moeller earlier that night for the appointment of a guardian and the issuance of an *ex parte* temporary restraining order, it was in Judge Moeller's living room in Meridian while his wife and children were washing dishes in the adjoining kitchen after a late supper.

In his Can't-Bust-Em' overalls and red plaid shirt rolled up to expose the white sleeves of a long-john-looking religious undergarment, the tall, white-haired, craggy-faced judge looked more like a sugar beet farmer than Moab County's lone jurist whose decisions were seldom questioned and rarely appealed. Over the clatter from the kitchen, Judge Moeller bade his visitors to enter.

The two lawyers — one hired by Stan to represent the guardian he wanted the court to appoint and other paid for by the county to represent David's interests as the ward — described David's medical condition, what was happening at the McQuade residence and how state law required new polio patients to be placed into a hospital for quarantine and treatment. Next, Judge Moeller listened as Stan, under oath, told of David's having been left on the floor by his father in the morning and having been refused medical care by his mother in the evening.

The judge pushed himself back into the cushions of his easy chair, pondered what he had just heard and then exploded. In a hell-fire-and-brimstone voice, he scorched Tom McQuade in person and damned Virginia *in absentia*. When he "GRANTED" the guardian-ship, he designated "Dr. Roberts, NOT Dr. McQuade and NOT Mrs. McQuade," to act as David's guardian. Emptying himself of fury, he went on to rule that, "This Court finds that the behavior of both biological parents has been shameful and has been inimical to the best interests of their son and the Court will, in due course, make a decision about the possible severance of their parental rights. The Court will follow the recommendations of Dr. Roberts, who is one of the most respected citizens in Moab County."

Immediately after leaving the Judge's residence, Stan exercised his authority as David's guardian *ad litem*. He directed the deputy to call Jean Wells and have her meet them at the McQuade residence with an ambulance. He picked up Lu and, with Tom and the deputy sheriff in separate cars, the three cars caravaned to Loah.

Once the papers had been served and Tom had slugged Jeff Fry and Jean Wells had transported David to the Loah Hospital, Stan summoned Tom, Lu and Virginia into the leadened quiet of the hospital x-ray room. It was past 3:00 a.m. The four sat in an exhausted circle and Stan, voice trembling, spoke. "I have known Judge Moeller my whole life," Stan began his monologue. "I don't think I've seen him more goddamned mad than he was tonight when he heard what happened to David today, or was it yesterday? But the judge can't be any more furious than I am. You're our closest friends and Dave is like a son to Lu and me."

Virginia dropped her face in her palms. Tom stared blankly at nothing in particular.

At that point, Stan blasted both of them. "I thought we had a deal at our Moab County Panmunjon Conference for a Trial Christmas that would work. Tom, you screwed up with the wine, the quiz and the belt and then you did something that I still can't believe any father or doctor would do: you . . .walked . . . out . . . on . . . your . . . own . . . paralyzed . . . son . . . and left him lying on the floor, unexamined, undiagnosed and untreated!"

Tom nodded in guilty assent.

"Then you, Ginny," Stan growled, "ignored what I explicitly told you about Dave's perilous condition and called in that pointy-headed preacher from Salt Lake while your son's life was at stake. I won't mince words: Dave would surely have died from pneumonia if we hadn't shown up tonight and gotten some antibiotics into him. How could you, a mother, do such a thing?"

Her face still cupped in both hands, Virginia sobbed.

"So, here's what we're gonna do and if I get any crap out of either one of you, I'll call Judge Moeller and tell him to sever your parental rights. He'll do it in a flash and you'll never see Dave again!"

Stan slowed his words and lowered his voice. "I'll be the attending physician and I'll get the best specialists down here from Salt Lake. Tom, you'll cover the night shift with Jean Wells as nurse. Ginny you'll do the day shift with Lu as nurse and me in charge. Any questions?" Nobody said anything. "Dave's gonna stay here in Loah for the quarantine period that, by law, will last at least two weeks."

Stan continued. "Tom, you'll move back up to the lake place. Ginny, you'll live in the Loah house and, if you want to pray and quote Mrs. Eddy, go ahead. But," he paused for emphasis, "I want your complete support for Dave's medical treatment and I'll have that Fry guy arrested if he shows his face in this County again. Are you with me?"

"Yes," came her tired answer.

"The best place in the world for Dave is Boston Children's Hospital. As you guys know from having lived there, it's right next to Harvard Medical School and, as I tried to tell you, Ginny, but you wouldn't listen, they've had fantastic results with kids like Dave using the Sister Kenny method. I'll make the arrangements to fly him there after the quarantine and I want both of you to go with him. In Boston, you do the same thing: Ginny, you'll do days and Tom'll do nights. Ginny, you can stay with the sister Tom hates but keep her the hell away from him. Tom, you can stay at the Copley Plaza Hotel. It's not far away. Do I hear any dissent?" There was none.

113

"Good. We'll know in a day or so if Dave's gonna get past the pneumonia and I think he will. Once he's in Boston, it'll take some weeks to see if he'll be able to walk again and I'm betting on Dave. When he takes that first step, you'll have to come back here, Tom, because I need help covering this hospital. Ginny, you'll stay in Boston until Dave's discharged and he becomes an outpatient. At that point, he can stay with your sister and you'll come back here, pack up your things and move back east."

Stan rubbed his eyes and continued. "When Dave's well and you two are permanently separated, Judge Moeller and I'll decide what's best for Dave. In the meantime, your collective job is to learn that forgiveness doesn't mean forgetting, it means going forward without letting your mistakes louse up your son or destroy each other. Do I hear any objections?" Nobody said a word. "Let's get some sleep."

Except for the period between the magic show and the Trial Christmas, David's two weeks of quarantine were the best days of his remembered life. For over twenty hours a day, he slept in a dreamy surcease without rules, nightmares, quizzes, perfection, pressure or parental discord. During the day, his mother hovered with Lu Roberts, Stella Benson, Stan Roberts and an occasional specialist from Salt Lake City. At night, his father and Jean Wells took his temperature, carried him to the bathroom, sponge-bathed him, brought him milk shakes and, every six hours, handed him gold-colored antibiotic pills to take.

At the end of the two-week quarantine, Stan gave David an injection which, with boosters administered by Tom in curtained-off spaces on three different airplanes, knocked him out until he woke up in the polio ward of Boston Children's Hospital on Longwood Avenue in Boston. The ward, divided between the girls and boys by a common wall, occupied an entire floor. Patients slept either in a row of cubicle beds or in a line of iron lungs that, like steam locomotives, hissed, hummed and, sometimes, thumped.

It was in Boston that David's dreamy heaven became a fiery hell. Eight times a day, his paralyzed limb was wrapped in a hot, heavy towel to bake for fifteen minutes before he was stretchered into the baths and boiled in a stainless steel tub while a physical therapist worked on him wearing insulated gloves to protect the therapist's hands from getting burned. Each blistering baptism was followed by a violent ritual in which David refused to swallow two, oversized salt tablets, requiring the orderlies to restrain him and, as he gagged and fought, force the dreaded chokers down his throat.

In time, the treatment worked. On a crisp morning in late March, David took his first, unsteady, unassisted steps between parallel bars. After covering no more than five yards, he threw himself, grinning, into the waiting arms of his physical therapist. Cheers went up from the children in the wards, tubs, cubicles and iron lungs and also from Tom and Virginia who were in the process of changing shifts. Twenty minutes later, the two of them were sitting across from each other in the hospital cafeteria where they toasted David's steps by klinking together heavy mugs of black coffee.

"They think he'll make a complete recovery," said an exultant Virginia. "The worst outcome might be a right leg that's a little weaker and slower than the left."

"He'll still beat Ted Williams' .406 batting average," Tom said and they smiled at his allusion to their time together in Boston back in 1941.

After an awkward silence, Tom confronted their marriage head-on. "I can't get over your magic show, the Fry guy or the night we showed up with the court order and I doubt that you've gotten over Maxine or the quizzes or the morning I left Dave on the floor. Am I right?"

"Yes," she said softly, "you're right."

"I thought stopping drinking would blot all that stuff out," Tom said. "But I've been off booze since Dave got polio and I still keep reliving what happened. Feeling both emotions at the same time, I shrivel with shame about myself and I overheat with anger at you."

Virginia said, "Whenever I'm not worrying about Davey, I think the same way."

"We can't live together or raise Dave in a houseful of recrimination," Tom said.

"I know."

"Stan was also right that we ought not hurt each other anymore."

Virginia sipped her coffee and said, "If things continue to go well here, Dave will be an outpatient by April. What'll we do then?"

"We'll do what Stan told us to do." Tom lighted a cigarette. "Tomorrow, I'll leave Boston and go back to Loah and start seeing patients again. Later, when Dave becomes an outpatient, you'll leave him with your sister and come out to Loah and pack up and move back here and we'll work out the legalities later. In the meanwhile, I have some requests."

"I think I know what they are."

"Tess," he started to say but Virginia finished his sentence, "won't raise David. You and I will. When he's well, I'll tell him everything so he knows the truth about *both* parents."

"And also, I —" Tom started to say when Virginia finished that sentence, too. "You want to see David and that will happen as well. You also want David to see a physician for any medical problem and I promise that, this time, it will happen with no exceptions."

"Thank you, Ginny. I'm sorry about everything."

"I am too, Tom." Her eyes glistened. "And Tom?"

"Yes?"

"There aren't many women in Moab County that would be suitable for a man like you."

"Oh."

"But, I think highly of Jean Wells."

Chapter Seventeen

SALK VACCINE

Tom put his office phone down and, before seeing his first patient of the morning, took a moment to inhale relief and exhale joy. The call had been from a resident at Boston Children's who told him that "David was getting around pretty well and would be discharged tomorrow and the prognosis was excellent."

A knock on the door interrupted his buoyance. It was Jean Wells. "Dr. McQuade, we're ready for you."

"Be there in a minute." Tom looked at his calendar. With David's discharge, Virginia would be back in Loah sometime around April 10 to pack. He'd have to move up to the lake before then. Still uplifted by the good news from Boston, Tom donned his white coat, picked up the patient file and strode down the corridor to examining room number one. He opened the door and saw Eva Lighthorse waiting for him and wearing blue jeans, cowboy boots, a turquoise concho belt and a hand-made sweater patterned with antlered deer front and back. Beneath the overhead florescence, her sun-darkened Navajo complexion contrasted sharply against the whites of the room.

Eva was not the type of young Navajo woman who drops out of reservation school to work the sugar beets in Utah and then has babies at the earliest biological moment. She was the only child of an elementary school teacher mother who had died of tuberculosis and of a hogan-born, self-educated father who was an Army "code talker" during World War Two. Eva graduated from the Phoenix Indian School with honors and, when the money wasn't there for college, joined her ailing father on Del Benson's Lazy M Ranch outside Loah. There, she nursed her father until he died and, after that, stayed on to do chores, raise horses, hire field hands, and, as the town wags put it, "keep Del company."

Dr. McQuade smiled and said, "Eva, the test came back and you got your wish. You're pregnant."

"Oh, Doctor McQuade, are you sure?"

"There's no doubt about it, Eva."

The high-cheekboned young woman beamed. "Thank you."

"Don't thank me, Eva," Tom laughed self-consciously.

"Del's at the ranch." She looked at the glazed glass in the window as if there were a view of the Moab Peaks. "He'll be thrilled, doctor, I just know he will."

Knocking and opening the door at the same time, Jean Wells squeezed herself into the examining room to give Eva the prenatal care lecture prescribed by the Utah State Department of Health. Over the nurse's shoulder, Stella Benson appeared in the hallway and said, "Doctor McQuade, Ruby's on the line and says somebody important's calling person-to-person for you from Ann Arbor, Michigan."

"I'd better take it in my office, Stella." Dr. McQuade stood aside, let the nurse have his chair, waved goodbye to Eva and left.

"Hello, this is Dr. McQuade speaking."

"Permission requested, sir, to use the word, 'shit.'"

Tom broke into a smile. "Wait a minute, Silverman, I got busted and you got promoted. Besides that, you became Surgeon General and generals outrank God."

"How'd you know it was me?"

"Easy. You're the only guy who would ask my permission to say 'shit.' How *are* you, anyway, Syd?"

"Just great."

"I read about you all the time in the *AMA Journal, Time*

Magazine and even in the Salt Lake papers. How's it feel to be famous?"

"Not much fun sometimes, especially when a Congressional Committee is chewing on your hind-quarters."

"You mean your ass, lieutenant?"

"Yes, sir."

"Lieutenant, I have a question for you: Having been Surgeon General of the entire United States of America and now the Dean of the distinguished University of Michigan Medical School, why are you calling a lame-handed medic in podunk Utah?"

Syd put off his answer until the subjects of Ginny and Dave had been exhausted and then started in on a long answer to Tom's short question. "As I'm sure you know, the only thing holding up the mass release of the Salk Vaccine is a report from our medical school here in Ann Arbor." He paused long enough for Tom's, "uh huh," and continued. "We're scheduled to make that announcement in two weeks, on April 12."

"Everybody knows about the pending Michigan report but hasn't Walter Winchell been ranting on the radio about how unsafe the vaccine is?"

"Winchell talks one minute about wife-swapping in Hollywood and the next he says the Salk vaccine contains 'live virus' and is a 'killer.' We think there's an anonymous, disgruntled Public Health Service employee who gave him information about an early, experimental batch of the vaccine and so, with respect to the current vaccine, Winchell's full of beans."

"'Shit,' lieutenant. Remember, you can use that word."

"O.K., fecal material," Silverman compromised. "Tom, I'm going to tell you something in the strictest confidence and it is something that America and the world are waiting to hear."

Suddenly, through the open door to Tom's office came the high-pitched shriek of a sick baby. He jumped up, slammed the door, sat back down, put a finger to his ear, and said, "Were you going to tell me the results of the Michigan study?"

"Yes."

"Holy Cow!"

"Tom, we expect over a thousand people here in Ann Arbor

on April 12 to hear me announce our findings. The National Foundation for Infantile Paralysis, or 'March of Dimes,' chose that date because it's the anniversary of the death of Franklin D. Roosevelt who, of course, is the most famous polio victim of all time. It'll be in Hill Auditorium and the place'll be packed with floodlights, newsreel cameras, TV cameras, radio announcers and press from all over the world. Eli Lilly's going to have the proceedings telecast live via closed circuit to doctors gathered in movie theaters all across the country."

"Why tell me?"

"Captain, would you please be patient?"

"Yes, general, sir."

"That's better," Silverman said. "On April 12, I'm going to declare that the first generation Salk vaccine is safe for a mass, national vaccination program and is 60 to 70% effective against Type I, the kind Dave had, and is over 90% effective against Type II, bulbar, and Type III, encephalitic."

"Dave could've used it. He almost died."

"With this vaccine, the odds are that kids like Dave and Presidents like Roosevelt won't get polio."

"How soon will it come out?"

"The March of Dimes has generated so much publicity that, after our report, the federal government will have to approve the vaccine immediately. Consequently, The White House has arranged for an open telephone line to run from Hill Auditorium to a blue ribbon advisory committee at an Ann Arbor Hotel and then to Washington, D.C. where Olveta Culp Hobby, the Secretary of HEW, and Leonard Scheele, the Surgeon General, will be standing in front of reporters and cameras to sign the licenses that'll officially release the vaccine to the public at large."

"Syd, I repeat: why are you telling all this to a lame-handed medic in podunk, Utah? What does all this have to do with me?"

"Excuse me for a second, Tom." For almost a minute, there were voices at the Michigan end of the line before Syd resumed their conversation. "Sorry, but believe it or not Edward R. Murrow just called for an interview. Except for Peleliu, I've never seen anything more frenzied than this."

"Gee, I could tell from the way you treated your own dysentery on Peleliu that you were headed for Big Time Doctoring," Tom tweaked his former subordinate.

"That's about as funny as a pulmonary embolism," Syd said. "But now to the point of my call which, incidentally, does have something to do with Peleliu."

"What are you talking about?"

"You saved my life on Peleliu and I've never forgotten it. I want to give you an historic opportunity to be in the world's spotlight."

"You don't owe me anything. Besides, we owe you. You're the one who hijacked the bus in Alabama,"

"Forget credits and debits, then. Regard this as an order from your commanding General and dear friend."

"O.K."

"Subject to a few conditions, you will be, on April 13, 1955, the doctor who will kickoff a nationwide vaccination program that the President, the March of Dimes, the press and the public are all clamoring for."

"Me?"

"You, Tom. Everybody from *Life*, *Time*, *Newsweek*, *Look*, Associated Press, NBC, CBS, Mutual and the whole world will be out there in Loah, Utah to watch you, interview you, photograph you and pester you to death."

"Jesus."

"Well, what do you say?"

"Sure, what are the 'conditions?'"

"First, comply with the instructions from the manufacturer. Eli Lilly, Parke Davis, Sutter Labs, Pitman-Moore, Sharp & Dome and Wyeth have all been approved and they've got large batches on hand already. I'll have Sutter Labs send you their vaccine since they're in California and closest to you."

"Fine."

"Next, the initial patients are restricted to two categories. The first consists of children from 3-13 because they're at the greatest risk."

"I'll have the Moab County Health Department round them

up."

"Good. Now, there is another priority category: young, pregnant mothers."

Tom laughed. "There's no shortage of young, pregnant mothers out here. This is Mormon country, remember? These days, I do more obstetrics than almost anything else."

"But there's something else that's extremely important, Tom. With the world watching, you've got to stick the first syringe of Salk vaccine into an arm that's brown or black. The Eisenhower Administration wants to show that it cares about minorities and, as you might infer from the Alabama hijacking, I also want the country to care about its minorities." Just last year, the Supreme Court declared segregation unconstitutional and yet the country has hardly done anything to improve the rights of minorities and their medical care is a disgrace."

"Syd, you may have forgotten but this is Mormon Country. The Mormon Church still thinks they're slaves and, besides, there aren't any Negroes out here."

"Isn't there anyone out there who isn't lily white?"

Tom stopped to think. "Well, part of the year Navajo Indians are here working the fields. But they're in Arizona on the reservation now and they won't show up until the sugar beet harvest starts."

"I thought sugar came from cane."

Tom didn't bother to educate Syd about sugar beets and went on thinking out loud. "Seriously, I don't know where in the hell I could round anybody up who's got more than a suntan, Maybe I'm just not your guy." Before Silverman could comment, Tom blurted, "Wait a minute. What about a beautiful, dark-skinned young Navajo woman I was examining when you called. She's PG!"

"Sounds perfect."

"Her name's Eva Lighthorse."

"Eva Lighthorse! Wow, I can just see Jim Hagerty, the White House Press Secretary, turn Ike into the 'Great White Father.'"

"Now, I've got a condition for you, Syd."

"What's that?"

"Tell me honestly, is the vaccine safe?"

"The short answer is yes, but you need a little history." Syd chuckled, "I just happen to be an overnight expert on the history of polio immunology."

Listening, Tom took out his Zippo and fired up a Lucky Strike.

"In 1908, an Austrian doctor, a guy named Karl something or other, confirmed that polio was a transmittable virus," Silverman lectured. "He envisioned a vaccine that would kill the virus, keep the patient well and stimulate the development of antibodies."

"I don't know zilch about this."

"I didn't either. But it's important because of the questions you may be asked by the press. Okay?"

"Okay."

"Later, in 1935, Dr. Maurice Brodie at NYU thought he had figured out a way to kill the virus with formaldehyde but he leaped to conclusions, rushed into clinical trials and vaccinated a bunch of kids. One died and three others were paralyzed in the arms that had been injected."

"Isn't that what Walter Winchell is predicting now?"

"Yes, of course. Which brings us to Jonas Salk who, in 1953, devised a different process for neutralizing the live virus with formaldehyde. He injected himself, his wife, his three sons and some 500 children in Pittsburgh. Nobody died or was paralyzed, and everybody developed antibodies. The results were statistically inconclusive so Salk went ahead, last year, with extensive, double-blind tests."

"Those were the tests that nobody knows the results of yet?", Tom asked and then corrected himself, "except you guys at Michigan and now me?"

"That's right. Obviously, no vaccine is ever 100% safe and it's always possible that a manufacturer might screw up a dose or two. The fact is that Salk's special use of formaldehyde kills the virus and stimulates the production of antibodies. So, the question is: Will you do it?"

"O.K., I've been so worried about Dave and down in the dumps about Ginny and me that maybe this'll pick me up."

"That's great, Tom, I'll make the arrangements."

Tom hung up. With the news about David and the call from Syd, Tom felt better that he had in a long time. As he walked back down the hall to his next patient, he found himself whistling a tune from *South Pacific*, "Younger Than Springtime."

Chapter Eighteen

BULBAR

*B*efore daybreak could silhouette the Moab Peaks, dozens of children and pregnant mothers had already jammed the white-tiled, low-ceilinged Loah Elementary School. The line circled the building, wound through the front door, and snaked among tables, chairs and stainless steel kitchen fixtures. Sandwiched in the crowd were March of Dimes representatives, public health officials, local politicians and twenty-seven reporters who had been bussed down from Salt Lake on a Trailways Bus leased by Sutter Labs to see, photograph and interview "the first doctor" and "the first patient" in America's nationwide program to eradicate infantile paralysis.

At exactly 8:15 a.m. on April 13, 1955, Jean Wells handed Tom a syringe loaded with Sutter Labs Salk Vaccine. While flash-bulbs popped and television and newsreel cameras rolled, Tom stuck the shiny, tubular needle into Eva Lighthorse's brown left arm and slowly depressed the glass plunger, injecting the dense gray liquid into her body. After he withdrew the syringe, placed a wad of alco-hol-soaked cotton over the puncture and looked up smiling, the crowd cheered. Tom McQuade handed the used instrument over to the curator of the Utah State Historical Society.

Before Eva could be interviewed, she disappeared into the throng. Before Tom McQuade could give the next shot, reporters pelted him with questions. "How'd it feel to give the first shot?" "How safe do you think this stuff is?" "Do you have any comment about the warnings Walter Winchell has been making about this vaccine?" Tom coped as best he could with the questions and then went on giving shots to kids and young women until late in the afternoon when the mobs and the media were gone and until nobody was left in the empty, cluttered cafeteria except the doctor, nurse and school custodian.

Jean Wells took charge of the clean-up, shooed Tom out the door and told him that he'd have to drive fast if he was going to get back to his lake place in time for the evening news. For a moment, Tom thought about driving the few blocks to the McQuade family residence where he could watch and listen to the news with Virginia who was packing up to leave but he decided not to. He missed her; he wanted to see her; but he didn't want to disturb the peace they had made in the cafeteria of Boston Children's Hospital or transgress Stan's official directives as David's legal guardian.

As it happened, Tom didn't get to the house at Fish Lake in time to hear or see what the rest of the country did. On NBC-TV that night, Dave Garroway proclaimed a "new medical era." At CBS, Edward R. Murrow staccatoed about the "permanent elimination of infantile paralysis from the planet earth." On Mutual Radio, Walter Winchell began the broadcast with his usual lead-in of Morse Code dots and dashes and greetings to "Mr. and Mrs. America from border to border and coast to coast and all the ships at sea." After reporting the straight facts about the vaccinations in Loah, Utah, he renewed his warning: "When talking about Salk Vaccine, I'm starting to feel like the mythical Cassandra, the daughter of the King of Troy, who had the gift of prophecy but foiled by Apollo never to be believed. There has been a rush to judgment and, despite what Dr. Silverman announced at the University of Michigan yesterday in Ann Arbor, the Salk Vaccine has still not been proven to be safe and we're on the brink of a catastrophe worse than the one precipitated by Dr. Brodie back in 1935 when one child died and others were paralyzed.

Later in the week, Tom unlocked the door to his empty lake house at around 6:00 in the evening. It had been a long day of assisting Stan with one operation after another in Meridian. Just as Tom reached into the refrigerator for a bottle of Natural Set-Up, the telephone rang. It was Jean Wells. She was at the Loah Hospital. Something was wrong.

Eva Lighthorse was there and her symptoms were nausea, soaring temperature, racing pulse, paralysis and difficulty breathing. As if that weren't enough, calls were coming in from the parents of vaccinated kids who were vomiting, running fevers and complaining about inflamed, aching arms. Jean had tried to call Stan in Meridian, but he had gone fishing. "I'll be there as fast as I can," Tom said and dashed to his Chrysler.

Thirty minutes later, Tom pulled into the Loah Hospital parking lot and saw Del Benson's red pickup parked in the space "Reserved for Dr. McQuade." Ever since the magic show, Del had not spoken to Tom and walked out of any restaurant, drug store or auditorium whenever Tom walked in. At first, it was unnerving; however, in time, Tom became philosophical about it because Del shunned all members of what town wags called "Maxine's Alumni Association." After all, Del had no right to fault Tom when Del had slept with Eva for years and she was even going to have Del's baby.

Taking the front steps of the hospital two at a time and throwing open the front door, Tom glanced into the waiting room and saw a seated, hunched-over Del Benson whose jaw was pressed against two clenched fists and whose eyes narrowed at the sight of the fast-striding doctor. When Tom reached the emergency room, Jean Wells and Stella Benson were hovering around a clear plastic oxygen tent that was draped over Eva's still, supine body.

Relieved to see him, Jean blocked Dr. McQuade's approach to the patient and rattled off what she knew in sentences that were not punctuated by pause, breath or intonation. "Del went out to The Lazy M to irrigate this morning and found Eva asleep and didn't wake her and came back after irrigating this afternoon and saw she was awful sick so he brought her in about three hours ago and he wanted Stan Roberts to come down from Meridian but Stan had gone fishing and when I mentioned your name Del went crazy and stomped around the hospital and cussed you out but when Eva got worse I told him we couldn't wait so I called your Lake place and . . . ."

Tom McQuade cut her off, "Forget Del. Tell me about Eva." She was lying motionless under the oxygen tent where Stella was nervously smoothing bed covers. Calmed by the doctor's large presence and commanding voice, the nurse picked up a clipboard at the bottom of Eva's bed and read, in measured tones, the jumbled history she had taken from Eva who could barely talk and also from a hyperventilating Del who, in rubber boots on his feet and with a .38 revolver on his belt, was dressed for irrigation.

"Yesterday morning," Jean recited, "Eva started vomiting but dismissed it as morning sickness. As the day went by, she came down with a fever, developed a splitting headache, felt pains up and down her spine, got dizzy and was incredibly tired. At about 4:30 p.m., she went to bed, slept and waited for Del to come out this morning to start irrigating at The Lazy M."

"She take anything?"

"Couple of aspirin at first but she couldn't hold them down. Nothing else."

"Mmmm."

"Del thought she had the flu and spent the day watering his beets. When he got back to the ranch house late in this afternoon, he could see she was in bad shape." Jean went on, "When Del brought her in here at 5:15 this afternoon, Eva could hardly move or get any air. Her temperature was 103° and her pulse was rapid, sometimes irregular." Tom reached under the oxygen tent, took Eva's wrist and felt her pulse thumping wildly.

"About 15 minutes ago, she started gasping so we put her under the oxygen tent and called you. Since then, she's been stable but listless, in and out of what seems to be a deep sleep and still having trouble breathing."

"Did she have any of these symptoms before the vaccine last week?"

"No and I asked her specifically. On that subject, look out, doctor." Jean glanced in the direction of the hallway and waiting room. "Del's been flying off the handle about you. Says you shouldn't have seen Eva about her pregnancy and shouldn't have, in his words, 'talked her into the goddamned polio shot.'"

Tom snapped, "Forget about Del, will you please?" He took the chart from her. "You mentioned calls about kids? Kids who received the vaccine?"

"There have been six calls. I took five. The first one came in this morning, just before noon." Jean looked at some telephone pink slips. "Margaret was on duty then and said that nine-year-old Johnnie Cushman, who lives down on the Nephi River Road, had a sore arm, was vomiting and had a fever. Margaret figured it was the flu, advised aspirin and bed rest."

The nurse went on talking about the other children with similar symptoms. As she spoke, Tom plugged a stethoscope into his ears, reached under the tent and, with eyes closed, listened to the rattling of Eva's lungs and the pounding of her heart. After that, he tested her knees, feet, arms and hands for reflexes that weren't there.

"The last two calls were just like that and I —"

"Jean," Tom barked. "Get Eva on an iv with saline solution and five million units of penicillin. Watch her like a hawk. Tell me the second anything changes."

He stepped away from Eva and beckoned Stella Benson to come close. "Call the state health department emergency number in Salt Lake. Tell them that we've got a gal in critical condition with bulbar polio and that there may be an epidemic going on here."

"Bulbar polio? But how in the worl —"

Tom stopped her with the flash of a vertical palm. "Tell them to fly in a portable respirator immediately and, with it, all the gamma globulin they've got. After that, have the sheriff try to find Stan, he's fishing the Nephi — I think he said he and Lu were going to Piute Bend — and get him the hell back here pronto. Call Arlin Brinkerhoff at the county health department, have him canvass every kid and mother who got the Salk vaccine and get anybody in here who's not feeling well."

"Doctor McQuade, Eva's choking!" Jean Wells' voice shot up an octave.

"Get going, Stella!" In four steps, he was back at the bed and saw, through the clear plastic, Eva's head yaw, her color darken and her pupils shrink into pin-points of airless panic.

"Quick, Jean, get me a tracheotomy pack." In seconds, he had the oxygen tent off, a hole bored at the base of her throat and a rubber tube into her lungs.

While the young Navajo woman coughed, sputtered, gasped and passed in and out of consciousness, Tom McQuade and Jean Wells spent the next six and a half hours trying to keep her from drowning in her own pulmonary juices. In taut, rapid motions, they suctioned fluid, forced oxygen and, using pillows under her abdomen, positioned her for postural drainage. Consumed by trying to save Eva, neither doctor nor nurse paid any attention to Stella Benson's sporadic reports that Del was drinking and that nobody had located Stan Roberts yet.

By one in the morning, a Kifa Cuirass Respirator had arrived from Salt Lake City and had been strapped over Eva's chest. It was connected by a black rubber hose to a power unit with wheels and, as Eva lapsed into a sweat-soaked sleep, the respirator compressed her upper torso with alternating surges of positive and negative pressure, pushing air out of her lungs and then letting it back in. For the moment, the crisis had passed and Tom stole 30 minutes away from the emergency room to examine six children and diagnose their symptoms, in each instance, as spinal polio.

At 1:30 a.m., he looked into the emergency room where Eva was stable but grave. "Jean, keep your eyes glued on her. I'm going to my office."

Off his feet for the first time in hours and yearning for a depth charge for the first time since the night of the magic show, Tom cranked the handle of his telephone. "Ruby? Get me Ginny. She's at home . . . yes, Ruby, the Loah house."

"Hello." Despite the hour, Virginia was still packing and wide awake.

"Ginny?" Tom's voice was weak.

"How's Eva?"

"You heard?"

"Everybody's talking about her and the sick kids and the shots."

Tom gave a deep sigh. "Eva's in terrible shape. I don't think she'll make it. Bulbar polio. I'm sure of it."

"Oh, how awful."

"Ginny, I gave Eva polio. I also gave at least six other kids polio, too. There may be more. The vaccine must have contained live virus."

"You didn't do anything, Tom. You gave them the vaccine that Syd and the Michigan Medical School and the federal government said was safe."

Then she heard something she had never heard before: the sounds of her estranged, oversized, combat veteran husband crying. "Ginny," he managed between sobs, "come . . . please . . . hold her hand . . . read the Bible . . . pray for Eva . . . help her . . . help me."

"Honey, I'll be there in less than five minutes. Hang on and I'll —"

A tell-tale click had come on the line and Virginia barked, "Ruby Nelson get off the line this very instant."

"Mrs. McQuade, I wasn't listening, really. A Doctor Silverman from Ann Arbor, Michigan said it was an emergency. He asked me to break into the line so he could talk to Dr. McQuade."

"Okay, Ruby," Tom said. "Ginny'll hang up and I'll hold on."

After some cracklings and clickings, Syd Silverman's voice came on the line. "Tom?"

"Goddammit, Silverman! I've got a Navajo girl near death and six kids in bad shape! All with polio! All of 'em got that fucking vaccine you said was so fucking safe!"

"I know," came a weary voice. "The Utah Health Department already reported your situation and the same thing is happening in California, Idaho and Illinois. Thirty-seven new cases so far."

"What in the name of Christ is going on?"

"Tom, it's past three-thirty in the morning here and I've been up all night talking with the Surgeon General, the Secretary of HEW, President Eisenhower and the health departments from eight different states. The real answer is that nobody knows for sure."

"Well, I know something for sure: a young woman is about to die from respiratory failure and six kids are in big trouble." He

131

exploded, "What the hell happened to them, Syd?"

Syd was silent for a moment and then, in a voice that got weaker by the word, said, "All I can say, Tom, is that each new polio case so far has involved Sutter Labs vaccine. Only an hour ago, Sutter Labs voluntarily pulled all of its vaccine off the shelves and away from everybody. Something must've gone wrong in the manufacturing process and the most likely theory is that, when the vaccine was in cold storage but before it was treated with formaldehyde, a sediment formed on the bottom of each vial and that sediment covered and protected some live virus from being killed by the formalin."

"Well that's just great for an ivory tower medical detective to theorize about," Tom shot back. "But what the hell do I do for Eva Lighthorse, Johnnie Cushman and five other cases of polio in my little piss ant hospital?"

Sounding washed out, Syd said, "Tom, the federal government's sending a Public Health Service team to Loah with all the gamma globulin, antibiotics, respirators and support you'll need. They're coming by military transport, already airborne, and they ought to be there in the next six to eight hours."

Tom shouted, "the girl may not make it even if every goddamn doctor in the whole fucking federal government were already here! Christ Almighty, I should've listened to Dr. Winchell."

"Tom, I'm deeply, deeply sorry . . . I didn't know . . . Nobody did . . . I feel awful . . . for you . . . and your patients."

Silverman's voice faded in a long distance decrescendo and Tom could hear his friend's quavering words, "My god, I'm so sorry, Tom."

Tom took a deep breath. "Syd, I shouldn't have screamed at you. It's not your fault. Maybe nobody's to blame. Right now, I've got to save this girl, if I can. I've got to get back to her."

"Tom, I know I speak for President Eisenhower when I say that everybody feels terrible about this tragedy. It may be the worst medical crisis this country has ever faced."

"Bye, Syd."

"Good Luck, Tom."

Tom dropped the telephone back on its cradle, pushed his

tired weight up from the swivel chair, stepped into the hallway florescence and glanced to his left in the direction of the waiting room
for any sign of Del Benson. Seeing nothing but a darkened front
entryway, he turned to his right and walked down the twenty-five
feet to the emergency room where Virginia was already seated next
to Eva and reading from The Bible. Quietly, Jean Wells was suc-
tioning fluid and Stella Benson was adjusting the I V.

Tom checked Eva's vital signs. She was losing ground and
so he increased the surges from the respirator. With the compressor
sounding like a washing machine and making the only noise in the
emergency room, the doctor, nurse, aide and faith healer maintained
their wordless vigil through the night.

By 6:42 a.m., daylight had illuminated the frosted window
and cast blurred shadows across the white emergency room floor.
From Eva's side, Jean whispered. "She's slipping away, Doctor
McQuade."

"I know and there's nothing more we can do about it. At
least she's not going out in panic or pain."

Twenty minutes later, Tom disconnected the respirator.
Virginia, head down, released Eva's lifeless hand. Jean Wells pulled
the sheets over Eva's body. Stella Benson started to dismantle the
'IV.'

"Stella, Del's your cousin." Tom said. "Go out and give him
the bad news. Try to get him to go home. Tell him we did everything we could." Stella nodded, dabbed her eyes with some tissue
and left.

Tom's voice cracked as he gently put his hand on Virginia's
shoulder. "I'm going down the hall to the x-ray room to be alone
and collect my thoughts. I'll be back in a few minutes."

She nodded. "Why don't you come over to the house and
sleep with me tonight?" She reached out and squeezed his hand.

He paused and looked into her eyes. "Thanks for coming,
and being here. I think I'll take you up on that offer."

Stoop-shouldered, he lumbered out into the hall, angled left
and made his way a few yards toward the back of the hospital to the
x-ray room which, with its lead shield, heavy door and lack of windows, was the quietest place in town. After he closed the door and

smelled the aroma of photographic chemicals, Tom dropped into a technician's chair and rubbed his bloodshot eyes.

All of a sudden, he faintly heard yelling in the hallway. Tom jumped up, threw open the door and stepped out into the florescent corridor, squinting. At the waiting room end of the hallway a drunken Del stood not quite forty feet away. In his unsteady right hand, Del aimed his .38 irrigation revolver at Tom. With his outstretched left arm, he kept an hysterical, flailing Stella at bay.

"Goddamn you, Tom McQuade!" the farmer yelled at the sight of the blinking doctor. "First you stole my wife." He paused to shove Stella back. "And now you've killed Eva and our baby."

"Del . . . Easy now . . . Put the gun down . . . We did everything we could for her . . . You're upset and I understand . . . But please don't do anything rash."

At that moment, Virginia stepped out from the emergency room and into the hallway. She saw the wavering gun and yelled, "No, Del!" Just then, Stella lunged at her cousin and the Colt fired a single round. At 680 feet per second, the bullet hit the left side of Virginia's upper chest and slammed her back against the emergency room door frame. Her mouth flew open; her legs buckled; and she corkscrewed down onto the floor.

Del dropped the gun and stumbled out the front door of the hospital. Stella Benson shrieked and jerked both fists up to her mouth. Tom shouted, "GINNY," and fell to his knees and untwisted her body. Cradling her head in his right arm, he cried, "Ginny, oh Jesus, Ginny." Blood spewed from a blackened chest hole several inches below her left shoulder, soaked her denim blouse and pooled out onto the white linoleum.

Through eyes glazed by shock and widened by pain, Virginia looked up at her husband. Gasping, she tried to say something, but could not as Tom sobbed and stroked her cheek. While Stella kept on screaming, Jean rushed into the hallway, saw what had happened and disappeared into the emergency room.

In seconds, the nurse was back, ignoring the hysteria and ministering to Virginia. With her left hand, Jean pushed a compress down hard against the crimson outflow and, with her right hand, gave Virginia a shot of morphine. "Doctor McQuade! We've got to get Mrs. McQuade into surgery, fast! Look at the color of that blood — it's bright red!" Next, she barked at her aide, "Stella get a stretcher!" Stella just stood there, alternating between hyperventilations and sobs. "DO IT NOW STELLA!"

Brought out of his daze by Jean's strident command, Tom spoke slowly at first and then picked up speed as he gradually focused on the emergency. "Keep her air passage clear. Tube her if you have to. Get the ether ready and find extra clamps. We'll need a chest retractor. Round up type O or A negative blood. We'll do an anterolateral thoracotomy and I'll close the wound to her heart or artery." Tom McQuade had not done heart surgery in Utah and he hadn't performed a thoracotomy like this since Peleliu.

At 8:45 a.m., deep-voiced moans and heavy floor-poundings could be heard from the dead-bolted x-ray room. The unbottled hurt ebbed and surged for the rest of the morning until, finally, Stan Roberts and a team of Public Health Service doctors broke down the door, found a blubbering Tom McQuade on the floor and injected a sedative. Before losing consciousness, Tom stretched accented vowels into a ghostly wail and cried, "Maaadame Fortuuunoo's dead, Stan . . . my Ginny's gone."

Six hours later, in his official role as Moab County Coroner, Stan Roberts performed an autopsy and filed his report which read in part as follows:

"A .38 caliber bullet severed the victim's thoracic aorta; there was rapid exsanguination; the pleural cavities filled with blood; and, despite the heroic surgical efforts of Dr. McQuade to perform an emergency anterolateral thoracotomy, the victim died from asphyxiation on the operating table of the Loah Hospital at approximately 8:42 a.m. on April 19, 1955. Virginia Russell McQuade was 45 years old."

Chapter Nineteen

SEVERANCE

Within a week of her death, there were two memorial services for Virginia Russell McQuade. In both, the pews were packed to overflowing. In both, the air was heavy with loss.

The first was held at the LDS Second Ward in Loah with Bishop Smith officiating. His eulogy was entitled "Mother, Magician and Miracle Worker" and it lasted, as rural Utah services sometimes did, over three hours without a break. Tall, erect, and commanding, Bishop Smith confessed his personal shame at having misjudged Virginia at first because of her racial heritage, magic, social work and "eastern" origins. In words that were visually accented by a powerful lower jaw and audibly suffused with emotion, Bishop Smith explained how unforgivably wrong he had been. She had, he said nearly in tears, saved his son's life with her healing, ended the drought with her prophecy, and helped her own son defeat polio with her mothering.

The other service was held four days later at the Ottawa First Church of Christ, Scientist and the speaker was Jeff Fry. Traveling by train, he had accompanied her casket from the Larsen Funeral Home in Loah to the plot where she was buried next to Molly Sykes in Ottawa's Memorial Cemetery overlooking the Illinois River. Thin to the point of gaunt and pale to the point of anemic, Fry started to recount how he had known Virginia since they were toddlers; but, breaking down at each personal reference, he turned to the religious. "Virginia died from a bullet fired by a man who, as Mary Baker Eddy wrote in *Science and Health*, was corrupted by the evils of the Mortal Mind and Animal Magnetism." He closed by telling the mourners that "better than anyone, Virginia understood our Christian Science faith because she possessed an Immortal Mind that could heal the sick, love the outcasts and even bring rain from the sky."

Nobody from Virginia's immediate family was at either service. Her father had died shortly after the McQuades had left for Utah. Her mother was in a nursing home, oblivious. Tess stayed in Boston to avoid any possible encounter with Tom. David was anchored to his aunt there. And Tom went on a depth charge bender that lasted from the time Stan had given him the sedative in the x-ray room of the Loah Hospital until after he woke up in the Roberts' guest house in Meridian almost a week later.

When the bourbon and beer eventually fell below flood levels, Tom's sotted brain began to process bodily sensations and gradually supplemented them with cognitive reasoning. The combination was a juggernaut of pain, nausea, dizziness and fundamental questions. *What happened? Am I dead? Am I alive? Where the hell am I?*

When he opened his eyes, he realized that he was lying on his back in a bed and felt sunlight shining on him from somewhere. With the ache and dizziness and without his glasses, he couldn't see a damn thing. Then he heard a familiar voice.

"Here're your glasses Tom," Stan said.

Tom sat up slowly and reached in the direction of the voice. He put on his glasses and, through the blur, tried to make out his surroundings. Gradually, the knotty-pined room came into focus as did the Navajo rugs on the floor and Lu's collection of early American copper pots and kettles hanging on the walls. Finally, he saw Stan sitting only a few feet in a black, antique rocking chair.

"How do you feel?" Stan asked as Tom sat up in bed to

accept a piping hot mug of coffee.

"Worse than dead," Tom mumbled.

"You almost were dead. If Lu and I hadn't gotten you out of jail and stomach-pumped and iv'd you two nights ago, you would've joined the Dead Depth Charge Club."

"I don't remember," Tom said, swallowing the hot coffee in grimacing gulps.

"I'm not surprised."

"Have you talked to Dave?"

Stan leaned over and, with a Thermos, topped off Tom's mug. "I have."

"What about Ginny?"

"Ginny is buried in Ottawa in accordance with her will. She was laid to rest next to somebody named Molly Sykes."

"And Del?"

"He's in jail, charged with first degree murder. Everybody, including me, wants the bastard to get the firing squad at Point-Of-The-Mountain Prison. If I know Judge Moeller, he won't disappoint us."

Tom went from gulping to sipping. "What do you know about Dave?"

Stan didn't answer him directly. "I've talked, maybe a dozen times, with Ginny's disagreeable sister, that Tess woman, and also with some pushy Boston lawyer for the *Christian Science Monitor*. Naturally, they blame you for everything. In fact, Tess thinks that you killed Ginny by having the affair with Maxine, giving Eva the vaccine and inviting Del's retaliation."

Tom took a deep breath. "I didn't do it that way but I did kill her."

"What in the hell are you talking about?," Stan said. "Del Benson killed Virginia, not you!"

"I understand that," Tom whispered. "It's a long story but, trust me, I killed Virginia in a way that was different from what Del did but just as real."

"You're crazy," Stan grumbled.

"No argument there. Now *please* tell me about Dave."

"He's fine, a bit weak but no lingering indications of paralysis. He's in school half time, was torn to shreds by what happened to his mom and asked twice about you and I lied and said you were O.K. when in fact I didn't know where in the hell you were until three days later when the sheriff called." Stan waited a moment before telling Tom the bad news, "Tess wants to adopt him."

"She what?"

Stan let the message sink in and then continued, "I'm Dave's legal guardian and I want to tell her to go to hell and order her to bring Dave back home to Utah where he belongs with you, Lu and me."

"Stan," Tom said in a weak voice, pointing at the Thermos. "Would you mind?"

Stan poured Tom another cup and said, "You're going to let me fight for Dave, aren't you? I've already talked to the best child custody lawyer in Salt Lake and he tells me that Utah's got jurisdiction over Dave, not Massachusetts. With Judge Moeller making the decisions, with you being Dave's natural father, and with me acting as Dave's legal guardian, we would win in a walk against that Boston bitch."

Tom shook his aching head. "No Stan, there's been enough fighting in the McQuade family. Because of me, Ginny's dead. Because of me, Dave almost died. Because of me, I'm pretty much dead myself."

"Are you out of your mind?"

"No, for the first time, maybe I'm in my mind."

"Tom, you can't just let Dave go. He's your son. You're his father. That Tess is a menace and she'll poison him against you for the rest of his life."

"I'm sure she'll do just as you say."

"Then let me get your boy back here!"

"Tess hates me and, frankly, the feeling is mutual. She loved Ginny and she can look after Dave in ways I can't." With watery eyes, Tom said, "I've got to put Dave's interest first and I've got to be realistic about me."

"Damn it, Tom, I won't let you do this."

"Yes you will. You yourself said that, when he got over the polio, Dave should live in Boston, not here."

"But that was with Ginny, *not* Tess."

"I know, I know. But until I can get over what I did in Peleliu to myself and what I did in Loah to Dave and Ginny, I can't be a father."

Stan didn't fully comprehend what his partner was saying but stuck to the subject at hand. "Then we'll negotiate with Tess and work out a short-term custody arrangement."

"No, Stan. Dave doesn't deserve any more fights, divisions, uncertainty. And I don't deserve him."

"Don't say that."

"Be a good partner and do as I say? Call Tess and tell her that you and I agree. Then inform Judge Moeller that it's alright to sever my parental rights and make Tess Dave's permanent, legal guardian."

"I don't want to do that."

Tom ignored Stan's objections and said, "But there are some stipulations."

"What are they?"

"First, Tess must promise, in writing and in the most legally binding way possible, that Dave will be treated by a medical doctor at the onset of any health problem."

"What else?"

"Next, she's got to promise, when he's old enough to understand, to give Dave a letter that you're going to write about the night his mom died so he'll get the straight facts."

"Is that all?"

"No, there's one more thing. Tell Dave in your letter that I agreed to the severance out of love and that I want him to come and see me when he's grown up and, when he does, I'll tell him the rest of the story that not even you know about."

"Have it your way, Tom," Stan said grudgingly. I'll call Judge Moeller. I'll write the letter. And I'll call that bitch, but, it'll break my heart."

"Mine's already broken."

It would be 40 years before Tom would see his son again.

Chapter Twenty

*W*hen his secretary's voice came over the desktop inter-com, David McQuade was at his desk in a corner office on the 38th floor of The Shasta Valley Natural Gas Company Building but his thoughts were not. They were lost in the faded reds, greens and yellows of an antique magic poster on his office wall, billing Harry Houdini and "The Devil's Death Chamber" at the Majestic Theater in Chicago, on April 17, 1918.

"Mr. McQuade, it's 10:00 o'clock. You wanted me to remind you."

That meant there was one hour for David to finish his preparation and get from the law offices of Franklin, Wolf & McQuade on California Street, through a December drizzle and to the marbled cavern in the Mission District where the Honorable Barry G. Wallendorf held court. This would be the fourth straight Monday David had appeared before the volatile, 72-year-old San Francisco federal judge who had the face of a Bassett and the temper of a Doberman.

David represented The Shasta Valley Natural Gas Company which hundreds of plaintiffs had sued for a gas pipeline explosion in the San Francisco suburb of Ridgemont. Two years earlier, on a brisk October morning in downtown Ridgemont, Shasta's underground trunk line had exploded with such fire and force that one square block of buildings was shaken into blazing rubble, 35 people were incinerated and 172 others were burned, disfigured, blinded or dismembered.

In the resulting lawsuit, the plaintiffs alleged that Shasta had been negligent and should pay them "$725 million for life, limb, property, pain and suffering." According to the plaintiffs, Shasta was negligent because, when its area troubleshooter shut down a branch line that was leaking, he should also have shut down the nearby trunk line that exploded less than a half an hour later.

In addition to the $725 million for their actual losses, the plaintiffs wanted a verdict for "billions of dollars in punitive damages to punish Shasta for willful and deliberate misbehavior." Since the now-defunct U.G.F. Metallurgy Company of St. Louis had manufactured both the branch line pipes as well as the trunk line pipes, the plaintiffs claimed that Shasta must have known about the trunk line danger as soon as it learned about the branch line leaks and must have knowingly delayed a shut down. Plaintiffs maintained in the litigation that Shasta delayed shutting down the trunk line to enhance revenues, contain expenses and strengthen its financial statement.

In its defense, Shasta blamed U.G.F. Metallurgy for the premature corrosion that had caused the leaks and also blamed a Bay Area earth tremor for the friction that had ignited the fumes. Shasta categorically denied any prior knowledge about the dangerous condition in the trunk line and, since there were miles of perfectly good U.G.F. pipe beneath Ridgemont, Shasta contended knowledge of leaks in the branch line did not mean knowledge of leaks in the trunk line. In short Shasta, could not be liable for corrosion it did not cause, leaks it did not know about or an earth tremor it did not have anything to do with.

Each of the previous pretrial hearings had gone the same way. The judge had pummeled David with loaded, run-on lectures disguised as questions and had ruled against Shasta so often that the ratio of his rulings was nineteen to one in favor of the plaintiffs. The only time the judge put any pressure on the plaintiffs' lawyers was when he hounded both sides to settle before the year-long jury trial began next week.

Since the judge had threatened David at the last hearing with contempt if he "presented another groundless motion" and since David was going to present another motion in less than an hour, he tried to imagine how this morning's hearing would go. In his mind's eye, he could see himself standing at the lectern in court and asking Judge Wallendorf to dismiss the plaintiffs' punitive damages claim. In his mind's ear, he could hear this unsettling colloquy that seemed so real it could have come from a court reporter's transcript:

> JUDGE: Mr. McQuade, I see that you have filed another motion.
> MCQUADE: That's correct, Your Honor.
>
> JUDGE: Didn't I say last week that I wanted a settlement from Shasta, not another motion?
>
> MCQUADE: Your Honor discouraged us from filing a "groundless motion" and this motion isn't groundless.
>
> JUDGE: I gather from this motion that you want me to dismiss the plaintiffs' punitive damage claims, is that right?
>
> MCQUADE: That's correct. The jury can't inflict punitive damages on Shasta unless there is clear and convincing evidence that Shasta actually knew about the problems in the trunk line and then, knowing the danger, deliberately refused to shut the line down.
>
> JUDGE: Mr. McQuade, the trial hasn't started yet and the plaintiffs haven't presented their evidence yet. Isn't your motion premature? Shouldn't you wait and move for directed verdict at the close of the plaintiffs' case?
>
> MCQUADE: Absolutely not.

143

JUDGE: Why not?

MCQUADE: Because discovery is over and the plaintiffs have not come up with any clear and convincing evidence that Shasta knew the trunk line was dangerous and should be shut down

JUDGE: But Shasta knew about leaks, Mr. McQuade! A citizen reported the smell of gas. Shasta sent out a troubleshooter. He found leaks in the branch line and he shut it down. Since U.G.F. Metallurgy built the branch line pipes as well as the trunk line pipes, Shasta's troubleshooter . . . Alex . . . whatshisname?

MCQUADE: Alex Cook.

JUDGE: Alex Cook must have known that the trunk line was leaking too.

MCQUADE: There are hundreds of miles of perfectly good U.G.F. pipe throughout Shasta's system in Northern California and, consequently, Cook's knowledge of leaks in the branch line doesn't mean he also knew about leaks in the trunk line.

JUDGE: Shouldn't the jury hear that evidence?

MCQUADE: Of course but only to decide whether Shasta was negligent and whether the plaintiffs should get a verdict for $725 million. The plaintiffs' gigantic, multi-billion dollar punitive damage issue should be thrown out now.

JUDGE: Wasn't Alex Cook at the trunk line shut off valve when the blast occurred and wasn't he killed there?

MCQUADE: That's correct, Your Honor.

JUDGE: Then Cook must have gone there to shut down the trunk line because he must have known it was dangerous. Isn't that also right?

MCQUADE: That's sheer speculation.

JUDGE: And wasn't there ample time for Cook to have shut down the branch line, quickly checked the condition of the trunk line and walked 400 yards to the main shut off valve?

MCQUADE: Yes, but Your Honor is making assumptions about what Mr. Cook did and knew before he went to that valve and also why he was there.

JUDGE: Since Shasta's written safety procedures required Cook to make a prompt report of what he did, can't we properly assume that Cook called Shasta headquarters and told them about the leaks in the branch line and the condition of the trunk line?

MCQUADE: There is no evidence that Cook checked the trunk line or that he called Shasta headquarters. Your Honor cannot speculate about such things.

JUDGE: And isn't it also logical to conclude that someone at headquarters who was worried about cash flow and replacement costs told Cook to delay a shut down for as long as possible because Shasta was only a couple of days away from its first profitable fiscal year in a long time? Isn't that why Cook didn't get to the shut off valve in time?

MCQUADE: Your Honor, you're engaging in unsupported surmise, speculation and conjecture and you've done this ever since the case was filed. Frankly, I think you want the billion dollar punitive damage claim to hang over Shasta's head like the Sword of Damacles to pressure Shasta to settle this case and to pay more money than Shasta can afford. To protect my clients, I must ask that you recuse yourself for bias and prejudice.

JUDGE: YOUR REQUEST IS IMPERTINENT AND DENIED AND SO IS YOUR PENDING MOTION WHICH IS GROUNDLESS AND YOU ARE HEREBY HELD IN CONTEMPT AND FINED $1,000.

With that, David's daymare ended, leaving his palms slick, armpits soaked and heart thumping. Immediately, he did what his psychiatrist preached as an antidote to anxiety attacks, "objectify, objectify, objectify." Mindful of the time, David took out a pen and jotted down his emotional trigger-points on a legal pad where they would be "objectified" for more clear-headed analysis.

"The judge hates me," David scribbled and then thought about what he had just written. The facts were that Judge Wallendorf was the butterball son of poor immigrants; he had earned his law degree at night from one of California's many unaccredited law schools; and he had ward-heeled his way into a federal judgeship that lasted for life but paid a salary that didn't go very far in San Francisco. Naturally, a judge like that would resent a Stanford-educated, big-firm lawyer like David McQuade who was rumored to make over a million dollars a year and who, at 54, was a lean six-footer with genetically tan skin, thick gray hair, obsidian eyes and an angular face stretched tight as much by emotional intensity as by obsessive weight-lifting.

"The judge is biased in favor of the plaintiffs," David wrote and then considered the realities. True, Judge Wallendorf had given the plaintiffs all the breaks and he had also expressed compassion for them in open court. Yet any judge would have compassion for these innocent victims whose lives, families and businesses had been permanently ended or terribly disrupted by the worst natural gas catastrophe in California history.

"The judge has it in for Shasta," was David's next entry. Of course he did and there were reasons for it. Shasta was a Fortune 500 Corporation; its shares were traded on the New York Stock Exchange, and it was the third largest gas utility in California.

Rather than taking full responsibility for its own ruptured lines, Shasta had hired a major San Francisco law firm to oppose the claims; blamed a bankrupt company in St. Louis for the explosion; and offered only $38 million to settle the case, telling the judge that Shasta was in financial distress and that its insurance company, Industrial Risk Underwriters of London, had balked at paying these claims. Like most judges, Judge Wallendorf wanted deserving plaintiffs to be compensated as soon as possible; he hated long trials; and he terrorized defendants who offered too little or plaintiffs who demanded too much.

"George Santos is an unscrupulous bastard," was David's last objectification and nearly every lawyer in town would have agreed with that unflattering assessment of the plaintiffs' lead lawyer. However, to be fair, "Big George" was a gifted trial lawyer with a history of record-setting verdicts for plaintiffs in personal injury cases. In spite of himself, David had to admire not just Santos' trial skills but also his media manipulations that scared Wall Street, sent Shasta's shares into a nose dive and gave Industrial Risk Underwriters a colorable excuse to deny insurance coverage for this disaster. With George's silo size, unabashed nerve and thunderous sound bites, he was a non-stop public relations machine promising Bay Area readers, viewers, listeners and potential jurors that he and his clients would get such a gigantic verdict that they would "end up with a controlling interest in Shasta and, for the first time in the company's history, it would be run at fair rates for consumers and in a safe manner for everyone." At the thought of Big George becoming the CEO of Shasta Valley Natural Gas Company, David lapsed back into his subjective cauldron.

Again, his secretary's voice came over the intercom. "Mr. McQuade, I'm sorry to interrupt, but there's a Dr. Roberts on the line from Utah. I told him you were about to leave for court but he insisted on speaking with you. Said he was your father's medical partner."

David immediately forgot about the Shasta case and said, "Put him through, Susan." He picked up the phone and heard the soft rush of a bad long distance connection. "Stan Roberts, my God, is that really you?"

147

"Hello, David. How long's it been?"

"At least forty years, Stan. How's Lu?"

"She's holding her own after a stroke three months ago and sends her love."

"Send mine to her. And what about you?"

"Well, I've gotten so fat that I've lost visual contact with my pecker and my ticker isn't keeping very good time these days either. But I'll be O.K. so long as the fish keep biting." Stan wheezed and asked, "And how are you, my boy?"

"Trying lawsuits, pissing off women, getting divorced, alienating kids, seeing a shrink and taking feel good pills. I'm right up-to-date, the complete modern man."

Dr. Roberts laughed and went straight to the point of his call. "I know you and your dad haven't talked in over 40 years, but yesterday his neurologist told me that your old man's got Alzheimer's and it's an unusually aggressive form."

" I didn't know he was sick."

"Of course you didn't."

"I'm sorry to hear it."

"Forget what happened in the old days. Come back to Utah and see him."

"I'm about to go to federal court in just a few minutes and I'm really up against it."

"Dave, please," Dr. Roberts stretched out his words. "Your dad's a physician. He accepts the disease. But he's also your father and he's losing lucidity and dying. He needs to clear the air and I'll bet you do too."

With the telephone squeezed between his head and right shoulder, David swung the leather armchair around and looked out at a soggy San Francisco. "I appreciate your keeping an eye on him but —"

"Dave," Dr. Roberts interrupted, "You've gotta bury the past, the magic show, the murder, all of it. Come back to Utah. Talk to him. Listen to him. Try to understand."

"You know the history between my father and me."

"I do and it's time for some new history. It's his last chapter."

"What could he and I possibly talk about?," David asked rhetorically. "Mom, who took a bullet for him? Maxine, who feasted on his whanger? What about Polio? Or maybe Eva?"

"Damn right, you should talk about all that stuff and more." Stan again lost his breath, slowly regained it and said, "I'll bet your Aunt Tess never gave you my letter, did she?"

"What letter?"

"That's what I thought. Just a couple of days after Del killed your mom, I sent a letter to you in care of your Aunt Tess and I described what happened the night of the murder and I explained how your mom and dad had come together in such a beautiful way. Your dad wanted you to read that letter when you were old enough to understand how human beings, like your parents, could hurt each other with so much hate and yet forgive each other with so much love."

"I never saw the letter or even heard about it from Aunt Tess."

"I also said in my letter that your dad wanted to see you when you were an adult so he could tell you things that not even I know about."

"Come on, Stan," David said. "That letter can't mean anything. Right after you must have written it, my dad filed a petition with the Moab County Court and severed his parental rights and you'd better believe I received a copy of that goddamned document which, in effect, says 'fuck off David.'"

"He severed those rights out of love, David."

"Bullshit."

"That's why you've got to come back to Utah right now!" Dr. Roberts wheezed some more and softened his pitch. "Your dad treated you plenty awful but there's a lot of good in him and he really cares about you, Dave. Hell, just the other day, he bragged about the case you won in the U.S. Supreme Court that was in all the papers and that nobody out here in Mormon country liked one damn bit — the one about homosexuals in the Army."

"He did?"

"Yes, he did," Dr. Roberts chuckled. "Your old man's a political liberal when he talks about you these days and, in Utah, that's conclusive proof of Alzheimer's."

"I'm headed into a year-long jury trial that involves billions of dollars and a major gas company. I don't have time for anybody now, not him, my kids, my fiancé or even myself."

"You're supposed to be in some big deal law firm. So let one of the other guys cover for you just like your dad and I did for each other."

Reflexively, David wanted to say that some of his colleagues weren't "guys" but let it pass. "Where does he live?"

Dr. Roberts explained that Tom McQuade lived in an apartment at the Sunrise Retirement Village overlooking the Nephi River and Uintah Canyon. "In general, he's done okay but he's got to move into the medical center for assisted living and the pig-headed bastard won't do it."

"Have you pushed him?"

"Pushed him? My God, Dave, I even threatened to baptize him into the Mormon Church after he died and that would force him to spend eternity without another drop of Jack Daniels."

David thought that was pretty funny because, in Mormon Heaven, prohibition lasts forever. Just then, his secretary handed him a note, "Judge Wallendorf's court in 20 minutes!" David nodded and waved her off. "What kinda shape's he in, Stan?"

"He's lost height and a lot of weight. He's often incontinent. Breaks down and cries when he's frustrated. Loses his temper sometimes. Has a pasty complexion. Stands lopsided. Wanders off and gets lost. Occasionally needs a cane."

"How's his mind?"

"Runs words together. Confuses names. Doesn't have much of a short-term memory. But, on the positive side," Dr. Roberts emphasized, "he has long stretches when he can carry on a perfectly normal conversation and, amazingly, he can remember details from as far back as when he was a little boy."

"I don't know," David said, wavering.

"I'll make you a deal. If you'll fly into Salt Lake, Lu and I'll take your dad up to meet you at the airport. With her stroke and my angina, we don't get around like we used to. But, God willing, we'll be there and we'll all drive back together to Sunrise Village which is only 15 minutes from our place in Meridian. Whenever you need to leave, just take the shuttle back to Salt Lake. In good weather, the trip takes just under two hours."

David McQuade frowned at his watch and, while holding the telephone between his head and right shoulder, stood up at his desk. "I gotta saddle up for court where a federal judge is going to take a chainsaw to my member."

"To hell with your member, I just told you that I haven't seen mine in years."

"Well," David sighed, "I've got to make a quick trip to London and, while Utah isn't exactly on the polar route, I guess I could stop by for a day or two. However," he quickly added, "I've got to stay in touch with my office so tell me what the phone situation is at my dad's place."

"Your dad's phone doesn't have an outside line for long distance."

"Why's that?"

"His phone bills started showing charges for calls to places like Japan and Sweden. The last straw was the $1500 worth of car wax he bought from one of those middle-of-the-night infomercials on television and so the phone's restricted and the TV's gone."

"Good lord."

"It's common for Alzheimer's patients to get confused by the TV and misuse the phone," Dr. Roberts explained. "If you're gonna stay in contact with your office, you'll have to do it from the pay phone in the main lodge."

"Stan, do me a favor. Call the retirement home. Have them temporarily activate an outside line from my dad's condo. Tell them I'll use it for e-mail and long distance and I'll pay the bill and have it disconnected when I leave."

"O.K., but your dad doesn't have e-mail and I doubt the main lodge does either."

"I'll bring a laptop. That's all I'll need."

"Lu will be thrilled to see you, Dave."

"And I'll be thrilled to see her too, Stan."

"When do you think you'll arrive?"

"I'll figure that out and have my secretary call you with the details."

"That's great."

"One more thing, Stan. Did you keep a copy of the letter you wrote to Aunt Tess, the one she was supposed to have given me?"

Dr. Roberts thought for a moment and said, "I might, I'll have to look."

"Please do. If you find it, would you FAX it to me? The FAX number is 415-395-9460 and I'll read it on the airplane."

"I can't wait to see you, Davey. Maybe we'll get a chance to drop a few lines in the Nephi. It'll be like ice fishing at this time of year but I've got some adult beverages that'll keep us warm."

David smiled broadly. "You don't know how good that sounds, Stan. I'll see you soon." They hung up and David buzzed his secretary. "Susan, what's going on tomorrow?"

"Let me see. Tomorrow morning you've got a trial-prep session with Fred Danielson upstairs in the Shasta Executive Suite and tomorrow night you're scheduled to have dinner with Leah."

"What about the day after tomorrow?" he asked, throwing papers into his briefcase.

"Your One Great Hour Of Suffering is from 11:00 to 12:00," she replied. Her reference was to the hour that David McQuade set aside each month when his three former wives and his two "former children" could call, FAX or e-mail their grievances, which were usually about him, and present their demands, which were usually about money. David named the hour after a local charity drive called, "One Great Hour of Sharing."

"Now that's an incentive to get out of town if I ever heard one," David said, rushing to put on his raincoat. "Anything else?"

"You're supposed to meet with Mr. Santos at 2:00 p.m. in his office to review demonstrative exhibits for the trial."

"Have Warren Stanfield cover that for me and be sure to tell him to wear hip boots and a gas mask. Is that all?"

"There's one more item on your calendar. The election of new partners will be held during lunch the day after tomorrow and Mr. Franklin has demanded, in writing, that every partner be present."

"That settles it. Get me tickets for Salt Lake City leaving the day after tomorrow. I'll spend two days in Utah and then fly to London to meet the chaps at Industrial Risk Underwriters and then hustle back here for the first day of trial."

"What about the election of new partners and Mr. Franklin's edict?"

"Send a memo to His Excellency. Tell him I don't care who becomes a partner around here anymore. We've got so many, there might as well be thirteen more. He's got my proxy."

"Do you really want to address Mr. Franklin as 'Your Excellency?'"

"On second thought," David said over his shoulder on his way to the elevator, "Change 'Excellency' to 'Grand Imperial Vizier.'"

Chapter Twenty-One

THE GOVERNOR

*B*y the time David unlocked the door to his gentrified three-story in Pacific Heights, it was past midnight. Groping in the dark for his computer, he was too preoccupied to notice the distant splendor out his back window of white headlights coming, red taillights going and stationary gold lights outlining the horizontal roadway and curved suspension cables of the Golden Gate Bridge.

Earlier in the day, Judge Wallendorf had ruled from the bench and, as expected, had denied Shasta's motion to eliminate punitive damages from the case. However, contrary to David's mid-morning anxiety attack, the judge was civil; there was no talk of contempt, and he even ordered Santos to turn over some recently-acquired evidence relating to the plaintiffs' punitive damage claim. In addition, the judge once again leaned on both parties to settle and David once again had to explain why Shasta could not offer more than $38 million to settle the plaintiffs' hard-dollar losses of $725 million.

For what seemed like the umpteenth time, David described how precarious Shasta's financial position was at the moment and how Shasta's insurance company, Industrial Risk Underwriters of

London, had refused to pay the plaintiffs' actual damages of $725 million because the policy excluded coverage for "knowing and reckless acts" and because the insurance company claimed that Santos had "credibly demonstrated that Shasta's deliberate behavior was the cause of the catastrophe." Although Shasta had filed a bad faith case against Industrial Risk for its refusal to pay the claims, that case would take years to resolve and Shasta needed the $725 million now. Besides, even if Industrial Risk did pay the $725 million, there would still not be a settlement because the plaintiffs also wanted billions in punitive damages and Industrial Risk's policy excluded coverage for intentional acts and, in bold capital letters, also excluded coverage for punitive damages.

Staring at his computer and thinking about Industrial Risk's denial of coverage, David smelled some Anglo-American rats. Although he could never prove it, he suspected that Santos had made a deal with the Brits whereby they would withhold insurance money so Santos could bomb Shasta with a giant verdict, take over the company and then settle Shasta's bad faith case against Industrial Risk for a song. At this stage, David couldn't do anything about the judge's denial of Shasta's motion, but he might be able to do something about Industrial Risk's denial of coverage.

David turned on the computer and clicked into his address book until he came to "Eastwood, Bryan K., Governor, State of California" and scrolled down to the telephone number listed for Eastwood's "Home, Private Line." It was rude to call anyone in the middle of the night, especially the Governor of the State of California; however, this was the perfect time for the kind of conversation David wanted to have with his former partner and law school classmate. He dialed the number in Sacramento.

After five rings, a groggy male voice came on the line, "Hullo."

"Bryan?" David asked.

"Who's this?"

"David, David McQuade."

"David? What the hell are you doing calling me at this hour?"

"A minor emergency."

155

"Well, if it's minor, call me at the frigging office!"

"Your office wouldn't be a good place to talk about the Bad Taste Party, Bryan." David's reference was to a bash thrown twelve years earlier by the junior partners of Franklin Wolf & McQuade at Bryan Eastwood's house in Atherton when his wife was away visiting her parents in Vermont.

Disturbed, the Governor rolled over in bed and away from his wife and, cupping his hand over both mouth and phone, hissed, "David, are you out of your mind?"

"Of course I am but my insanity has nothing to do with that party where, if I recall correctly, you appeared as Nero in a loose toga over a leopardskin jockstrap. By the way, Bryan, I've been meaning to ask where you got that jockstrap."

"Jesus Chris, David," the Governor growled, trying not to wake up his wife. "I can't believe this conversation is actually taking place."

"It is taking place, Bryan. And a good thing, too, because I've got happy news."

"Happy news?"

"It's about the video tape you've been worried might surface someday that would crater your political career and bust up your marriage to Brenda." David was talking about a video tape that had been taken at the Bad Taste Party but he didn't have it and didn't know where it was or whether it even still existed.

"Are you referring . . . ?"

"Yessiree, I am. Since I assume Brenda's in bed with you and you can't talk about this touchy subject at your end, I'll confirm that it *is* the videotape of *the* Bad Taste Party at *your* house," David lied.

"How do you know?"

"Well," David lied again, "before I paid $3,000 for it, I watched it on my own TV-VCR and, oh my, you had such a good time that night, stripping down to your hunky altogether; chug-a-lugging anything alcoholic; fucking the brains out of a young nymph in the hot tub. Also, Bryan, there's a swell scene of you sniffing some white —"

"So you've got it?" the Governor interrupted.

"Yes, my liege," David lied yet again.

"Any copies running around loose?"

"No, but if there are, the vendor knows she will be professionally vaporized and probably indicted." That was another lie.

"Who had it?"

"A young lawyer we both know who isn't so young anymore. Two days ago, she came to me in a panic needing money to put back into a client trust account about to be audited. It seems she had been, shall we say, 'borrowing' money from the trust account to finance a nasty heroin habit."

From Sacramento came an audible sigh of relief and then, "That *is* happy news and I will immediately reimburse you."

"Forget about the money, Bryan."

"Thank you, my old friend, loyal partner and political supporter. I'll be in the City next week and I'll buy you and that pretty doctor friend of yours the best dinner in town, any place you want, just name it."

"I appreciate the offer, Bryan, but I've got to decline." David dropped any trace of fraternal jocularity and got down to serious business. "However, there is something you can do but it's got to happen in three days."

"What's that?"

"I'd like you to have the California Department of Insurance FAX a letter to Industrial Risk Underwriters of London and advise them that the Department is considering a full scale audit of all its policies, premiums and payouts in California."

"Are you nuts? I can't do that."

David ignored the Governor's resistance and went on. "Bryan, I'm not asking you or the Department to actually conduct such an audit or even to actually *threaten* to conduct one. Just have the Department tell the Brits that such an audit is being considered."

"But David, the Department is not considering any such audit and I'd certainly know about it because Industrial Risk Underwriters has a huge presence in this state. It probably insures hundreds of billions of dollars of risk here."

"Then tell the goddamned Department to 'consider' it, Bryan, and, while you're at it, tell them to FAX the fucking letter!"

"You know very well I can't do that. As far as I know, Industrial Risk hasn't violated any state regulation and hasn't been the subject of any complaints."

"Then I'm afraid I can't keep the video from going to every newspaper, radio and TV station in San Francisco, LA and Sacramento, Bryan." That was another lie.

"You're extorting me, aren't you, David?"

"I can't extort you, Bryan," David said with some truth because he didn't have the video. "I'm also not asking you or the Department to do anything illegal or fraudulent."

"The hell you aren't."

"Get real, Bryan. There are bound to be complaints on file against a mammoth carrier like Industrial Risk and it's inevitable that any big insurance company has violated at least one of the Department's thousands of regulations. Besides, there must be somebody in that vast bureaucracy who has considered or will consider an audit of Industrial Risk."

There was a strained silence at the Sacramento end of the line. "No promises. No *quid pro quos*. If the letter goes out, it won't be part of any deal with you or anyone else. Do you read me?"

"Of course."

"I'll see what I can do."

David hung up and smiled to himself. When muckrakers get irate about undue influence in government, they usually jump all over corporations and unions and special interest groups but rarely do they criticize major law firms with their unseen connections, lobbyists, wealth, clients, alumni, and power. David yawned, turned back to his computer, and clicked into his e-mail.

E-mail from Leah Pedrini, M.D., to David McQuade:
David, your secretary left a message for me to meet you for dinner at Tadish's Grill tomorrow night at 8:00. It is about time that I hear from you and I'm down in the dumps about that and several hundred other things too.

E-mail from David McQuade to Jake Reid, M.D:

I realize that I've missed so many sessions that the only one who knows the exact number is your billing person. However, I'm leaving town the day after tomorrow and I need a refill on the Zoloft. I've got some extra Prozac from two years ago when you had me on those green and white smile-makers but I don't want to mix Prozac with Zoloft for fear I'll become a serial killer. Besides, Zoloft generates more sunshine, squelches my libido and decommissions The Little General. Although I lay off the Zoloft when I'm with Leah, I don't want any more marriages, kids, divorces and alimony.

Believe it or not, I'm going to Utah to see the man you've heard me curse and cry about for years — my father, Thomas D. McQuade, Jr., M.D. After severing his parental ties to me more than 40 years ago, he has come down with Alzheimer's and, according to his old partner, wants to see me to "clear the air" and tell me "the rest of the story," whatever that might be. I suspect he wants to confess his sins and get some priestly forgiveness before embracing eternity. I can't imagine dispensing any forgiveness but I'm willing to listen.

After two days in Utah, I'll fly to London for a day and then fly back here in time for the Ridgemont trial. I know you don't want me to try that case but the client is faced with extinction and I can't not do it. You know me, I never back down.

Chapter Twenty-Two

FRED DANIELSON

When David McQuade was in law school and until he started practicing law at what was then called Franklin & Wolf, he had assumed that witnesses simply showed up cold to testify at depositions or trials and they answered the questions put to them and that was that. As he soon learned, that happens in the United Kingdom but not in the United States.

Routinely, American lawyers meet with their clients and friendly witnesses in advance and prepare them to testify by refreshing their memories with calendars, photographs, diaries, printouts and letters; alerting them to anticipated questions they will likely be asked; and suggesting ways to answer those questions truthfully but, of course, helpfully. Yet, there is always a fine line between preparation that prepares and preparation that suborns perjury, and most American lawyers believe that, to stay on the ethical side of the line, all they have to do is say the words, "tell the truth."

Which is how David McQuade began his early morning discussion with the CEO of Shasta Valley Natural Gas Company, Frederick M. Danielson, in the deep pile expanse of his office on the top floor of the Shasta Building. "Do I have to remind you to tell the truth, Fred?" David asked, almost as a joke.

"I don't think so, David," Fred said with a knowing smirk. Runner thin, golfer tan and clubman smooth, 63-year-old Fred Danielson was as cold-blooded as he was narcissistic. So much so that, at a recent Franklin Wolf & McQuade retreat, David had told his partners, "When Fred Danielson was born, he was wearing an Armani suit and looking for a throat to cut."

The two men were seated across from each other at a heavy oak work table with a silver coffee service and china cups and saucers in the middle. Ten yards of thick carpet and floor-to-ceiling windows away sat a massive desk that proclaimed power and, a few feet beyond it, hung dozens of famous photographs that proclaimed connections. Danielson liked to describe his office as "too large for a board meeting but too small for a shareholders meeting."

"Fred," David said, "let me repeat something that I've mentioned dozens of times in the past. Big George and his clients are going to get a verdict for $725 million for loss of life, limb, property, and income because the jury is almost certainly going to find Shasta liable for negligence, whether the fault was Shasta's cuts in the budget for safety inspection programs or Alex Cook's apparent decision not to immediately shut down the trunk line after he found leaks in the branch line."

"You've been a broken record about that, David, and I've been a broken record about something else," Danielson said, sipping coffee and raising his eyebrows to see above the rim of the cup. "Without insurance money from Industrial Risk, Shasta cannot pay more than $38 million to settle. Not a farthing more. Consequently, since we can't settle or win the trial, I want you to stretch the case out into infinity with as many motions and appeals as there are pieces of paper in that big law firm of yours."

"Fred, I'm going to London to lean on Industrial Risk for some farthings so forget about all that for the moment, Okay?"

Danielson nodded.

"What scares the hell out of me," David said, "are the billions of dollars in punitive damages that Santos wants for his clients and for his megawatt ego. Fred, I don't like him and I don't trust him, but Big George is a master at turning juries into lynch mobs."

"So you've said, many times."

"In one of the few rulings that His Honor has made in Shasta's favor, he yesterday ordered Santos to give us the recently-acquired evidence that purportedly shows Cook or someone else at Shasta knew about problems in the trunk line and knew about them in time to have shut the line down before the blast."

"What 'evidence' does Santos have to support this fantasy?"

"Part of it we already knew. Part of it we didn't. However, it's not going to matter how weak his punitive damage evidence is if we can't pay off the $725 million. The judge will be so pissed off at us that he'll send everything to the jury, including the punitives and, at that point, we might as well bend over and kiss our asses goodbye."

"Pull the shroud away, David," Danielson said, irritated. "What the hell is Santos' evidence?"

"Telephone records."

"Telephone records?"

"Four calls. One we knew about. Three others we didn't." David pushed a computer printout across the table to Danielson. The four calls were highlighted in yellow, sequentially showing day, time, length, numbers called from and numbers called to. Danielson put on sleek, wire-rimmed reading glasses and squinted at the colored rows of data.

"Hmmmm" was Danielson's only audible response.

"We knew about the first one," David said. "It was from an anonymous caller from a pay phone in downtown Ridgemont. Alex Cook took that call and drove straight to the gas line nearest the pay phone. That turned out to be a point in the branch line about 400 yards downstream from the trunk line. After the usual check, Cook found premature corrosion and also verified a leak. His log reflects the call, the trip, the corrosion, the leak and the immediate shut-down of that line which, by the way, served a residential neighborhood."

"Poor Alex. He was such a good man," Danielson said looking out the window at nothing in particular. "By closing off that line, he saved thousands of lives. A genuine hero."

David went on, "Then there's the next call. It was from Alex on his mobile phone to your private line in your office. I hope you know something about that call because I don't."

For a split second, Danielson flinched then quickly recovered. "Oh, yes, I remember that call from Alex."

"Why didn't you tell us about it?"

"I did."

"You did?"

"Well, maybe not to you or Warren but to one of your paralegals."

"Which one was it?"

"I don't remember the name."

"Denise? Joel? Mary? Freida?"

"David, I don't keep track of all the Franklin, Wolf & McQuade gnomes that swarm around here."

"Well, they sure as hell didn't pass this information to me or Warren."

"Then fire them, David," Danielson said, buying himself some time while he thought of something to say.

"Fred, we can't fire all four paralegals on the Shasta case when you can't even tell me which one you told about this significant and, I must say, surprising information."

"Then let me tell you directly, without any paralegal middle-man-or-woman, what Alex told me on the phone because it will make you a happy lawyer."

David had not known about this call from Cook and, until recently, Santos hadn't either. Since Cook was dead, Danielson was free to say anything he wanted without fear of contradiction and so David braced himself for what Danielson was about to say. "All right, Fred, make me a happy lawyer."

"Be glad to." Danielson poured himself more coffee and said, "Alex called me and sounded relieved and exhausted. He said that a gas smell call had come in from Ridgemont and that he had responded. He said he was shocked to find the branch line corroded because those pipes had not been in the ground long enough to be corroded."

So far, so good, David thought as Danielson paused to sip more coffee.

"He verified a leak, and then he shut the entire branch down on the spot." Then Danielson digressed. "Since natural gas is so vital to so many people and businesses and institutions, our field personnel do not have authority to shut down lines, especially major ones, unless they have actually verified a leak or unless they have gotten approval from me or from another senior executive."

David asked. "Did Cook say anything about the trunk line?"

"As a matter of fact, he did," Danielson said, putting the cup down, leaning back and steepling his fingers. "He told me that, since U.G.F. Metallurgy had manufactured both the branch line and trunk line pipes, he was naturally concerned about the safety of the trunk line because the pipes could have been part of the same defective batch. Consequently, he made a number of checks at various points along the trunk line and didn't detect any corrosion, leaks or danger. As a result, he saw no reason to shut the trunk line down and I concurred and thanked him for his good work and that was it."

"But, that wasn't it, was it?" David said. "Because the trunk line turned out to be a linear powder keg."

"Unfortunately yes. And that's why Alex was probably negligent because, as good a troubleshooter as he was, he should have found the problems that were obviously in the trunk line. If he had verified a single leak, then he had the authority to shut down the trunk line right then and there. Also, if he had found any serious corrosion and if he had told me about it, then of course I would have instantly told him to get over to the valve and close off the flow."

"Let me see if I've got this straight," David said, more suspicious than confused. "Cook called you and reported the branch line corrosion, leaks and shut down?"

"Correct."

"And Cook said that he ran a number of checks at different locations on the trunk line but didn't find anything to worry about."

"Yes."

"So he didn't ask for your approval to shut down the trunk line?"

"That's right. There was no reason for such a request as far as he was concerned."

"Then why was he at the shut down valve when the blast occurred?"

"I have no idea, David," Danielson said with an air of uncontradictable confidence. "The most logical explanation is that he went there to check the pressure gauges because, with the branch line closed, the trunk line volume would have increased substantially."

David tried not to sound dubious. "Which brings me to the third phone call that we didn't know about."

Danielson squinted down at the printout again.

"It's a call from Alex's mobile FAX machine in his truck to the FAX machine located just outside your office in the Executive Suite. Santos tells me that it lasted just long enough for a one-page document to have been transmitted."

Danielson's retort was swift and sharp. "David, after Alex and I talked on the phone, I never heard from him again and I certainly didn't get a FAX from him. If those telephone records are correct, then our FAX machine must have been out of paper or out of order."

"Is there anybody else around here who might have picked up a FAX from Alex?"

Danielson got huffy and said, "*All* members of the executive staff get their FAXes from that machine, David. That's why it's in the suite and not in my office. But they would've given me anything from Alex Cook."

"Calm down, Fred, I'm not saying that anybody got anything."

Danielson cooly took off his glasses, folded them and put them back into his inside coat pocket. "Let me repeat myself. If Alex had verified even a single, tiny leak, he didn't need approval from anybody. But, as he told me, he checked the trunk line up and down and didn't find the latent problems that apparently were lurking there."

"I understand all that and so does Santos," David countered, not believing a word Danielson had said. "But what if Alex had quickly checked the trunk line and had detected corrosion but no leaks? Wouldn't he have needed somebody's approval to shut down the trunk line under those circumstances?"

Danielson pushed back his chair, signaling that their session was about to end. "Yes, but we don't have to speculate about that because Alex Cook told me on the phone that he checked the situation out thoroughly and everything looked good. Point, game, match."

Danielson rose to leave as David said, "There's one more call we didn't know about. It was from Alex's mobile phone immediately after the FAX and shortly before the explosion. It was to his home phone and it lasted for almost three minutes."

"So he called his wife or kids, so what?"

"So maybe nothing, maybe something." David spoke very slowly so Danielson would understand the importance of what he was about to say. "Santos theorizes that Cook told you he had found the same corrosion in the trunk line as he had in the branch line. Cook didn't have time to look for leaks in the trunk line but the situation was grave enough that he wanted your authority to cut off the gas flow. You didn't give him that authority; instead, you told Cook to wait for a few days until the end of Shasta's fiscal year but he objected and sent you a FAX to cover his flanks. After that, he called his wife and told her what had happened, and, without your permission, he went over to the valve to shut down the trunk line when all hell broke loose and he was killed."

"That's bullshit!"

Realizing he was going to be stuck with Danielson's story, David said, "Well, whether its bullshit or bullion, you can relax. Assuming the call was with Cook's widow, Santos can't talk to her or call her to testify about anything she and her husband said to each other on the phone. It's called the husband and wife privilege."

If Danielson was relieved, he didn't show it. Checking his watch, he said, "I'm late for a meeting with some Wall Street brokerage houses to plot how we're going to pump value back into Shasta's stock with this lawsuit hanging over our heads."

"Fred, before you go, let me ask you one last question: did you talk to Mrs. Cook about the disaster?"

Speaking with testy articulation, Danielson said, "Of course I did. I sat next to her at Alex's funeral and spent the better part of an afternoon explaining all that Shasta was going to do to make sure that she would always be comfortable."

"Well, did —"

Danielson finished David's question with a hostile edge in his voice. "Did I ask her what she knew? Damn right I did and she didn't know shit and I trust that my word is enough for my lawyers on that score so *my* lawyers won't go out there and traumatize a grieving widow with a barrage of questions about the worst day of her life." Danielson walked toward the door and, without looking back, said, "Understood?"

"Understood," David said and smelled another rat but this time it was his rat. Which, in practical terms, meant that he would follow Danielson's orders and not talk to Mrs. Cook or involve her in the case in any way. After all, David didn't want to be burdened by what she might say. His job was to win the case, not look for facts or truths that could hurt Shasta. He would live with his own rat and it wouldn't be the first time.

When Danielson reached the door, he stopped, turned and said, "By the way, John Franklin tells me that you're taking a family trip to Utah. Is that right?

"I'm going to see my dad for a couple of days."

"I don't like the idea of Warren Stanfield here all by himself while this case ramps-up to trial. I would like you to reconsider the Utah trip and stay here to deal with Santos and pick the jury."

"Fred, I've got to go to London to put the squeeze on the Brits for $725 million in farthings, remember? According to the map, Utah is between San Francisco and London."

"London's fine but I want you to reconsider Utah."

E-mail from Jake Reid, M.D., to David McQuade:

I'm not happy about it but I will refill your damned Zoloft. However, I am pleased that you will be seeing your father. Go there as if you were a cultural anthropologist to gather data and stay there as if you were a loving son to give comfort. Before you see him, remember the analysis we've been over many times:

A.   When we were kids, we were little, vulnerable, weak. We had to adapt to circumstances and develop patterns of behavior to cope with our environment. Those patterns get ingrained.

B.   When you were a kid, your father ordered you never to back down and always win, never lose, be the best and you did all of that to stay on his safe side. Not surprisingly, you took on all comers; you won; and you didn't lose

C.   Your mother didn't protect you from him or from their marital storms. Instead, she made an Oedipal alliance with you that hurt him, lowered her and damaged you. The magic show you and she engineered was a terrible thing for everyone concerned but an even worse thing to involve a little boy in. She shares responsibility with you and with your father for who you are today.

D.   When you became an adult, you unfortunately continued to see and react to the world as you had as a child. You continued to think that you couldn't back away from any fight and that you had to be perfect, always win, and never lose. Eventually, you developed a form of the "imposter syndrome," thinking that perfection and exhaustion were what had made you a successful trial lawyer and, therefore, you couldn't let up lest you fail and be exposed as an overachieving imposter.

E.   Of course perfection is impossible and of course there are battles that should be left unfought. Grown-ups know that kind of thing but you didn't and don't still. Instead, you take on every challenge, strive even harder to win, exhaust yourself even more and hate yourself for being human. It has gotten so out-of-hand these days that you'll do anything to win and that includes breaking promises, splitting hairs, and lying. Even when you do win, it isn't enough anymore.

F.   When you see your father, do not seek moral conquest and do not indict him for what sounds to me as very
human behavior that you couldn't understand as a kid but
that you can as an adult. Nobody except your father knows
what happened during the Battle of Peleliu but we do know
something today that nobody knew back then: that Post
Traumatic Stress Disorder is devastatingly real, especially
for people who suffer from depression or who have family
members, like your lobotomized grandfather, who suffered
from depression.

G.   There is something else: Don't try that Ridgemont
case! The last mega-trial you handled — the oil spill
calamity in Alaska — you won and yet ended up, two weeks
after the verdict, getting depressed, boozed up and wrapping
your car around a bridge abutment on the Bayshore Freeway.
That victory may have brought you headlines but it cost you
a concussion, lacerations and a fractured pelvis. The next
one could cost you your life.

Chapter Twenty-Three

LEAH PEDRINI, M.D.

David preferred dining at noisy eateries in the Financial District where waiters wore white aprons and patrons jostled each other at the bar and had to shout over the clattery din to be heard. In those venues, the talk was usually business and the subjects were usually impersonal. David's objection to the quiet, romantic restaurants on Nob Hill was that they were quiet and romantic. They made him feel obliged, especially when he was with a woman, to reveal inner truths and he didn't like to talk about inner truths.

So it was not by accident that David selected Tadish's Grill to have dinner with Dr. Leah Pedrini. Although he told her that his choice of restaurants was because "Tadish's has the best Petrale Sole in town," she knew his *modus operandi* and was already one glass of chardonnay ahead by the time he waved from the doorway and weaved his way back, dodging busboys and waiters and diners, to the last wood-paneled booth in the back.

They exchanged "Hi's" and a lip peck. David motioned to a familiar waiter for a single malt scotch on the rocks and said, "I got your e-mail. What's up, doc?"

Uncharacteristically, Leah Pedrini stared at the chardonnay, inert and blank-faced. For as long as he had known her, Leah was never inert or blank-faced. Invariably, her moods were projected by rapid talk, enhanced by emotional expression and dramatized by exaggerated, Italianate gestures. Tonight, though, she was inanimate, her dark hair a shroud and her olive-skin face a mask.

Leah was the first female physician in a long line of physicians, first in Italy and later in the United States. She was born in San Francisco, educated at Vassar and took her medical training, internship and surgical residency at the University of California Medical School in San Francisco. The combination of Mediterranean beauty and operating room skill had opened doors to opportunities she thrived in as well as to older male physicians she fell for.

David was the first, non-medical man she had dated since college and, although he was constantly embroiled in bare-fisted litigation, his cases were exciting and often in the news; he was a magician who could tell people the names of their pets when they were children or geometric designs they were thinking of at the moment; his looks, while not of the slick-back movie star variety, were a gravitational combination of physical, emotional and intellectual intensities, and, most important of all, he listened to Leah with his eyes. With him, she could say or confess anything and feel heard, safe, and, if necessary, forgiven.

"David, I'm about to cross the Rubicon."

"An appropriately Roman expression from a nice Italian girl," was his flip response.

"By that I meant leaving and never coming back."

He knew what she meant but, while sounding the internal alarm for his emotions to take battle stations and for his nerves to close their bulkhead doors, he asked, "You mean leaving San Francisco?"

"No David, I meant leaving you."

"Oh."

Frowning, she launched into a practiced monologue. "I'll begin at the beginning, with the time we met for the first time at the Butlers' house on Big Sur. You were so different from the doctors I had dated, married or had affairs with that I fell like a stupid school girl for you and, after that, our times together have been wonderful but they've also been sporadic, disjointed, and almost never for the purpose of just being together, the two of us."

She took a deep breath and said, "So here's a summary of us. Geneva where you spoke at an international law conference; Washington, D.C. where you gave a magic show for a NAACP Legal Defense Fund benefit dinner; Anchorage where you were in trial for sixteen months in the oil spill case; Dallas where you hob-nobbed at the American Bar Association Convention; L.A. where we entertained bigwigs from Southern California Edison; Sacramento where your partner was sworn in as Governor; and, of course, San Francisco where I left my surgical group to become a free-lance, assisting surgeon so I could be available for you at client dinners and sporadic sleepovers wedged in between depositions, partners meetings, court hearings and crises with Julie, Jim and your ex-wives."

Leah fell silent long enough for the waiter to deliver David's scotch and then resumed, talking faster and getting more animated with every word. "Do you see the pattern? If we were married, it might be different. Or at least it might mean something. But you won't discuss marriage. Every time it comes up, you get lawyerly and say 'we'll address it at a later date and that's a promise.' After all this time, I know it isn't a promise but a dodge and, if I may say so, a lie." As if delivering a formal lecture, she took a throat-clear-ing drink of water and said, "To add insult to injury, you go around fraudulently proclaiming that I'm your fiancé which I'm not and which I've never even been asked to be."

David took a full-mouthed swig of scotch and felt his emo-tions on full alert and his nerves safely sealed. He felt nothing and was ready for anything.

"While you were in Philadelphia, *incommunicado*, taking depositions for that more-important-than-me Shasta case, Roger Kellog asked me out for dinner and I went. He's the brain surgeon I was having an affair with when I met you. A month ago, he got a divorce and said that he did it to be free for me."

"I know him," David said in a flat voice. "He's the skull-sawing son-of-a-bitch who testified for the plaintiff in the St. Martin's Hospital case. I cross-examined that lying sack of neuro-matter for six hours. If you'd like to see his dick, I cut it off while he was on the witness stand and it's back at my office in a bottle of formaldehyde."

"That's funny," Leah said, seething with retaliatory intent. "I've seen a lot of Roger's dick since then and it's still attached, fully functional and, if I may say so, one of the largest I've encountered."

At battle stations, David couldn't be hurt or insulted. Her dig meant nothing. He drank more scotch.

She took two deep breaths to calm herself and went on. "Roger and I had a good enough time at dinner but all I did was think about you and, afterwards, raced straight home from the restaurant to see if you had called and, of course, you hadn't." Slowly, her anger subsided and her lower eyelids glistened. Meanwhile, David felt nothing, said nothing and stayed with his scotch.

"So this is what happened," she gulped down the rest of her wine and her voice dropped to a near-whisper. "Roger called and asked me to go with him to Maui for a medical meeting. After nine straight days of not hearing from you, I went with him to make you jealous but you never even knew that I had left town. On the way back, Roger asked me to marry him." The glistenings spilled onto her cheeks.

David was numb, just the way he felt whenever a jury came back and filed into their seats and announced, through the foreman, that they had arrived at a verdict. At such moments, David was so well armored that it didn't matter what the jury decided any more than it mattered what Leah was saying right now.

"To hurt you, to get a companion, to have a life, I wanted to say 'yes.' But," she sobbed, "I said 'no.'"

At the word, "no" David's emotions stood down from their battle stations. "Thank you, Leah," he said, trying to sound as if he meant it because he did.

She reached across the table for his hand and he took it in his with a gentle squeeze. "I love you, David, and I don't know what you're trying to prove by the way you live."

David cupped her hand in both of his and looked straight into her eyes. "You sound like Jake."

"He doesn't want you to try the Shasta case, does he?"

"No."

"Neither do I."

David nodded and kept on listening and staring at her.

"David, I don't know if I can hang on for a whole year while you wage war eighteen hours a day, seven days a week in that godawful Shasta trial. I'm already as lonely as I can possibly be and my job as a surgical assistant is a dead end."

"I understand what you're saying and I wish the situation were different. I wish I were different."

Leaning toward him over the table, she said, "I'm afraid of what this trial might do to you but even more afraid of what it might do to us. Please, for you, for me, for us, don't do it."

David stared into his scotch and said, "I'll have to think about that, Leah."

She sat there, pondering what he had just said. After a few seconds, she realized that David McQuade was going to try the Shasta case no matter what she or anybody else said and no matter what it did to him, her or them. When that epiphany sank in, she felt a spasm of loss in her stomach followed by the sensations of acceptance, release and detachment throughout her body. "Susan told me you're going to see your father in Utah and then fly to London."

"That's right."

"I think seeing him is one of the most important things you can do for yourself, David. He's haunted you for decades."

"Huh huh."

"Does Jake think it's important?"

"Yes, very much so."

"Are you angry about me and Roger?"

"Not at the moment," David said shaking his head. "When it sinks in, I'll probably want to strangle the bastard."

"I'd like that," she smiled. "If jealousy is what it takes for you to love me more than litigation, then I'm all for jealousy."

"The only thing is," he said, "I wish your Maui fling had been with a better human being."

"Tell you what," she joked. "Next time, I'll run off with a

Nobel Prize Winner."

He laughed and, in the softest voice he could summon, asked "Would you spend the night with me?"

"Yes."

E-Mail from David McQuade to Jake Reid:

Leah is in the shower and is going to spend the night here at my place. I don't know how much longer she and I will last. For good reason, she feels a distant thousandth to my practice. I'm sick about it but she's suggested that the price I have to pay to keep her is to withdraw from the Shasta case and that's out of the question and maybe there's a biochemical explanation for why that is.

You've often said that I'm addicted to adrenalin and that may be true. For me, it's a potent antidepressant and it must have been for my father too. He never knew what to do with himself when he wasn't at the hospital or on a housecall. So, when he wasn't rushing around being a doctor and when his adrenaline level was low, he would fill his tank up by drinking depth-charges, screwing Maxine, fighting with my mother or asking me to multiply one four-digit number by another.

Jesus, Jake, the more I think about it, I'm turning out to be just like him and I don't even have a war wound to blame. When I compare him to me, I realize the things he did that hurt and infuriated me are the same things I've done too. I work to exhaustion and so did he; I've struggled with booze and so did he; I've cheated on wives and so did he; I've been a shitty husband and so was he; and I've failed as a father and so did he.

My God, the older I get, the more I hear him come out of my mouth when I talk. And the closer I get to Utah, the more I feel like a shameful hypocrite.

Chapter Twenty-Four

WARREN STANFIELD

*B*ecause Leah Pedrini was a surgeon and accustomed to late night calls, her eyes flew open on the first ring and, immediately, poked David in the ribs to wake up and answer the telephone. After groping in the dark and knocking an alarm clock over onto the floor, David finally found the phone and grunted a deep-voiced, unfriendly "hullo."

"David, I'm sorry to call you like this but we're on the eve of Armageddon." The familiar voice belonged to David's young partner on the Shasta case, Warren Stanfield. When David's groggy brain finally recognized the voice, David said, "Warren?"

"Yes."

"Why the hell are you calling me this time of night?"

"Because it's very, very important."

"Didn't you know that only drug-crazed psychos call at this hour?"

"Is that what the Governor told you last night?"

David couldn't think of a comeback but the dig woke him up. "What's this Armageddon crap, Warren?"

"Armageddon, from the Book of Revelations, the apocalyptic show down between good and evil. That's where we are in the Shasta case."

Warren's upbringing as an Evangelical Christian loaded him with so much Biblical knowledge and high-minded morality that David called him "Reverend" and maintained that Warren "had been born again one too many times." Although the young man's religiosity bugged David, Warren Stanfield had set records at UCLA Law School; he was a rising star at Franklin, Wolf & McQuade; and, in court, he could be as charming as a door-to-door Bible salesman or as thunderous as an Old Testament Prophet.

"To repeat, why in the hell are you calling me at this hour?"

"Because I knew you were leaving for Utah first thing in the morning and I read your report about the meeting you had today — I guess it's yesterday by now — with Fred Danielson. David, Danielson's a liar who's going to get us into big trouble." When it came to the Commandment to "love thy neighbor," Warren made an exception for Fred Danielson who, in an antitrust case against Shasta two years earlier, had ordered David to remove Warren from the case because "Stanfield is a Christian waterass." David had refused and Warren went on to win the case, without an apology or a thank you from Danielson.

Incensed at Warren's answer, David barked into the phone, "You mean you called me in the middle of the goddamned night to tell me that Fred's a scum-bag? For Christ's sake, Warren, I've known Fred was a scum-bag from the instant I met the bastard sixteen years ago!"

Warren quickly said, "I didn't call just to tell you that. I called because Fred lied to you in your prep session."

"What do you mean?"

"I mean Cook did send Danielson a FAX as the phone records show and Danielson did in fact receive it. In the FAX, Cook said that he had made one quick check and immediately saw that the trunk line was as badly corroded as the branch line. Since Cook didn't have time to verify any leaks, he had called Fred for authority to shut down the trunk line."

"Hold on, Reverend. Did you see this FAX?"

"Yes."

"Where?"

"In Danielson's office a little while ago."

"IN DANIELSON'S OFFICE?" David shouted as the doctor next to him went on sleeping, oblivious to the telephone commotion.

"That's correct."

"HOW IN THE HELL DID YOU GET IN?"

"The same nice lady who cleans my office at 9:30 p.m. also cleans Danielson's office between midnight and one-thirty. She forgot to lock his door after she finished. Mistakes happen."

"Warren, that's an illegal entry and a criminal offense so WHAT IN THE NAME OF GOD WERE YOU DOING IN FRED'S OFFICE?"

"Pursuing a higher moral purpose."

"YOU WERE WHAT?" David yelled again and still Dr. Pedrini didn't stir.

"When I received the telephone records Santos gave us and saw that Cook had called and had even sent a FAX to the machine right outside Fred's office, I knew something was wrong and I'll bet you did too."

David was noncommittal as Warren plunged ahead. "There were barely fifteen minutes between the time Cook shut down the branch line and the time Cook called Fred. That was enough time, at most, to make one check of the trunk line but not enough time for Cook to do what Fred claims Cook said he had done; that is, make a number of checks along the trunk line to assure himself it was safe. Also, although our engineers tell me that it's awfully difficult to reconstruct pipe that has been blown to smithereens, it appears that the corrosion was uniform throughout the trunk line so Cook would probably have discovered it on the first check. The point is, Danielson lied through his teeth to you."

With his head spinning, David said, "Proof that Fred lied to me is not proof of what Cook did or what Cook knew or of what Cook told Fred, Warren. Punitive damages have to be established by clear and convincing evidence, not by inferences stretched from inferences, remember?"

"Of course, but when Cook's FAX and Danielson's lies surface in court, Wallendorf's going to nuke Shasta and give you and me lethal injections." Warren added, "I checked the maintenance records for the FAX machine outside Fred's office and it's never been out of order. Shasta has a service contract and a guy comes in twice a month to maintain all the FAX machines."

"What about the paper supply?"

"David, that machine is a super-duper model that always has paper in it. This is the executive machine, for heaven's sake. It can print two thousand FAXes without a reload."

"I don't like this."

"I also talked to the office services person who oversees every detail in the executive suite and she said that machine gets reloaded every morning at 5:30 a.m. and it's NEVER out of paper." Warren had found the rat that David had smelled.

"Did you make a copy of Cook's FAX to Danielson?"

"I was going to but I heard voices from down the hall and got out of there as fast as I could."

"How did you know to look in Fred's office in the first place?"

"I had a nonchalant chat in the cafeteria at lunch with Suzy, Fred's secretary. She said he kept his 'super-secret stuff' in the credenza behind his desk."

"I can't believe you did this."

"It gets worse, David."

"What gets worse? You or the story?"

"The FAX gets worse because, in it, Cook estimated the replacement cost on the trunk line to be between $19 and 20 million and the revenue loss to be between $3 to $5 million."

"Warren, it's late. Spoon feed me. Why is that worse?"

"Because Fred wrote on the FAX, 'Told Alex to defer trunk shut down for three days. Alex pissed.'"

"Sweet Jesus."

Warren could hardly contain himself. "Obviously, with the fiscal year only two days away and with Shasta on the verge of its first profitable year in a long time, Fred didn't want anything to surface that might cost $19 or $20 million which, if accrued, could go on that year's books and wipe out profits, dividends and the golden parachute the Board had promised him if he turned the company around."

"Shit-fuck," David said.

Warren raced on. "Fred probably figured that a three day delay wouldn't pose much of a risk because Cook had not found leaks, only corrosion. Since Fred's handwritten note says Alex was 'pissed,' what probably happened was exactly what Santos now suspects happened: Cook must have disagreed with Fred, hung up, FAXed Fred the shut down request to cover Alex's butt, and then made tracks to the valve to shut off the trunk line when the quake hit and he was killed."

David's mind flashed to the other call from Cook's mobile phone. "But before he charged off to the shut down valve, Alex must have called his wife to tell her what Fred had said, what Alex had faxed and what Alex was going to do."

"That's how I figure it," Warren said. "Which explains why Fred was so adamant about keeping Alex's widow out of the case."

"As I said, shitfuck."

"David, we've got to go straight to Judge Wallendorf and tell him the whole sordid tale."

"ARE YOU OUT OF YOUR EVER-LOVIN' GOD-DAMNED MIND, REVEREND?" David ranted. "I can just see it now. There you are, standing at the lectern in court and telling our sweet-tempered judge, 'Your Honor, I was burglarizing my client's office the other night around 12:30 a.m. and, in the course of my felonious conduct, I found an incriminating document that I didn't have time to steal or make a copy of and that my client whom I detest and who detests me now says doesn't exist but he's lying because I saw it with my own eyes in his credenza and, since the memo doesn't exist any more, that contemptible client must have destroyed it and obstructed justice. Not only that, Your Honor, this document demonstrates that this sub-human client knew, before the disaster, that the trunk line had the same dangerous corrosion as did the leaky branch line and this heartless bastard deliberately delayed the shutdown so that Shasta could make a profit and its shareholders could get a dividend and he could get a golden parachute for himself while exposing the innocent citizens of Ridgemont to a megaton explosion. This also means, Your Honor, that the plaintiffs should automatically get their $725 million for Shasta's negligence and, on top of that, they also should get a few billion in punitive damages for Shasta's gross, wanton and deliberate misbehavior. As if that weren't shitty enough, Your Honor, these facts also mean that Industrial Risk had the absolute contractual right to refuse to pay anything under its policy," David paused and said, "You're a fucking genius, Reverend."

Chastened, Warren said, "That doesn't sound like much fun to me either but I'd like to keep my license to practice law and stay out of jail. If you have any better ideas, what are they?"

"With tonight's burglary, you've done piss poor job of trying to stay out of jail and hang on to your license, Reverend."

"O.K., O.K., but what'll we do?"

David could sense a meltdown at Warren's end of the line and tried to sound avuncular. "I don't know, Reverend. Go to bed and get some sleep and I'll think of something and e-mail it to you from Utah."

"Thanks, David."

"Reverend?"

"Yeah?"

"Sometimes it's best not to know certain things. This was one of those times and Cook's FAX was one of those things."

E-mail from David McQuade to Warren Stanfield:

Reverend, I'm so agitated that I can't go back to sleep and so I've stayed up thinking about what you just told me and here's what we do about Cook's FAX and Fred's lies: nothing, absolutely nothing. That means no more nocturnal burglaries; no more middle-of-the-night telephone calls to me; no contact with Cook's widow; no accusations against Danielson; no confessions from you; no word to anybody about this; no more Armageddons; and no more *Book of Revelations.*

Warren, don't ever again do anything for a "higher purpose." Typical of religious zealots throughout history, you thought you were doing God's work rooting out evil when in fact you were just getting even with Danielson for his "Christian waterass" accusation in the antitrust case, a couple of years ago.

We are lawyers. Our job is not to pursue "a higher good." Our job is to represent Shasta Valley Natural Gas Corporation and its shareholders and employees and hope like hell we can do enough damage control so that, by the end of the day, the company will survive, its shareholders will keep their investments and its employees will still have their jobs. In practical terms, that means we've got to get $725 million from Industrial Risk in London and then get rid of Santos' billion dollar punitive damage claim in court.

Fred lied to me but so what? Clients lie all the time to their lawyers and that's not a crime like, for example, your cat burglary was. Moreover, if you go back and read Santos' deposition of Danielson, you'll see that, because Santos hadn't yet known about the phone records, he didn't ask Fred any questions about those calls and Fred didn't perjure himself. Fred cetainly would have lied under oath if Santos had asked the right question but he didn't.

We aren't the keepers of Fred's fetid conscience. We aren't cops, priests, ministers, rabbis, ethicists or ombudsmen. We're lawyers.

E-mail from Warren Stanfield to David McQuade:

I can't go to sleep either and I just read your e-mail that arrived ten minutes ago. As instructed, I will do "absolutely nothing." Therefore, I won't go back into Danielson's office; I won't breathe a word of this to anyone; I won't call Cook's widow; and I will stay the course you have charted. Even if I don't "do" anything, I still want to say something which is this:

1.   I may have crossed some kind of line by going into Danielson's office in the middle of the night without his knowledge or consent. However, I didn't sneak into or break into Danielson's house; I entered an office that is called "his" but he doesn't own it. Shasta Valley Natural Gas Company owns it. I doubt that I "burglarized" anything. Besides, I am a Shasta lawyer and I even own 50 shares of

Shasta stock. I don't think what I did was all that wrong.

2.   Even if I did something that may have been technically illegal, my "higher purpose" was to root out Danielson's deception and bring the whole truth to the court's attention. For a long time, lawyers have been committing lesser crimes to dramatize greater crimes. Just look at the civil disobedience lawyers engaged in during the civil rights struggles in the 1960's.

3.   I respect you enormously but I have to point out that, within the past 48 hours, you yourself lied to the Governor of the State of California and extorted him to achieve a higher purpose, which was to squeeze Industrial Risk out of $725 million for Shasta.

4.   What makes that stratagem even worse is that, given Cook's FAX, we now know that Industrial Risk does not have to pay anything under its policy because Fred deliberately put off shutting the trunk line down and Industrial Risk didn't insure intentional acts and, in its policy, explicitly excluded punitive damages. Obviously, had Fred given Cook authority to shut down the trunk line, Cook would have had the time to get to the valve and shut it off without wasting time with the FAX to Danielson or the call to his home. In short, if you're successful in wringing $725 million out of Industrial Risk in London, that could be a criminal act done for a higher purpose or, depending on how you look at it, a lower purpose.

5.   I understand the conflicting ethical considerations here and I'll walk every step of this dangerous road with you. I hope Utah goes better than the Shasta case. I'll pray for both of us.

E-mail from John P. Franklin to David McQuade:

Fred Danielson called me today and, in one of his patented rages, howled about your going to Utah and, Warren's appearing at the final pre-trial conference and picking the jury. Of course, I'll support whatever you do. However, you need to know that, according to Fred, he's "OUTRAGED AT FRANKLIN, WOLF & MCQUADE." So what's new? Have a good trip.

Chapter Twenty-Five

SUNRISE VILLAGE, UTAH

*F*or almost two hours, David McQuade was trapped in a window seat on American Airline's Flight 215 from San Francisco to Salt Lake City by a florid hot water heater salesman who, at close range and in a beer breath, rattled on about how "we've licked the sediment problem." Before the salesman could finish his unrequested diagram of a "filtrater" on a cocktail napkin, the fasten seat belt sign flashed on; the jet roar eased into a hiss, the McDonnell Douglas Super 80 nosed downward, and the captain alerted passengers to some momentary turbulence coming off the Wasatch Mountains and a good view of the Great Salt Lake on the left side.

Throughout the flight, David pored over a smudged carbon copy of the letter Stan Roberts had sent Tess Russell in 1955. It didn't surprise him that she hadn't given it to him because she hated Tom McQuade and wanted him permanently demonized and Stan's letter spoke of how Tom and Virginia had come together "with hearts full of love" in the wake of Eva Lighthorse's death; how Virginia had been the accidental victim of Del's bullet; how Tom had heroically tried to save her life, and how neither Tom or Virginia had been saints. Stan's letter changed the landscape of David's mind, planting doubts where there weren't any before and raising questions he hadn't asked before.

As the jet banged its way down through the unsettled air, David wondered what the protocol should be upon seeing his father at the airport after decades of strained silence. A handshake? A hug? Never, even in the best of times, had they ever said anything to each other resembling, "I love you."

Once out of the jetway and inside the gate, Dave spotted him. Always a big man who carried his bulk as if he were well exercised and who intimated those around him with a powerful and resonant voice, his father was now strikingly different. In his late 80's, Tom McQuade had shrunk, lost weight, stood lopsided, was pasty, and resembled a dying tree. After bringing David gradually into focus, he moved stiffly with a cane toward his son and then, swallowing each word, said something that David did not understand.

At close range, Tom resolved the protocol issue, extended his right hand as far as his arm would push it and put on that disapproving expression he always seemed to reserve for his only child. David mumbled something that had the word "sir" in it and, shaking his father's hand, wondered if they were about to climb back into the ring for another round of father against son or, now that circumstances had changed, son versus father.

As the rest of the San Francisco passengers streamed past them into the terminal, the McQuades stood there, avoiding each other's eyes and not saying anything. From behind them, a man yelled, "Looky there, it's the best damn fisherman on the Nephi!" David turned toward the voice and was bear-hugged by Stanley Joseph Smith Roberts. When they broke from the embrace, David recognized the ruddy complexion, thick glasses and jolly smile but little else. After decades of steaks, eggs, biscuits, gravy, beer, potato chips, chocolate chip ice cream, and gravity, Stan had gone from wide to double-wide, from thick-shouldered to sloped and from full-faced to puddled.

Seconds later, David felt a softer set of arms around him and heard the stroke-slurred words, "Praise the Saints that you've come back to us, Davey!" It was Lu Roberts, whom Stan had married when he was at the University of Chicago Medical School and she was in nurses' training. Now a frail, thinly-haired, stick-figure of a woman, Lu had as many wrinkles as her husband had pounds. Despite more than 60 years of being married to a Mormon husband, raising five Mormon children and living in all-Mormon Moab County, she was still a Chicago convent girl who, until her stroke, drove all the way to Salt Lake City for Mass every Sunday.

The foursome made their way down the concourse past color posters of goggled skiers cutting through deep powder at Park City, Alta and Snowbird. Tom hobbled with a cane, leaning to his left and saying nothing. Stan wheezed and hefted his arthritic weight forward, step by labored step. Lu inched along chatting, smiling and clutching David, whose mother had been her closest friend and the only other "Gentile" woman in Moab County.

From the airport, Stan squinted through the mud-spattered front window of the four-door Buick Regal and, at speeds that varied between too fast and too slow, negotiated the freeway system around downtown Salt Lake City and Temple Square. With the Roberts in the front jabbering and the McQuades in the back fogging up the side windows, the Buick followed signs to "Cheyenne" and "Denver," turned onto Interstate 80 and headed east, climbing up and into the frigid Wasatch Mountains.

At an exit marked "Meridian — Uintah Canyon," the Buick left I-80 and turned south onto newly-plowed, two-lane State Route 51. On one side, it wound along the rocky, partially frozen Nephi River and, on the other side, it hugged steep, snow-drifted embankments. Mile after winding mile, the Roberts talked and the McQuades didn't and time passed and so did thick stands of Douglas Fir as well as oncoming drivers who recognized the doctor's red Buick and waved. After almost two hours, the Buick approached a "Y," in the road, where the sign said "Meridian" to the right and "Sunrise Village" to the left.

Sunrise Village was laid out in a three hundred yard semicircle that ran along a crescent-shaped bluff overlooking a bend in the Nephi River. Financed with Texas oil money in the 1970's, the lodge, main dining room, chalets and medical center looked as if they had come out of a Hansel and Gretel story with their woody browns, canopied roofs, rhythms of half-timbers and gingerbready ornamentation. Within the wide ellipsis formed by the curve of the buildings were a parking lot, pool, recreation center, putting green and criss-crossings of heated, enclosed ramps and walkways. Except for the medical staff and administrators, employees wore alpine attire. Except for a wealthy few from Salt Lake City, residents were predominantly out-of-state flatlanders who came for the majesty of the Rocky Mountains and the coziness of an ersatz Swiss Village.

There were, in the apartments and facilities facing the Nephi River, floor-to-ceiling windows so residents could lie, sit, eat, and even die looking out on the wide water below and the Denver & Rio Grande railroad tracks along the far shore. During daylight hours, hawks, deer, eagles, elk and an occasional big horn sheep came within sight of the Village. At night, powerful arc lights from the main lodge bleached the river, canyon walls and passing trains with an artificial brilliance.

Stan parked the Buick in front of chalet 28 and turned off the ignition. After a few seconds of uncertain silence, he looked at his wife and then shifted his weight to address his backseat passengers. "Lu and I are going to have dinner with my cousin from Ogden tonight. So we've got to leave you two and get to Meridian. Tom," Stan said glancing at his old partner, "Dave came, he's here, don't blow it. Dave," Stan turned his voice but not his bulky frame toward the younger McQuade directly behind him in the backseat, "You stay cool, understand?" Neither father nor son said anything.

After the Buick drove away, Tom held the door open for his son and pointed down a narrow, unlighted hallway. David groped for a light switch and, wondering what his father's silence had meant during the past two hours, found the spare bedroom and put his garment bag and overcoat down. After unpacking his shaving kit and swallowing a Zoloft, he picked up the laptop case and made his way into a darkly shadowed living room where his father had turned on a lone floor lamp and was already seated in one of two Naugahyde, LA-Z-BOY recliners that were side-by-side, facing floor-to-ceiling windows and the wintry scene outside. Cautiously, David sat down.

The arc lights from the main lodge were already on, illuminating the Nephi River, D&RG tracks, rock walls and gnarled, undersized pine trees rooted in protruding ledges near the canyon mouth. For almost 20 minutes, father and son stared at the frigid landscape and listened to the thermostatically controlled blower on the electric furnace start and stop. Finally, David turned away from the windows and, with what little light the floor lamp could throw off, surveyed the living room. Squinting, he noticed crocheted doilies on the dinner table, a collection of miniature glass ballerinas in a china cabinet, frilly pillows on the sofa, and, on the mantle over a small brick fireplace, a color portrait of a smiling, thin-faced, elderly woman wearing a wide-brimmed straw hat. "Who's that? She looks familiar."

"My wife."

"Your wife?"

"Yeah, Jean Wells."

"The nurse?"

"Uh, huh."

"You married Jean Wells?"

"Uh, huh."

"I didn't know you remarried. When'd you do that?"

"Four years after your mom died."

"What happened to Jean?"

"Cancer."

"When?"

"Last year."

David paused and turned back toward the partially-iced windows. "Stan called me a couple of days ago in San Francisco."

Tom didn't acknowledge the statement.

"Dad?"

"Huh?"

"Stan called me and said that you had been diagnosed with Alzheimer's."

"Nobody's sure."

"According to him, you're in pretty good shape, considering, and that you've come to terms with it."

"I'm not eternal. I accept that."

"Yeah, well, that's not exactly what I came here to talk about."

"Oh?"

"The reason I'm here, dad," Dave drew an exasperated breath, "is because he said you wanted to talk with me."

"Did he?"

"As a matter of fact he did and, ever since I landed in Salt Lake, I've wondered what in the hell he was talking about and why in the hell I came here. Frankly, you haven't said a damn thing to me." The furnace blower started up again.

Tom broke the tension. "Please."

"Please?"

"Please," he ran his words together and swallowed some vowels. "Please-get-us-two-drinks-stiff-ones-the-liquor-cabinet-is-over-there-then-come-sit-talk." Tom pointed to a wet bar in the far corner of the living room.

Once his father's blurred request registered, David made for the bar and poured a Jack Daniels and water for his father and an unknown brand of straight scotch on the rocks for himself.

Tom brightened at the sight of a drink and began talking in distinct, well-spaced words again. "Mormons didn't want us to have booze at the Village. But there are old farts here from all over the country and they're Episcopalians, Presbyterians, Catholics, even a couple of Jews. We outvoted the bastards; formed our own private club." His father smiled. "First time I ever bested the Brigham bunch."

"Congratulations," David toasted his father's religious victory.

Tom raised his glass in a return and sipped the sour mash beverage. "Thanks, Syd."

"Dad, you called me 'Syd'."

"I did?"

"Yeah, you did."

"Oh, God. Stan says I've been calling him 'Syd' too."

"Who's 'Syd'?"

"Must be Sydney Silverman. Helluva guy. Great doctor. You knew him when you were a little guy in Morro Bay. Served in War Two with me. I saved his ass and he saved mine."

"I think I remember you and mom talking about him. Was

he the one who became Surgeon General?"

"Yeah, Syd's the best."

After being called "Syd," David studied his father and focused first on Tom's partially paralyzed left hand — the one he variously claimed had been "hit by a Jap sniper" or "smashed in a Jeep door." Since the old man's skin had lost its color and had become partially translucent, David could make out the subcutaneous metal splints connecting the left hand to the lower three fingers that were immobile, permanently curved, and nerveless.

Then David noticed, when his father checked the time for ordering dinner, he had two watches on his left wrist. For a few seconds, the old man couldn't find the glass of bourbon that was right in front of him. Next, David saw that his father wore a brown sock on his left foot; a red sock on his right; and neither matched his plaid slacks or pink shirt with dribble stains down the front.

Tom broke his son's scrutiny. "Go over to the desk. Get my prescription pad. Top drawer."

After hesitating at being bossed around, David did as he was told and watched his father scribble out three different prescriptions and then hand them over. Sounding doctorly, the old man said, "Here, get 'em filled, tomorrow, in Meridian. Your peptic ulcer's over. Immediate relief. I guarantee it."

"But, dad, I don't have a peptic ulcer." David saw that one of the prescriptions was written upside down.

"Better yet," his father broke in, "I'm gonna pee and, while I'm in the bathroom, I'll get you some professional samples. We'll lick that damned tummy thing tonight." Rising up slowly from the LA-Z-BOY, he hunched his way, lopsided and caneless, into the dark. Left alone and still wondering why he had come back to Utah, David stared outside at as much of the panorama as the night would yield to the arc lights from the lodge.

Momentarily, David heard the bathroom door open and the approach of shuffling feet. He turned and recoiled at the sight of his father whose right hand tendered a glass of water, whose left hand offered an unidentified pill, and whose curved, fleshy penis hung down, exposed and dangling. The old man had forgotten to put it away after urinating.

"Thanks, dad, but I really don't have anything wrong with me."

"Take the pill, dammit. It'll help," his father said in a dictatorial voice that David had heard thousands of times growing up.

David hesitated.

Then came a softer, more caring tone that was new. "Please, son. Get well. Feel better. Swallow."

"O.K." David gave in to the old man's ministrations and put the mystery pill into his mouth, sliding it down between his cheek and lower gum. It tasted fishy — like cod liver oil — and he worried that it would dissolve before he could ditch it. "Dad," David said, pointing to the old man's penis.

His father glanced down and, without embarrassment, tucked himself in, forgot to zip up and sat back down in the LA-Z-BOY with his fly open. His speech pattern reverted to the swallowed, the unspaced and the run-on: "Tell-me-the-minute-you-feel-better-damned-tummy-thing-should-already-be-healing-that-medication-is-brand-new."

David feigned improvement. "Yeah, as a matter of fact, I already feel better, thanks." He covered his mouth, coughed and secretly spit the slippery orb into his right hand.

"What's that Dave?" His father pointed at the laptop.

"Oh, that's a computer."

"The-hell's-it-for?"

"It's an electronic gizmo that'll let me type, read and stay in touch with the office. I've got a giant case about to go to trial; that means I'll have to leave here in a couple of days and fly to London and then back to San Francisco."

Abruptly, Tom's curiosity ended and both men fell silent. From the illumination thrown off by the arc lights, father and son could make out windless snowflakes fluttering down and, in the distance, sheets and chunks of ice floating downstream and disappearing into the darkness of Uintah Canyon. Time passed and both men watched Amtrak's "California Zephyr" come winding into view on the opposite shore like a moving string of Christmas lights.

Slowly, father turned to son and, with an expression David had never seen before, said "I wasn't much of a father to you, Dave.

I made some horrible mistakes." Then, "I'm sorry."

"That's all right, Dad. It really is O.K. I've made my own mistakes and they've been plenty horrible too."

"Let's turn in. We'll talk tomorrow. Good to see you, son."

"It's good to be here, dad."

E-mail from David McQuade to Leah Pedrini:

Remember I told you at Tadish's Grill that I would think about not trying the Shasta case? This probably won't surprise you but I can't do that. Ethically, I'm too far in to get out. Emotionally, I can't back off, quit or give up. It's just not in me.

However, before you rush out and run off with a Nobel Laureate, let me say this as categorically as I possibly can: Within two days after the Shasta trial is over, you and I will get married and I will take a year's leave of absence from the firm, the law, and my current self. At the end of that year, there won't be a me or a you, only an us. Officially, you are now my fiancé and, finally, I am now an honest man. I love you and there aren't enough adverbs in the English language to enhance the description of my sincerity.

P.S. My dad and I got off to a slow start but, just before we retired for the night, things warmed up. The Alzheimer's makes talking difficult at times but not all the time. We'll have the next two days to figure out what happened to us.

E-Mail from Governor Bryan Eastwood to David McQuade:

We checked into the situation you and I discussed the other night. As it happens, there were some complaints in the file; there were also a few violations awaiting administrative adjudication; and there were also several Department Examiners who thought it would be a good idea to consider an audit. Consequently, the Department of Insurance FAXed a letter to London four hours ago and they've already been besieged by lawyers, both British and American.

The Department will stand behind the letter for the next four days. Unless I hear something from you earlier, the Department will at that time settle this infuriating flap and will drop the letter in return for some pissant word changes in Industrial Risk's future policies.

E-mail from Susan O'Shea to David McQuade:

I hope your flight to Utah was pleasant and that you and your father were able to catch up after all these years. During your "One Great Hour of Suffering," you received messages from ex-wives numbers two and three but not from number one. You also heard from both of your children. I've listed them in the order their messages came in:

> 1.   Lois FAXed a note that said, "When you walked out on me two years ago, you promised you would pay to fix up the Menlo house at your expense whenever the time came to sell it. That time has come. I've gotten bids and I've selected one for $85,339 and I've told the contractor to bill you."

> 2.   Joanne called and sounded furious. She wanted me to tell you that, "If I don't hear back from David in three hours about paying last year's taxes on the gains from the sale of the Baytrain Bonds, I'm going to get a new lawyer and this time it won't be a wimp that Franklin, Wolf and McQuade can intimidate."

> 3.   Jim left a voicemail and said, "Hi Dad. The job at Tower Records didn't work out so I won't be able to pay back the money I borrowed just yet but I've got a new band and I'm hoping for some gigs and coin soon. Hope all's well."

> 4.   Another voicemail was from Julie who sounded upset. She said, "I'm not getting along with Tad anymore, and I want to live in your guest house."

5.   There was also some office news. Three Franklin, Wolf and McQuade associates were elected partners. Ten candidates were passed over and, of those, rumor has it that six will be "elevatored out." Mr. Franklin said your absence was noted. He likes being a Grand Imperial Vizier and wonders "if Viziers wear fezes?"

E-mail from David McQuade to Susan O'Shea:

1.   Call Lois and tell her to read our Property Settlement Agreement, which I now know almost by heart. At page 38, or maybe it's 39, she'll see she got an extra $27,000 from my 401(k) plan because of the Menlo house fix-up flap. I don't owe her anything, anymore, ever.

2.   Send Joanne this letter by Fed Ex and sign my name: "You've hired and fired virtually every domestic relations lawyer in the Bay Area. Why don't you look somewhere else for a lawyer to harass me? May I suggest Istanbul? When you call Turkey, find out whether Viziers wear fezes (an inside joke)."

3.   Call Jim and say "hi" in return. Don't mention the loan, the job, Tower Records, the band or the "coin."

4.   Julie's boyfriend's name is not "Tad." It's "Tat," as in "Tat's Tenderloin Tattoos" and the guy's got wallpaper for skin. She can't resist young men with wild names, unsuitable occupations and pharmacological dependencies. Tell her she can live in my guest house but only *after* she's been tested drug free, provides proof of that and has dumped her scuzzbag friends for good.

5.   I'm amazed that wife one didn't call. When you talk to Jim or Julie, ask if anything's happened to Beth. I'm actually worried about her but, for the life of me, can't imagine

why.

6.   Finally, advise John P. Franklin that I think Vizier's wear fezes but that I've asked one of my ex-wives to research it.

Chapter Twenty-Six

CONFESSIONS

"Gutenmorga" the cheerful hostess said as David and Tom appeared for breakfast at the main dining room in the Sunrise Village Lodge. To enhance the Swiss Alps atmosphere, the staff was instructed to use Swissdeutsch words that had obvious English cognates, like "good morning."

"Two please," David said.

The hostess gave them a broad smile and, with menus in hand, guided father and son to a table for two next to the panoramic windows that ran from one end of the dining room to the other. Outside lay a frozen still-life of canyon, mountain and river where the only movements were from a solo hawk in a fixed-wing glide above and a slow-moving coal train on the D&RG tracks below.

So far, it had been a difficult morning. After waiting for what had seemed too long for his father to get dressed for breakfast, David peeked into Tom's bedroom and, to his astonishment, saw his father standing in front of a full-length mirror and staring quizzically at himself with a wide wet spot covering the front crotch region of his pants and vertical streaks running down both pant legs. Tom had put his boxer shorts on backwards with the fly facing to the rear rather than the front and had urinated in his pants but couldn't figure out how it had happened or what to do about it. Twenty awkward minutes later, David had his father cleaned up, dressed and ready for breakfast.

At the table, Tom was embarrassed but had already forgotten the reason why and David was quietly wondering how to revive the warmth of last night. Silently, both men stared at their menus until a perky young waitress in an Alpine costume appeared to pour them coffee and take their orders. "It'll be right up," she said, gathering menus and walking away.

"Syd, is your Aunt Tess still alive?" Tom asked.

Wrong names didn't faze David any more. "No, she died in 1971. It was sudden, probably a heart attack but nobody knows because there wasn't an autopsy."

"She have a doctor?"

"Of course not."

"You have doctors?"

"I did," David said. "Mom must have really laid down the law to Aunt Tess about doctors and religion before she left for Loah because I never attended the Christian Science Church and I always saw doctors whenever I needed them, which, after the polio, wasn't very often."

"What did she do about religion?"

"Sent me to a Presbyterian Church around the corner."

"I was a Presbyterian once," Tom said. "They teach you how to feel guilty and hate Catholics?"

"All about guilt. Nothing about Catholics."

Swallowing vowels and running words together, Tom said, "So-what-was-it-like-living-with-her?"

"Not easy. In some ways, you were just a warm-up for the main event."

"How's-that?"

David sipped his coffee and said, "When you were at the hospital or on housecalls, you weren't around giving me quizzes or demanding perfection. But Aunt Tess was after me, almost full time, calling me from her office even when I was in school."

"About-what?"

"Academics."

Tom's word mushing vanished as fast as it had appeared. "Didn't I hound you about academics?"

"Not like Aunt Tess," David laughed. "I never thought I would miss our quizzes but I did."

"Why's that?"

"Your punishments – the beatings and the spankings – hurt but they were always over in a hurry. But when I made mistakes in Boston, Aunt Tess forced me translate Latin and it always took hours."

"You're joking?"

"I'm not joking at all, dad," David said. "These days, any time I hear or see the name, 'Virgil,' I get nauseated."

"Who's Virgil?"

"Just an old Roman I learned to hate."

"What about sports?"

"Aunt Tess didn't give a damn about sports but I did, though not for the right reasons like having fun or being fit."

Momentarily, the subjects of Virgil and sports confused the old man and he asked, "Wasn't Virgil the first baseman for the Red Sox in 1941?"

"I have no idea, dad."

"I had a Virgil as a patient once and I think his last name was something like Jensen or Hansen."

In an effort to bring Tom back to reality, David pointed out the window to the coal train that was still inching its way along the Nephi River and asked, "Where does all that coal come from, dad?"

The question worked. "From the other side of Price where there are some huge coal deposits. So you played sports in Boston?"

"I was a second team, all-city linebacker and I hated every minute of it."

"Why'd you play then?"

"Polio."

"I don't get it."

"After the polio, my right leg was shorter and slower than my left and the doctors at Boston Children's Hospital told me I wouldn't play sports again and so I had to play sports again and, as you and Aunt Tess taught me, I had to be the best and it bothered the hell out of me that I was on the second team and not the first."

The waitress arrived with their breakfast and refilled their mugs with coffee. When David started to butter his wheat toast, he noticed that his father had picked up a fork and was studying his scrambled eggs, motionless and perplexed. "What's wrong, dad?"

"What's this?" his father asked, looking at the fork.

"Come again?"

"What is this thing?," Tom asked again.

David laughed and said, "It's a fork, dad."

"O.K., a fork. But what's it for?"

David realized that this was another Alzheimer's symptom and quietly said, "Let me show you." He moved his chair next to his father's and gently guided the old man's hand and fork into the scrambled eggs and then up into his mouth. David repeated this motion several times until, suddenly, Tom pulled his hand away and smoothly started eating and said, "I get it."

"Good for you, dad."

"Good for me?" Tom repeated rhetorically, back in command of his brain. "Why? Because I figured out what to do with a fork? Because sometimes I piss in a toilet not in my pants? Because sometimes I call you David? Because I can remember Syracuse, Morro Bay and Loah but not yesterday or this morning?"

Still at his father's side, David put his hand on Tom's shoulder while the old man went on with his soliloquy. "I wanted to die fast, like LaRoux, not mindless or in diapers, like my father. All my life, I've been terrified of what's happening to me right now." Tom dropped his fork, put his face in his palms and, without self-pity, said through his fingers, "My father was a vegetable and I'm turning into one myself. I've tried to kill myself but there's nothing around here that I can do it with. I'm sorry, David. I'm so awfully sorry that, after all these years, you have to see me like this." Behind his hands, Tom sobbed. "I'm so, so very sorry."

"There's nothing to be sorry about," David said in a soothing voice and put an arm around his father's shaking shoulders. "I suspect you and I are going to use the word 'sorry' a lot before I leave for London."

Tom nodded.

David said, "What I feel the sorriest about is the magic show mom and I put on to hurt you as much as we could."

Tom thought about that confession for a moment and then trumped it with one of his own. "What I feel sorriest about was leaving you on the floor, paralyzed with polio. When I've got all my marbles, I beat on myself for walking out on you as a father and as a doctor."

"You can stop beating on yourself as of now, dad. Nobody will ever know where the McQuade family's disintegrations come from."

"I know," Tom mumbled.

"What are you talking about?"

"It started with me."

"What do you mean?"

Tom tried to say something but it came out in a series of wet, unintelligible sputterings that drew stares. When Tom had regained his composure, he looked around and said, "Let's get the hell out of here. These old geezers give me the creeps."

As they got up from the table, David said, "I'll go buy a newspaper."

"You do that. I'll visit the men's room."

"Don't forget to unzip and then rezip," David said as a quasi-joke.

"Thanks for the advice," Tom laughed. "I think I've got the hang of it."

"I'll see you in the lobby."

"Right."

After they parted, Tom headed toward the "Restrooms" sign but, on the way, he got befuddled, lost his bearings and started walking with the outward appearance of purpose but without the inner realities of direction, location or destination. Meanwhile, David bought his paper at the sundries store; glanced at the front page for a few minutes, checked his watch, returned to the dining room, looked into the men's room, walked quickly back to the apartment, and, with no sign of his father, called the Village hotline.

"He's done this before," the person at the other end of the line said. "What we do is put all staff on alert; search outside first because it's below freezing out there, and then, if necessary, we go apartment-by-apartment-and-broom-closet-by-broom-closet. We'll find him, don't worry."

Three hours later, a maid found Tom in the central laundry room buried beneath a pile of dirty linens that had apparently dropped on top of him from an overhead chute. The old man was dehydrated, terrified and crazed. After she dug him out from under the sheets, Tom charged his rescuer and, in a rage, beat on her with his right fist until the bewildered young woman was able to escape and call for help. Moments later, three male orderlies gang tackled Tom and, during the melee, unintentionally overdosed him with repeated stabs of liquid tranquilizer. Immediately, Tom went limp and they carried him straight to the Village Medical Center.

With his head spinning with concerns for his father and doubts about himself, David spent the rest of the day and much of the night sitting next to his drugged, unconscious father. After the doctor assured David that Tom would be all right and that the tranquilizer would wear off by early the next morning, David dragged himself back to the apartment. All he had the energy to do was turn on his laptop and click into his e-mail.

E-mail from Beth McQuade to David McQuade:

Today Jim was involved in a car accident in Tiburon. He has multiple lacerations and a badly broken arm that will require surgery. Jim's driver didn't have insurance; the other driver didn't have insurance, and, of course, Jim doesn't have insurance because you terminated it three years ago. So, he's at County Hospital as an indigent and I want him transferred down here to the Stanford Hospital where the surgery and the care will be first-rate and where I can, from Los Gatos, be close by.

I expect you to make the arrangements and cover the costs. If I may say so, it's time for you to stop being a lawyer long enough to be a father.

E-mail from David McQuade to Beth McQuade:

Beth, you've caught me at a very bad time but our son made

a series of bad decisions like quit college, be a rock musician and live a dead end life. You didn't do that. I didn't do that. He did and it's time, actually it's overdue, for him to live with the consequences of his own mistakes.

I took Jim and Julie off my payroll after they each ditched college and became chronological adults. Neither one of them was eligible to remain on the firm's health insurance plan once they were out-of-school and had reached 21. He will be well cared for at County Hospital and I'll ask a surgeon friend of mine to make sure that happens.

If I understand your e-mail correctly, you think that I would be acting like a father if I paid for him to be transferred to Stanford Hospital. What pains me is that defining parenthood in terms of paying money is something that you and I have done for a long a time. What I never understood until last night is that parenthood is more than paying for things. It involves something I did little or none of — talking, listening and telling our kids my truths, sins, and realities.

As it happens, I'm in Utah with my own father whom you never met, and I'm thinking a lot about fatherhood. Of course, I should have spent more time with Jim, Julie and you and less time in the courtroom. However, the courtroom generated big bucks for all four of us to enjoy the best of everything except for the best in ourselves.

I don't exactly know what to do about these deficiencies now but I suspect that talking honestly and openly with both kids would be a good place to start. At least I'm going to try.

E-mail from David McQuade to Leah Pedrini:

Jim is in County Hospital with a broken arm from a car wreck and needs a good orthopedic surgeon. Could you please make that happen?

I realize that, in my earlier e-mail, I made the grand assumption that your answer to my question to marry me and be my fiancé would be "yes." I didn't mean to be presumptuous but, in the terrible chance that your answer is "no," find out from Susan when I'll be over the Atlantic Ocean and then radio your negative answer to me and I'll jump out from 35,000 feet. By the way, I'm a lousy swimmer.

Seriously, the more I think how close I came to losing you the more frightened I feel. Leah, you are already number one in my Feelings Department and, as soon as the Shasta trial is over, you will be number one in my Departments of Time, Energy and Life. Stay away from Nobel Laureates and please hang in there for me. I love you.

E-mail from Susan O'Shea to David McQuade:

Julie came here to pick up the keys to your guest house and she swore that she was off drugs and that she got rid of "Tat." However, she looked terrible and so did the guy who was with her, somebody named "Natcho."

I hope all's well in Utah. Warren says that it was "pure hell" dealing with Mr. Santos concerning trial exhibits. Only three of the thirteen lawyers eligible were made partner. Five others were offered positions as permanent associates and the last five were, as some have cruelly put it, "elevatored out."

E-mail from David McQuade to Susan O'Shea:

Jim's in County Hospital. Please send or smuggle a six-pack of Anchor Steam Beer into him each day. Keep track of what's going on there and e-mail me current status reports. Get the firm's travel department to send him brochures about salmon fishing trips in Alaska and have him pick one out that he and I will take as soon as I'm rid of the Shasta case.

Julie conned you, just as she has conned everybody else including herself. She's obviously still on drugs and, if "Natcho" is the guy I think he is, his real name is "Ignatio" and he's an ex-con who's in a cartel with the Hell's Angels to monopolize crystal meth sales in the Bay Area.

Julie has always loved Beth's brother, George LeClair, who's a determined but talentless artist and who lives with his funky wife outside Taos, New Mexico and his number is in my computer. Please call George and ask him, for Julie's sake, to fly to San Francisco and, if possible, to take Julie back with him to New Mexico. I'm told by Dr. Reid that there are some good drug treatment centers in New Mexico but right now she needs love and understanding before she can go through drug detoxification and God knows she hasn't gotten much, if any, love and understanding from me.

Tell George he has a blank check from me to do whatever it takes. Since he's always broke, you should make all the travel arrangements on my credit card and then have the firm's accounting department send him a check for $5,000 drawn on my account.

I would call him myself but he has never approved of me or Beth. Now that I think about it, he probably has some pretty good reasons.

E-mail from Warren Stanfield to David McQuade:

I just got off a conference call with a chorus of hostile voices that yelled at me in British, American and Scottish accents. It seems that Industrial Risk Underwriters received an unsettling letter from the California Department of Insurance and the guys at Industrial Risk are out of their minds. Evidently, they've talked to George Santos (surprise, surprise) and Big George nominated you as his number one suspect behind the letter (surprise, surprise).

They are demanding a "full explanation" from you and they wanted you to know that, if Big George is right, "You won't get away with this bloody behavior (or is it spelled behaviour?)." Also they demanded to speak to you "IMMEDIATELY" and I told them that was impossible but that they wouldn't have to wait long because you would be in London in a couple of days.

George told them that Governor Eastwood was once a partner here. I confirmed that and, as you instructed me to say, I also told them you and Bryan were also old friends going back to Stanford Law School days. They smell an American rat and that's what you wanted in their nostrils.

That said, I've still got knots in my stomach and qualms in

my conscience about what we're doing. I'll pray for us both.

E-mail from David McQuade to Warren Stanfield:

Thanks for the update about the Brits. I want them to sus-pect but not know what's happened because I want them to fork over the $725 million in return for my best efforts to intervene favorably on their behalf through the Governor to the Department of Insurance. Of course, the Department is going to diplomatically back away from its letter no matter what I do but the Brits won't know that and, from their perspective, $725 million will be a cheap price to pay to avoid a full-scale audit in California.

Now, about your stomach, conscience and prayers: I under-stand and I'll take complete responsibility for everything we do or don't do in this Shasta mess. If there is ever a question about any-thing, I'll tell whoever asks that you were following my orders and that you fought me at every turn.

I know that two wrongs don't make a right but sometimes they do cancel each other out. Remember, Industrial Risk had no basis at all to stonewall Shasta on the insurance policy. Just because we later learned from the FAX in Fred's credenza that Industrial Risk unknowingly had a contractual basis for dishonoring its policy doesn't redeem the Brits whose intentions were evil and who have been happily spending Shasta's premium checks for years.

Take care. Cool down. Onward Christian Soldier.

Chapter Twenty-Seven

REVELATIONS

$\mathcal{A}$fter a fitful night on the outskirts of consciousness, David finally fell into a REM-stage sleep at about five-thirty in the morning and found himself in the middle of a bizarre, technicolor criminal trial. In it, David was handcuffed and flanked by two police officers. Leah was on the witness stand, crying. Tom, apparently the prosecutor, was asking her questions. On the bench, black-robed and acting as if she had never seen her son before was Virginia Russell McQuade. Just as David started to tune into what was being said, a telephone rang and kept on ringing until David couldn't integrate it into his dream and had to wake up, climb out of bed, stumble to the dresser at the far side of his father's guest room and answer the noise.

It was a nurse at the Sunrise Village Medical Center and David could hear his father yelling in the background. Without an apology for calling so early, she got straight to the point. "Mr. McQuade, your father has had a difficult night and we need your help."

"What happened?"

"The tranquilizers your father got yesterday apparently set off a cycle of sedation, agitation, more sedation, and more agitation

207

until he's reached the point that he's a danger to himself and others and we don't have anybody here at this hour who can contain him and so we need your —"

Her voice was drowned out by Tom McQuade's screaming, "GET ME THE GODDAMNED HELL OUT OF HERE!"

"Did you hear that?" she asked.

"Yes."

She said, "A few minutes ago, he broke one bed restraint and, while there's still a leather strap across his legs, his arms are free to hit and throw things. He just ripped out the built-in light fixture above his bed and threw it at one of our aids."

"My god."

"We couldn't get a hold of our medical director so I called Dr. Roberts who prescribed another type of tranquilizer and he told me to call you to ask if you could come over here —"

"I'M A DOCTOR AND I DEMAND TO BE DISCHARGED," Tom ranted.

"— to hold him still long enough for one of us to inject him with what Dr. Roberts just ordered. Would you please?"

"I'll be there as soon as I can but, nurse?"

"Yes?"

"How can a tranquilizer cause violence?"

"I have no idea but some Alzheimer's patients can be really scary. They're usually tough guys and they're most dangerous when they're coming out from having been snowed under by a general anesthetic or heavy tranquilizers."

"Thanks, I'll be there shortly."

As David hustled down the hallway and approached his father's room, he could hear the bedlam inside and could see three white-outfitted women cowering outside. Just before he walked in, an iv bottle came flying out the door followed by "I'LL KILL THE NEXT SONOFABITCH THAT TRIES TO GIVE ME A SHOT."

David walked in and saw medical debris — bed pan, iv tubes, cups, straws, pills — scattered everywhere. Most visible was a florescent reading light smashed and in pieces on the floor.

"MY SON'S A LAWYER AND HE'LL SUE THE SHIT OUT OF THIS PLACE."

"No he won't," David said, making straight for his father whose legs were strapped to the lower half of the bed and whose arms were flailing and grabbing at the leather restraint. David leaned over the bed and said, "I'm here, Dad. It's going to be all right now."

Momentarily, Tom stopped his thrashings and, through eyes of a cornered beast, looked up at David. Suddenly, he grabbed David's shirt with his bad left hand, pulled his son's head down to bed level and started pummeling him with Tom's usual weapon, a fisted right hand.

David jerked himself upright, startled but not hurt, and instinctively cocked his own right fist for a counterblow and stopped himself with a, "JESUS, DAD." Instead of following through with his right hand, David threw both hands onto his father's shoulders and pinned the old man back into the bed. Meanwhile, the room filled with white uniforms and a nurse, carrying a loaded syringe, ran to the other side of the bed.

WAIT!" David yelled at the nurse and, panting, said, "just . . . please . . . please wait . . . please . . . I think he's had enough . . . I'll try to calm . . . him down . . . if you'll . . . just excuse us . . . for a while."

Perplexed but dutiful, the nurse retreated to the hallway as David's hands went from pressing against his father's shoulders to stroking the old man's wrinkled neck and sweat-streaked bald head. Once there was calm, David reached down, unbuckled the lower restraint and put a cup of warm herbal tea up to his father's lips that one of the aids had handed him. With David holding his father's head and tilting the cup, Tom sipped the warm liquid and, before finishing, fell into a sleep so deep that he was unaware of the sponge bath, and change of clothes, covers and sheets. With David at his bedside, Tom slept for the next eleven and a half hours and woke up, slowly and refreshed, in time for a peaceful supper of soft food and more herbal tea.

"How do you feel, dad?"

"Pretty good, how about you?" Tom had already forgotten about getting lost in the laundry room, raging in the hospital and punching his son. "What are you doing here?"

"Oh, I just dropped by to see if you would like to sleep in your own bed tonight. I've made the arrangements."

"Damn right," the old man said, bright-eyed.

After an orderly had wheeled Tom back to the apartment on a gurney and David had helped him undress and put on his pajamas, David hoisted his father up into bed, propped him against two large pillows and handed him a snifter of brandy. With the hospital battles behind them, Dave sat down in a nearby rocking chair, swirled the carmel-colored liquid around in his own snifter and raised the first of several topics that needed airing.

"Dad, I want you to move into the life care facility for assisting living. Stan tells me it's essential. The people here say its essential. And, after what you went through yesterday and today, I think its essential."

"I'm staying put."

"I know you don't like the idea, but you're not going to be able to manage around here by yourself."

"Next-door's-that-old-bag-Harriet-she'll-give-me-a-hand-Syd."

"Dad, her name's Judy. She's a nice lady. But with her gout and cataracts, there's no way in hell she can take care of you. Christ, I'm only in my fifties and lift weights and yet I could barely do what needed to be done a little while ago."

"Still-say-no."

"Well, as I sometimes have to tell clients and opposing lawyers, there's an easy way and then there's a hard way. The easy way is obvious. So let me tell you about the hard way."

Tom took a slug of brandy, looked away from David and, pouting, pretended not to listen.

"Remember when I had polio and you and Stan went to Judge Moeller to get a guardianship?"

Tom didn't answer.

"Well, there's another judge there now. Name's Judge Gibbons. He's a good guy and I've already spoken to him. It'll be a piece of cake to get myself named as your guardian and have you physically moved into life care whether you like it or not."

Suddenly clear-eyed, Tom McQuade flared with biting fluency. "It won't be life care, it'll be death care but the death part of it doesn't bother me. In that place, I'll be a goddamn vegetable but I'll be worse than a vegetable because vegetables don't forget, don't cry, don't let their peckers hang out, don't slobber, don't get lost, don't fly off the handle, and don't pee or poop in their pants." Tom's snifter tipped over onto the bed and the brandy ran onto the covers as the old man started blubbering, "I-don't-want-to-be-a-vegetable . . . don't-let-it-happen . . .please."

Dave dashed into the bathroom, grabbed a wet towel, came out and sopped up the brandy while tears ran down his father's cheeks in multiple rivulets. "I won't but you can't stay here on your own."

Tom gave his son an appreciative look.

"After I leave tomorrow morning, Stan and Lu and a staff person will be here to help you move."

"Leave?"

"I've told you there's a huge trial about to start in San Francisco and I've got to go to London first and then fly straight back to California."

"When're you leaving?"

Exasperated, David said, "I've told you already, dad, tomorrow morning. I'm scheduled for the early shuttle and I'll be gone by the time you wake up."

"Don't-want-you-to-go," Tom said and started to cloud up again.

"I'll call every chance I get and I'll come straight back after the trial is over, dad. You can count on it."

"You will?"

"I will."

The old man looked at his empty snifter and brightened up. "Let's have another nightcap."

"We've both had enough, dad. Plus, I want to talk about a few more things before we turn off the lights."

"Like what?"

"Like, whatever happened to that Fry fellow?"

"Sonofabitch-sued-me-cuz-I-broke-his-jaw."

"That's Christian forgiveness for you," Dave laughed.

Peter D. Baird

Tom smiled and said, "Judge Moeller fixed his wagon."

"What'd Judge Moeller do to Del?"

"Sentenced him to a firing squad."

"They executed Del Benson?"

"No, the LDS Church couldn't stand the idea of a Benson being executed so the Governor commuted his sentence to life in prison."

"And Maxine?"

"She divorced Del and sold the ranch and moved with her daughter to New York City. Rumors had it that she married a millionaire and moved to France."

David let some time pass so he could work up the nerve to ask the most difficult questions of all. Then, in a voice louder than he had intended, David said, "According to Stan's letter, you think you killed mom. Was Stan right about that?

"Yes."

"What the hell did you mean?"

"I could have saved your mom after Del shot her."

"Stan told me you did everything possible to save her."

"He's wrong."

"He said that even the best surgeon in the world couldn't have stopped the bleeding from a bullet wound like that."

Tom's eyes were as pallid as his skin and yet he was in more control of his faculties than David had seen him since coming to Utah. Without swallowing as much as one vowel or running two words together, Tom said, "In Peleliu, I saved Marines who were wounded worse than your mom."

"I don't understand."

"Any skilled surgeon could have saved her. Stan knew that."

"But you were exhausted. You had been up for over 24 hours straight. Eva had just died from a vaccine the government said was safe and a madman had just shot your wife in the chest." There was irritation in David's voice. "At the time you tried to save her, you weren't just any skilled surgeon. Come on, dad."

Tom continued. "Stan's coroner report was right. Your mother died from a penetrated thoracic aorta, exsanguination and asphyxiation." In a voice that was strong and unaffected either by

212

Dave's irritation or by his own Alzheimer's, Tom said, "The bullet had only grazed her aorta."

"What in the hell are you trying to say?"

"What I'm trying to say is that, in the final analysis, what killed your mom wasn't Del's bullet."

David was the one agitated now. "If Del's bullet didn't kill her, then what did?"

"This." He held up his misshapen left hand and then, in a sad monotone, said, "I had a scalpel in it. I must have had a spasm that I didn't feel and the blade must have moved sideways and severed her aorta. Before I knew it, blood had flooded her chest cavity and she was gone. I can't remember why, at that point in the surgery, why I would have been holding a scalpel at all." He looked away from his left hand and directly into his son's eyes and said, "So now you know."

"But you can't blame yourself for your left hand!" David insisted. "You got shot in combat so blame the Japanese or blame the war!"

"That's not true either and that's the most important thing you need to know about me. Open the bottom drawer next to you. There's a manila folder in there. Take it out."

Hands trembling, David did as he was told, removed a dusty folder and opened it up on his lap. In it was a fragile carbon copy of an official U.S. Army document, a Judgment from a Court Martial held on board the hospital ship *The Mercy* dated October 12, 1944. The caption read, <u>The United States Army v. Captain Thomas McQuade, Jr.</u>

"Read it out loud, son."

Slowly, tentatively, David read what a Judge Advocate Officer had written more than fifty years earlier:

On September 18, 1944, Captain McQuade was outside the marine-field hospital on the Island of Peleliu during hostilities. Captain McQuade has little or no memory of what happened but he thinks a Jap sniper may have fired a single shot that seriously wounded Captain McQuade's left hand. He required immediate surgical attention, hospitalization and removal from the front.

No Jap sniper could be found. All hostile forces had been cleared from the area hours before. Captain McQuade's .45 was found nearby with one round fired. In light of the evidence of malingering and of a self-inflicted wound, this proceeding was convened to determine whether Captain McQuade should be found guilty and, if so, what his punis ment should be.

We find the accused guilty as charged and the evidence to be overwhelming. Malingering — inflicting a nonlethal wound to create a "million dollar injury" to avoid combat — is a cowardly act that undermines morale, is unworthy of any American soldier and is one of the most odious of military crimes.

However, we were moved by the testimony of Lt. Sydney E. Silverman, who told of Captain McQuade's heroic hand-to-hand fight in the foxhole in which Captain McQuade killed a Jap night fighter and saved Lt. Silverman's life. Lt. Silverman also explained how Captain McQuade then proceeded to operate on dozens of wounded Marines for some 72 hours until he became delirious from the heat, loss of fluids, salt depletion, sleep deprivation and exhaustion.

Lt. Silverman also said that Captain McQuade will pay a terrible professional price for having shot himself in the hand. Apparently, Captain McQuade is a gifted surgeon whose medical career will be permanently stunted by this injury.

Under these circumstances, Captain McQuade should not be criminally punished and he should not be given a dishonorable discharge or even a general discharge. However, the Army never tolerates any form of malingering and, in this theater of the war, a demotion in rank is the automatic consequence, regardless of mitigating circumstances. Thus, this Court concludes that Captain McQuade should be demoted to the rank of First Lieutenant.

In view of Captain McQuade's distinguished service record as a brave combatant under enemy fire and as a tireless surgeon in the South Pacific campaign and in view of the recommendations from his officers and men, and yet, at the same time, recognizing that malingering must always result in a sanction,

IT IS HEREBY ORDERED:

Honorably discharging Captain McQuade in the ordinary course; demoting Captain McQuade to the rank of First Lieutenant; preserving his monthly entitlement for disability compensation at the sum of $15.50 a month; and directing the Prosecuting Officer to prepare a form of Judgment that is not inconsistent with this Order.

When David had finished reading the document, his father said, "I was a fraud. When people asked about my hand, I lied. For years, I falsified reality. It wasn't a Jap sniper or a Jeep door. It was me. I was the coward who shot himself, violated military law, and ruined my own career. I'm the one who lied about it and hauled us all off to Utah and drank like hell and resented your mom's faith healing and laid Maxine every chance I got and terrorized you with quizzes and left you on the floor with polio and made myself Del's target and, worst of all, failed your mom on the operating table when she needed me the most and when both of us wanted each other the most."

David tried to quote the exonerating language from the Court Martial Order. "But dad, it says here —"

"It says there that I was a coward and that I lied at my own trial and that I single-handedly ruined my own surgical career and brought shame upon myself that I couldn't face or admit —"

"JESUS, DAD, STOP IT!"

Tom didn't heed his son's directive. "Then, when I got back from the war and realized that my injury was permanent and there wouldn't be a cardiac fellowship at Mass General for me or a life in Boston for your mom, I made everything worse."

With lips quivering, David stood up, moved over to his father's bedside, and sat down next to the old man who then lost all composure, broke down and, through tears and spittle, wailed words that were drowned in his blubberings but sounded like "Virginia," "left hand," "lies," "polio" and "Peleliu." For the next thirty minutes, David held his father until the sounds of two men crying became the sound of one man snoring.

Wobbly and dizzy, David made his way into the living room where a floor lamp was on and where he carefully lowered himself onto one of the two empty Lay-Z-Boys. He drew a series of deep breaths, struggled to collect his emotions and felt himself drenched in sweat. Not knowing what else to do, he mindlessly turned on the laptop and read his most recently received e-mail. The electronic message was from Leah and, as David read it, tears poured from eyes already wet and pain drowned a soul already flooded.

E-mail from Leah Pedrini to David McQuade:

I received your e-mail in which you told me, beautifully and lovingly, that you and I were engaged to be married after the Shasta trial was over, maybe next year sometime. As I tried to get across to you at Tadish's, I'm lonely and I can't wait and wait and then wait some more. I know you meant it but your contingent request to marry me re-confirmed my secondary status in your life. David, I need to feel more important than anything else in your life and I don't.

My grandfather was a doctor from Milan and was the wisest man I ever met. Before my first marriage, he told me *"L'Amore e' auito. Di spasarsi e' lavoio."* Roughly translated, it means "Love is support. Marriage is work." After I met you and for the first time in my life, I tried to love someone by giving him support and I was prepared to work every day with you on a marriage. Now, that cannot be.

Roger and I were married yesterday and tomorrow we leave for Italy. I delayed sending this to you until after the ceremony. That way, I couldn't change my mind.

I've left a lot of men. There have been two husbands, a number of live-ins and a string of boyfriends. Each time, I was happy to get out and, each time, I found myself singing Ray Charles' version of 'You Don't Know Me,' because none of those men knew me. How could they when I didn't tell them who I was? Maybe I was afraid they wouldn't love me if they knew that I wasn't the Goody-Goody-Pretty-Face-Doctor I pretended to be.

You were different because you knew me, inside and out. No matter what I confessed to, you listened, understood, and never thought any less of me. You knew my fears, fantasies, sins and drugs. You also knew about the young woman who died because I made an unforgivable surgical error and then covered up my mistake.

Yet, I didn't know you. No matter how hard I pried, you shut me out with deflections, silence and, the most effective technique of all, burying yourself and your feelings in the courtroom. I don't know what's inside you. I don't know your needs, sins, mistakes and fears. Knowing has to be mutual, symmetrical. Otherwise one is vulnerable and the other isn't. One is in the know and the other isn't.

Of course, Roger doesn't know me and he never will. But there will be mutuality because I'll never know him either. We'll spend our time on each other's margins, like 99% of the other couples in the world. We'll have money and the same social circles. We'll have the same conversations, denouncing HMOs, insurance companies, Medicare and the price of a new Lexus.

There will also be some support that might not sound like much but it is. Yesterday, he helped me get an interview with a first-rate surgical group. If I get the job, I'll be out of the free-lance assisting business.

I realize that you disapprove of him and I grant you that he is no Nobel Laureate. However, by marrying Roger, I've chosen something all the time over nothing some of the time. I wish someday that you will find peace. Maybe then you will also find love.

Chapter Twenty-Eight

THE FINAL PRETRIAL CONFERENCE

*B*lack's **Law Dictionary** defines "venue" as "the particular county or city in which a court with jurisdiction may hear and determine the controversy." In the Ridgemont case, San Francisco was the venue, Barry G. Wallendorf was the judge and the courthouse was at Seventh and Mission. Built in 1905 in a neighborhood considered even then rundown, the federal building was an early example of the American Renaissance/Beaux Arts style that embodied, in its orderly grandeur and monumental beauty, the vision of an American century. By the late 1990's, its sandstone was pocked, streaked and grimy; its classical facade of arched windows, colonnades, cornices and balustrades faced a shabby Greyhound Bus Station across the street; and its reflection of American optimism faded on a front sidewalk where derelicts urinated, panhandlers begged and darkly suited lawyers came and went.

On the morning of December 18, 1995, lawyers in the Ridgemont case cleared metal detectors, packed themselves into an antique elevator cage, got out on the third floor and filed into Courtroom Number One. At exactly 11:00 a.m., the bailiff banged his gavel and commanded, "ALL RISE." A side door opened and out came a scowling, roly-poly judge whose toupee was slightly off-center and whose only exercise for the past 27 years had been climbing up four steps to the bench and bouncing up and down on his seat cushion whenever he was agitated.

With everyone standing, Judge Wallendorf enthroned himself and looked out from his authoritative elevation at a marbled courtroom surrounded by paired Corinthian columns and arched panels over mosaic murals. Behind him was a waterland mural entitled, "The California Delta." From the back of the courtroom, the squat, hunched-over, black-robed judge looked like a dark toad which had hopped out of the Sacramento River.

The bailiff, clerk and court reporter were seated below the judge at their own elevated stations. Ten feet from them, centered in the well of the courtroom floor, was a lectern where trial lawyers stood to address the court, examine witnesses, talk to the jury, and grovel with, "Thank you so much, Your Honor" and "Good Point, Your Honor." Behind the lectern were two long, wooden tables for trial counsel and off to the judge's right was a jury box beneath a mural of the San Joaquin Valley entitled, "California Agriculture." Beyond the railing or bar was the gallery, consisting of eighteen pews filled that morning with plaintiffs, lawyers and press.

"PLEASE BE SEATED" was the bailiff's next directive. Everyone did as they were told and, after the momentary sounds of resettlement, the courtroom was quiet.

In a scratchy, high-pitched voice, Judge Wallendorf said, "Mr. Stanfield, I see that Mr. McQuade still has not graced us with his presence."

Warren stood up at counsel table where he was flanked by Shasta's CEO, Fred Danielson, and two other Franklin, Wolf and McQuade lawyers. "As we have explained —"

Judge Wallendorf broke in. "Mr. Stanfield, Rule 16 requires the presence of the lawyer who will try the case and that is Mr. McQuade, I believe?"

"That's correct, Your Honor, Mr. McQuade will be lead counsel. However, as I started to say, Mr. McQuade is in Utah with his father who has Alzheimer's. We expect him back tomorrow for trial."

Warren's statement wasn't currently correct because, at that moment, David was on his third scotch in the first class cabin of a British Airway's 747, flying from London to San Francisco. Earlier in the day, David had met with a hostile group of Industrial Risk executives and solicitors at the Browns Hotel where David was deliberately late so as to allow the caterers to do as he had instructed and go heavy on the whisky and light on the hors d'oeuvres.

What made the gathering a success wasn't the whisky, but rather these unspoken realities: the Brits knew but couldn't prove that David had arranged for the letter from the California Insurance Department and David knew but couldn't prove that the Brits had made an unholy alliance with Santos to refuse coverage for the Ridgemont explosion. Proclaiming this to be a "convention of sinners," David agreed to drop Shasta's bad faith case against Industrial Risk and to use his "good offices" with his close friend the Governor to get the audit letter rescinded in return for a $725 million check from Industrial Risk. With vulgarities that sounded odd when expressed in BBC English, the President of Industrial Risk handed over the check after David called Sacramento.

Instead of drinking to celebrate a successful strategy, David drank to numb himself against the actual loss of Leah and the expected loss of his father. Leah had been there for him, wanting him and now she was gone, wedded to another man. His father had been there for him, wanting him and he would soon be gone too, turned into a vegetable. To have had so much and then to have lost it was beyond the power of David's brain and body to comprehend. Eventually, he fell into a scotch-soaked sleep over Newfoundland.

Back in San Francisco, Judge Wallendorf was addressing both sets of counsel. "Magistrate Evans informs me that a jury has been picked. Is that right?"

Immediately, Warren was on his feet. "We objected during the voir dire and we must object again today because Mr. Santos repeatedly asked the panel such conditioning, bias-building questions as, 'how do you feel about corporations that burn innocent people?'"

"A 'yes' or a 'no' will do nicely, Mr. Stanfield," the judge said. "My question was simple: has a jury been empaneled? At that point, Judge Wallendorf turned to George Santos whose swollen rhetoric about pain, suffering and bereavement had paid off handsomely for him in seven-figure contingent fees, private jets, horses, and women. The darkly-complected Santos lifted his heft up from counsel table; tossed back a shock of moist, black hair; hunched his shoulders in exaggerated deference; and spoke with an oiliness that always worked with Judge Wallendorf. "Thank you, Your Honor. The jury has been selected and has been qualified for a twelve-month trial. If I may say so, the jurors appear to be an unusually intelligent group."

"I'm happy to hear that, Mr. Santos. However, it is an immense imposition upon the jurors, my staff, me and litigants in other cases who need their day in court to have this case consume us for one week let alone fifty-two!"

The burly lawyer smiled at his colleagues flanking him and then, shamelessly sucking up to the black robe, oozed, "You Honor is absolutely right and we agree 100%. It is such a waste of judicial resources for you to endure a year-long trial and so cruel for the victims to have to wait so long before they can receive their just compensation." He signaled the importance of what he was about to say with a deep sigh, "Unfortunately, Shasta has only offered a pittance to settle and so you and we have no choice but to drill until we finally strike justice."

"What is Shasta's current posture on settlement?" the judge asked.

Warren rose and said, "The company wants badly to settle. However, since Industrial Risk denied coverage and we've had to sue them for bad faith and since the company is on the financial ropes, $38 million is still our best offer."

With a blend of frustrated resignation and angry portent, the judge said, "Well, if Shasta wants a long trial then we'll give it a long trial. Is there anything else we need to take up today?" Nobody spoke. "We'll begin with opening statements tomorrow morning at 9:00 a.m., with or without Mr. McQuade."

"ALL RISE."

Chapter Twenty-Nine

TRIAL

The rule about opening statement is that lawyers should simply tell the jury what they intend to prove during the trial. No argument, no emotion, just unvarnished expectation. The next morning, when Santos began his opening statement, it was immediately apparent that he had no intention of following that rule and the judge had no intention of holding him to it. For over two hours, he growled and clawed like a Kodiak bear on its hind legs. "Shasta burned my clients alive," he thundered. "That gigantic corporation was negligent; it was also reckless; and it must have known about the leaks before the victims were napalmed into ashes and scars."

Repeatedly, Warren objected and each time the judge said, "overruled."

Santos coordinated his verbal onslaught with scenes that a technician projected onto a large screen in front of the jury, showing charred bodies, disfigured survivors and acres of rubble. "To compensate and make the plaintiffs' whole, you must, at the end of this case, render a verdict in the amount of $725 million against Shasta for negligence because, once Shasta knew that the branch line made by U.G.F. was leaking, it should have shut down the trunk line that was also made by U.G.F." At that moment, a multi-colored pie graph appeared on the screen, dividing $725 million into different sized slices for death, pain and suffering as well as for property, medical and income losses.

Santos let the $725 million figure sink in for an extended moment. Then, slowly pounding the lectern in rhythm with his words, Santos said, "But Shasta was more then negligent . . . it . . . must . . . have . . . known . . . about . . . the . . . dangerous . . . condition . . . of . . . the . . . trunk line . . . and . . . must . . . have . . . decided . . . against . . . a . . . safety shutdown . . . to . . . make . . . a profit . . . declare dividends . . . and . . . get . . . Shasta's President . . . a golden parachute . . . worth millions . . . in severance pay . . . And you . . . must . . . do . . . more . . . than . . . award . . . $725 million." Another pause and then more pounding and more syncopation. "You . . . must . . . punish Shasta . . . and teach it . . . and all of corporate America . . . that these heinous acts . . . will not be tolerated . . . by folks like you . . . who trust public utilities . . . to put your safety . . . and the safety . . . of your loved ones . . . ahead of their bottom-line profits . . . and million-dollar executives."

This time, the screen showed Shasta's net worth which was, according to Santos' accounting, $98 billion. "To send a message to a company this large, you must render a verdict for $725 million and another verdict, one for punitive damages, in the sum of at least $5 billion! That's right, $5 *billion* because anything less would be a financial slap on the wrist."

Santos was hitting his stride when the courtroom door opened and he turned away from his outline to see David McQuade walking in, carrying a briefcase and looking wan. Santos went back to his outline but, by then, he was out of synch with his projectionist. Rather than get flustered, the consummate trial lawyer smiled and said, "Let me welcome Mr. McQuade to these proceedings and close with one last slide that needs no explanation from me and that can never be explained by Mr. McQuade." As David approached, Santos' technician flashed up a sunless cemetery scene where rows of dark coffins, each slick with rain, faced rows of open graves. George Santos sat down, smiling and satisfied.

David made straight for the lectern. "Ladies and gentlemen,

my name is David McQuade. The first thing I ask of you, Judge Wallendorf and Mr. Santos is to forgive me for being late." Nothing from the judge or Santos suggested forgiveness.

"I won't mince words. My client is the Shasta Valley Natural Gas Pipeline Company which owned the pipeline that took lives, injured innocent victims, destroyed property and devastated livelihoods. On behalf of Shasta's thousands of employees and hundreds of thousands of shareholders, I want you to know how horrible they feel about this tragedy and how much they want you, me, Mr. Santos and Judge Wallendorf to do the *right* thing."

David cleared his throat and then announced, "Shasta . . . will pay . . . for *all* loss . . . *all* pain . . . and *all* suffering." The courtroom stirred. "The plaintiffs want $725 million to compensate them and Shasta will pay every penny of that $725 million with its deepest regret."

At that, David reached inside his coat pocket and removed the certified check for $725 million check from Industrial Risk. "This," he held up the multi-million dollar piece of paper, "is a certified check made payable to the Ridgemont pipeline disaster victims in the sum of $725 million." Judge Wallendorf's eyes bulged as David emphasized that, "This check is unconditionally payable at the conclusion of this trial, no matter what your verdict might be."

At that point, David chose his words with lawyerly care. "Shasta does not concede liability and submits that the U.G.F. Metallurgy Company of St. Louis company defectively manufactured the pipes and caused leaks that were ignited by friction from one of our earth tremors. Nevertheless, Shasta wants to be a good citizen and knows that the right thing to do is to pay this money so that, whether they win or lose — the victims will be made whole and be compensated at the end of this trial."

The jurors riveted on the check. "Your Honor," David asked, "I know we have not reached the testimonial stage of this trial; however, may I approach the clerk and have her mark this $725 million certified check as Shasta Exhibit Number One?"

"Of course, you may," the judge said, warming to this lawyer whom he had disliked for decades.

Instantly, Santos knew what was happening. Somehow,

David had wrung $725 million from Industrial Risk and he was using that money now to transform Shasta into a company with heart that the jury would be reluctant to devastate with punitive damages. But that was not all. Since the $725 million check would only be payable at the end of the trial, Santos would be the one blamed for prolonging these proceedings and delaying distributions to the victims and so it would be Santos, not McQuade, who would become Judge Wallendorf's whipping boy and be under pressure to settle for $725 million, distribute funds to the victims and end the trial.

Yet, Santos had no intention of settling the case for $725 million or abandoning it now. He already had enough money for himself, of course, but what he didn't have was control of a Fortune 500 corporation with its power, prestige, perks and jets. Since he and his clients were already assured of getting $725 million the minute the trial ended, there was nothing to lose by going forward except time and the use of the money. All-in-all, Santos believed that pressing on for punitives was the professionally correct thing to do, despite how much the judge might bellyache.

There was still the problem of proof, not just any proof but clear and convincing proof that Cook knew about the corrosion in the trunk line; that Cook told Danielson about it; and that Danielson instructed Cook to delay a safety shutdown. Before David showed up in court with the $725 million check, Santos was the Good Guy and could have gotten a verdict for punitive damages without pre-senting hard evidence or breaking a legal sweat. But now, he was the Bad Guy and, as such, he needed clear and convincing proof of deliberate misbehavior. The more he thought about it, the more Santos suspected that Cook's widow knew the true story but, of course, he couldn't talk to her. Yet, a lot can happen in a long trial; Santos had already "won" $725 million, his calendar was clear for the next twelve months, and so he decided to soldier on and see what happened.

David handed the clerk the check and said, "Please mark this as Shasta Exhibit One."

"Shasta Exhibit One will be received in evidence," the judge said, smiling.

Turning again to the jury, David said, "I didn't hear what Mr. Santos told you before I arrived but I'll bet the amount of Exhibit One that he wanted a lot more than just $725 million, didn't he?" Two jurors nodded. "I'll also bet that he asked you for billions of dollars to punish the very company that just handed over that $725 million check, didn't he?" More of them nodded. "One more wager: Mr. Santos didn't tell you that anyone at Shasta actually knew about the leaks in the trunk line before the calamity, did he?" Almost to a person, they nodded.

Then David proceeded to break the same rule Santos had already broken that forbids emotion or argument during opening statement. "When he asks you to award billions on top of the $725 million that Shasta has now just paid, Mr. Santos is asking you to give out free money that won't teach anyone a lesson and, instead would bankrupt a public utility you depend on for natural gas; it would throw hard-working employees out of work, and it would destroy the retirement savings of hundreds of thousands of people just like you whose pension funds are invested in Shasta stock."

"Objection, argumentative and move that what Mr. McQuade just said be stricken from the record and the jury admonished to disregard it," Santos interjected.

"Overruled and denied."

"But your honor," Santos whined.

"I said, overruled and denied, Mr. Santos!"

When Judge Wallendorf had finished roughing up Santos, David sat down with a quiet, "Thank you."

With both counsel having finished their opening statements, Judge Wallendorf summoned McQuade and Santos to the bench for a whispered, side-bar conference out of the jury's hearing. "George, let's end this thing right now so your clients can get their share of the $725 million and start rebuilding their lives."

"Afraid I can't do that, Your Honor," Santos said in a low rumble. "Shasta knew about the trunk line leaks and we are entitled to punitive damages." Jabbing a thumb in David's direction, Santos said, "I don't want to delay my clients' getting their money or to prolong this trial any more than you do, judge; but David won't offer me a dime for punitives."

"Are you crazy?" the judge hissed at Santos. "That check for $725 million, minus your 1/3 fee, will go to the victims right now, without wasting a year while you try to bankrupt a public utility that, for better or for worse, we all depend on around here."

"Then tell David to come up with a billion dollars in punitives and we'll all go home."

Standing there, David knew the truth and knew what Cook's FAX said and knew what Danielson was told and knew what Danielson had done and knew, if those facts came out, why Shasta deserved to be walloped with punitive damages. Consequently, David did what lawyers often do and, that is, tell the literal truth while implying a broader message that was false: "Your Honor, George has no proof, none, that anybody at Shasta knew about the trunk line explosion before the blast. None at all."

"You'd better convene your clients," the judge growled at Santos. "Let them make their own settlement decision."

"I don't have to, Your Honor," Santos pointed to his briefcase beneath counsel table. "I've got their written powers of attorney, authorizing me to settle this case at the time and on the terms I deem most advantageous."

"You're in a box, aren't you George?" the judge seethed. "You promised the world a mind-boggling punitive damage verdict that'll put you in control of our gas company and that's the reason you won't settle, isn't that right?"

Santos ducked the question. "I believe, in my best professional judgment, that Danielson knew about the trunk line corrosion in time to have prevented this disaster but didn't do so for reasons of personal and corporate greed and therefore Shasta should be punished with punitive damages."

"Do you have clear and convincing evidence of that?," the judge shot back.

"Yes, but it'll take some months to develop."

Chapter Thirty

VERDICT

$\mathcal{M}$onth-in and month-out, the trial dragged on until courtroom Number One seemed like a science fiction time chamber where hours slowed to an agonizing standstill and days stretched into weeks of hopeless incarceration. Five days a week from 9:00 to 12:00 and from 1:30 to 4:00, the jury snoozed, stared at the ceiling, doodled on their notepads and lost themselves in out-of-body experiences. Meanwhile, the judge fumed, sustained objections from David and hectored Santos to "move on."

While Winter, Spring, Summer and Fall crawled from the future, through the present and into the past, Santos projected dozens of videotapes; lugged in thousands of medical records, photographs, computer printouts, financial documents, police reports, and dying declarations from those who lived only long enough to tell of their agony; and put on the stand metallurgists, chemists, geologists, physicians, psychologists, firemen, policemen, paramedics, morticians, priests, ministers, rabbis, and survivors who had been burned, disfigured, traumatized and dispossessed.

On cross-examination, David McQuade and Warren Stanfield took turns asking only one question of each witness Santos put on the stand: "Do you have any personal knowledge that anyone at Shasta knew of corrosion or the leaks in the trunk line pipes before the explosion?" Every witness answered, "No."

Each night, David called Utah and heard, from his father's increased garble and decreased lucidity, the progressive ravages of Alzheimer's. Sometimes, the old man thought he was back in medical school. At other times, he wanted to "see LaRoux." He called David "Syd" or "Stan." He complained that Harry Truman was "socializing medicine." He would put the telephone down in mid-conversation, walk off, forget about the open line. By mid-September, Tom had been moved from assisted living into the locked-down Alzheimer's ward where patients couldn't take or make calls. From then on, all David could do was call and hear a staff member report that his father was "doing as well as can be expected."

After Tom was moved into the Alzheimer's ward, David tried, night after night, to call Stan and Lu Roberts for more information but nobody answered. Finally, his persistence paid off in October when, after a trial day of Santos' getting blocked and blistered by the judge, David heard a voice from Utah answer the phone and say, "This's Stan."

"Stan, this is David, where've you been? I've been calling you guys every night for weeks." In a somber voice, Stan said, "Lu had another stroke. This one was massive. She's still in the hospital in Salt Lake and I've been down there with her."

"Oh, God. Is she going to be all —"

"No," he said matter-of-factly. "She's paralyzed. Can't talk. Still in intensive care and she won't ever leave the hospital."

"Are you okay?"

"No," he said, again in a matter-of-fact tone. "But without Lu, I don't want to be okay."

"What's going on with you, Stan?"

"Same old cardiac crap but it's worse now. The doctors want me to have surgery and I've told them to go to hell."

"How does Lu vote on your surgery?"

"She voted 'no' by blinking her eyes twice yesterday. We've both had a great life together and now it's time."

"Time?" David asked, knowing exactly what Stan meant.

"Time to resign, check out, die. It's easy. Thousands of people do it every day." There wasn't a trace of self-pity in his voice.

"You don't sound that upset."

"Oh, it's inconvenient but your dad's the one I feel sorry for. At least Lu and I still have our wits left whereas Tom has lost his brain, bowels, bladder and dignity at the same time and he would despise the condition he's in. If he had a choice, he would've ended it right after he saw you."

"I'm hoping to have this trial finished by late November or early December. Right after it's over, I'll fly straight to Utah and do everything I can for you, Lu and dad."

"There's nothing you can do for Lu and me."

"Are you sure?"

"Absolutely, young man. And thank you from the bottom of my infarcted heart for coming back to Utah and seeing your dad. It meant the cosmos to him and the world to me."

David said, "It meant even more than all that to me, Stan. Thank you for getting me back there and helping me find my father, my mother and maybe, just maybe, myself."

By the afternoon of December 5, Judge Wallendorf had had enough. "Tomorrow morning, this case will end," he announced.

"But Your Honor," Santos bleated.

"Do not, Mr. Santos, bring any more computer printouts or C.P.A.s or videotapes or geologists or engineers or doctors or photographs in here to bore us. Instead, bring in some clear and convincing evidence that someone at Shasta knew about the danger and deliberately refused to shut the trunk line down. Otherwise, I'll grant Shasta a directed verdict, the victims will finally get their share of the $725 million that's been waiting for them all these months and the jury can be set free." The jurors broke into applause.

The next morning, as David sat at counsel table, waiting for the trial to resume and thumbing through an airline guide for flights from San Francisco to Salt Lake City, Warren jerked him up by the shoulder and shoved him to the back of the courtroom and into the relative privacy of a coat rack alcove. "What the hell's going on, Reverend?"

"Dave," Warren gasped. "I just heard that, last night, Santos met with Alex's widow, Bonnie Cook, who told Santos that her husband had quickly checked out the trunk line for leaks and found some awful corrosion and had called Danielson for authority to shut it down because he didn't have time to actually verify any leaks and Danielson wouldn't let him and so Alex FAXed Danielson a cover-his-ass shut-down request and then called Bonnie and went to the valve to close off the flow without Danielson's authorization." Warren was panting.

"ALL RISE."

Both lawyers scrambled to get back into their seats.

Santos stood at the lectern and said, in a confident voice not heard in months, "Plaintiffs call Bonnie Cook to the witness stand."

A short, hair-in-a-bun, plainly dressed woman in her late 50's came through the door escorted by one of Santos' investigators. The bailiff met her, guided her to the clerk for the oath and then ushered her to the witness stand where she settled in nervously behind the microphone.

Santos said gently, "Please state your name."

"Bonnie Cook," she peeped.

"Mrs. Cook," Judge Wallendorf said in a kindly tone, "Please pull the microphone closer so we can hear you."

That done, Santos launched into a series of leading questions. "Your husband was Alex Cook? He worked for Shasta? He was the troubleshooter for the Ridgemon t area? He died in the explosion? Did he call you shortly before the explosion? What did he say?"

Before she could answer, David was on his feet. "Your Honor, may I *voir dire* the witness?"

"You may."

"Mrs. Cook, are you here by subpoena?"

"No."

"How did you come to be here today?"

"I was told it was my duty."

"Who told you that?"

She hesitated and then looked up at the Judge. "I'm not supposed to answer that, am I?"

The judge looked puzzled. "Yes, you should Mrs. Cook. Why would you think otherwise?"

"Well, because of what that gentleman told me," she said, pointing at Santos.

"What did Mr. Santos say?"

"Something about how the law made my meeting with him confidential."

Santos leaped to his feet and said, "Your Honor, I can explain."

"Sit down, counsel," the judge snapped. "Mr. McQuade, you may proceed."

"Was it Mr. Santos," David asked, "who told you it was your duty to come here today?"

"Yes."

"You mentioned a meeting with Mr. Santos, when was that?"

"Last night."

"Where?"

"In my living room."

"How did he happen to be there?"

"He knocked on my door at about 8:15 . . .and . . . said he wanted to talk to me . . . real bad . . . about . . . about Alex." She momentarily lost her composure.

"How did he introduce himself?"

"Objection," Santos interrupted. "This is cross examination, not *voir dire.*"

"Overruled."

"Well, he said he was an officer of the court and he had come to ask me some questions."

"An officer of the court?"

"Yes."

"Did he explain what that meant?"

"No."

"What did you think it meant?"

"FBI, police or something like that."

"Somebody who worked for the government whose job it was to gather facts for a trial?"

"Objection, leading."

"Overruled."

"Well, that's what I thought," she said meekly.

"Did he lead you to believe you had a duty to talk to him?"

"Yes."

"Did he tell you he was one of the lawyers for the plaintiffs in this lawsuit?"

"No."

"Did he tell you that it was unethical for him to talk to you without having a lawyer present from your husband's company?"

"Obj —"

"Overruled."

"Did he tell you that anything your husband said to you in private was protected by what is called the marital privilege and that you had no obligation to tell him what your husband said?"

"No . . . he . . . he didn't."

"Did he tell you that you didn't have to come here and testify until Judge Wallendorf amended his pre-trial order and until a subpoena was served on you and you were paid a witness fee?"

"Not really. He told me that, normally, there were some formalities but this was an emergency."

David turned toward Judge Wallendorf. "Your Honor, we move that Mrs. Cook be excused without further examination from Mr. Santos and the reasons are many. First, it was unethical for Mr. Santos to contact the wife of a Shasta employee without calling us and making sure we were present at any conversation with Mr. Santos. Second, Mr. Santos did not tell her about the marital privilege which he knew about and she obviously didn't. Third, Mr. Santos should've properly identified himself as the lawyer for the plaintiffs and not mislead Mrs. Cook by telling her he was an "officer of the court," which all lawyers are but which does not make us the F.B.I. or the police. Fourth, he never listed Mrs. Cook as a witness and your Honor ruled months ago that no additional witnesses would be allowed unless you explicitly permitted it in advance. Finally, Mrs. Cook had no duty to be here without a subpoena and a witness fee."

Santos made for the lectern saying, "I can explain everything, your Honor."

"Not now, you can't," the judge hissed. He then turned to the witness and said, "Mrs. Cook, you are excused. Thank you for coming. You have my condolences."

"Thank you, your Honor," she said as she stepped down.

Santos wasn't rattled, not in the least. He never expected that Mrs. Cook would be allowed to testify to what her husband had told her in private. Of course, Santos didn't like to cut ethical corners and get caught at it and be scolded by a federal judge. But it wasn't the first time and, besides, it was worth the humiliation because, at long last, he now knew the truth which, happily, was far more damning than he could possibly have imagined. That truth, that fabulous truth, meant billions.

Santos had called Mrs. Cook to the stand so that Danielson, McQuade and Stanfield would know that he knew what Cook had told Danielson by phone and by FAX. Since they now knew that he now knew, they would have to come clean with the truth. With an expectant smile, Santos boomed out, "Plaintiffs call, as an adverse witness for cross examination, Frederick Danielson."

That hit Fred Danielson like a bolt of lightening. Seated between David and Warren, Danielson had frozen into an ice sculpture when Mrs. Cook was on the stand and then, just as quickly, had thawed into a puddle of relief when she left and blessedly took the truth with her. Now, Santos called him to the stand and, again, Danielson was fast-frozen.

David leaned over and whispered, "Get up there and tell the fucking truth, Fred." He nodded, stumbled out from behind counsel table, stood before the clerk and promised to "tell the truth, the whole truth and nothing but the truth so help me God."

Throughout the trial, Fred Danielson had followed his lawyers' strict instructions "to show up looking like an insurance salesman from East Dubuque." Today, he was not the same man who had, for months, worn off-the-rack polyester suits, scuffed oxfords, wrinkled wash-n-wear shirts and wide silk ties with cable cars on them. Since he had expected the judge to throw out the plaintiffs' punitive damage claim and end the trial today, Fred had indulged himself with an early morning manicure and a contoured haircut and had come to court wearing an Armani suit, a monogrammed white shirt, a Versace tie and high-sheened shoes with tassels. Indeed, he had begun his day feeling great and now, on the witness stand, he had never felt worse in his life.

"State your name," Santos said looming behind the lectern.

"Frederick M. Danielson."

"You're the Chief Executive Officer of Shasta Valley Natural Gas Company?"

"Yes."

"And you were the CEO when the Ridgemont explosion occurred?"

"Tragically, yes."

"Mr. Danielson, did Alex Cook call you shortly before the blast?"

"Yes, I have already testified that he did."

"As you just heard, I spoke to Alex Cook's widow last night and learned some interesting information."

"Objection."

"Sustained."

Santos had expected that objection and that ruling.

"Isn't it true that Mr. Cook told you he found corrosion in the trunk line and it wasn't safe but, since he didn't have time to verify any leaks, he needed your approval for the shut down?"

"No."

"No." As if Danielson's answer had been a blow to the head from a heavy-weight boxer, Santos just stood there, dazed by something that he didn't expect and that he knew was false. Seconds later, he pulled himself together and asked, "Didn't Alex Cook send you a FAX and ask for authority to shut the main trunk line down?"

"No sir, he did not."

Santos was shocked. Danielson had to know that Santos knew the truth. McQuade and Stanfield had to know that Danielson was lying. Weren't they worried about perjury or the obstruction of justice or disbarment? Santos was so flustered that he asked the kind of question trial lawyers never ask unless they've got proof in hand to show that the witness is lying: "Are you sure?"

"I'm positive."

Just as Santos was about to ask the same question again and

get lied to again, the judge broke in and said, "Mr. Santos, unless you have evidence that will impeach what this gentleman has just said, you're finished."

"But your Honor," Santos pleaded. "If you had let Mrs. Cook—"

Judge Wallendorf exploded, "YOU TREATED THAT LADY ABOMINABLY AND CONDUCTED YOURSELF UNETHICALLY, MR. SANTOS. YOU'RE ALL DONE, THIS CASE IS OVER, YOUR CLIENTS WILL FINALLY GET THE MONEY THEY SHOULD'VE HAD LAST YEAR. Do I hear a motion for directed verdict?"

David sat in his chair, pressing a row of lower teeth into his upper lip and staring at the table. Warren elbowed his partner. "David, make a motion."

"Mr. McQuade? Mr. Stanfield? Somebody? Do I hear a motion for directed verdict?" Judge Wallendorf looked like a jack-in-the-box behind the bench.

After more sputterings at his inert partner, Warren rose stiffly and said, "So moved, Your Honor."

"Motion granted."

The bailiff banged his gavel. "ALL RISE."

Chapter Thirty-One

JOHN P. FRANKLIN

*I*t took a gloomy David McQuade over an hour to extricate himself from the unwelcome hand shakes and back pats at the court-house before he could catch a cab and, through a heavy December downpour, reach the California Street offices of Franklin, Wolf & McQuade. Wet, tie loosened and feeling the opposite of jubilant, McQuade knocked on the corner office door and heard an ebullient voice say, "Come on in David."

John P. Franklin's office was like its occupant: large and dis-tinguished. Through his expansive windows, the stately, six-foot, four-inch, 76-year-old lawyer could, on a fogless day, see both bridges spanning San Francisco Bay and, with Wagnerian Operas playing in the background, liked to report the occasional sighting of a "Valkyrie escorting heroic trial lawyers up to Valhalla above the Golden Gate Bridge." Opposite the windows was one wall devoted to Yousuf Karsh photographs of each United States Supreme Court Justice since 1945, all personally dedicated to John P. Franklin. Built into the other wall were shelves filled with books, articles and speeches written by his favorite author, John P. Franklin.

When David entered, Franklin was standing behind his desk,

silhouetted by a background of low-hanging rain clouds pierced by the distant spires of the Golden Gate Bridge. "Congratulations! The single malt has been poured and I am already, as you magicians are fond of saying, one ahead." Franklin pointed to a waiting glass of sherry-colored scotch whiskey and bade his victorious partner to sit. "You made $725 million appear and billions of dollars vanish! I'd say that was Big Time Magic!"

Stiff from months of trial, David sat down with arthritic effort. He had occupied that same chair hundreds of times in the past when the two partners, one junior and the other senior, shared "Vespers" at the end of each business day — drinking, confiding and plotting. "Thanks," David muttered without meaning it.

Over a chinless face that sloped at a dignified angle into his bow-tied shirt collar, Franklin beamed at the younger man whom Franklin had taught at Stanford and had mentored at the firm. David had rocketed beyond Franklin's highest professional hopes but, to his regret, David had never found marital harmony or personal peace. While ice cubes bobbed in Franklin's bonded bourbon, he said, "David, you just raised Shasta from the dead."

"Sonofabitch lied, John. That's how we won. Save your congratulations."

Franklin sighed. "Warren called me from the courthouse and told me the whole story. It's a terrible thing that Fred did. It'll be on his conscience for the rest of his life. It was absolutely deplorable." Franklin meant every word.

"John, it's more than deplorable, it's a felony."

"I'm sure you instructed Fred to tell the truth."

"Of course I did."

"Then, it's not your problem. You aren't responsible for Fred's mendacity."

"Perjury, not mendacity," David leaned forward on the desk, forming a tent over his scotch with elbows tilted and hands locked. "John, I think I have an ethical obligation to disclose the perjury and get the truth out in the open." He got up, walked over to the bookshelf and pulled out a thick, blue-bound volume that contained the California Business and Professions Code For Lawyers. He returned to his seat and thumbed to Ethical Rule 3.3(a)(2). "Listen to this," he read out loud, quoting. "If a lawyer knows a client has rendered materially false testimony, then the lawyer must remonstrate with the client to tell the truth, withdraw from further representation or, if necessary, disclose the instance of false testimony to the court." Finished reading, David chuckled sarcastically. "It looks like I'll have to write a letter to my new buddy, the Honorable Barry G. Wallendorf."

"I'm surprised at your lack of thoroughness, David." Franklin reached across the desk, took the blue volume in hand and, from the same page, read a footnote to his partner. "Rule 3.3(a)(2) is the Model Rule which has been proposed by the American Bar Association but which has not yet been adopted by the State of California." Franklin looked up at the younger man. "Most states have adopted the rule you just quoted, but *not* California."

He turned a page. "Let me read the statute that governs you in *this* state at *this* time and it's found at § 6068(e) under 'Duties of Attorneys.'" Franklin cleared his throat and read out loud the awkwardly-worded statute in question. "It is the duty of an attorney to maintain inviolate the confidence, and at every peril to himself or herself to preserve the secrets, of his or her client."

David gulped down the rest of his scotch. "Fuck Section 6068(e)! I'll stand with the Model Rules and do the right thing."

Franklin spoke in crisp, authoritative words. "If you 'do the right thing' in accordance with the Model Rules that do not apply in California, there will be hell to pay. You could be disbarred. Wallendorf would surely permit George to retry the punitives which, with the Cook memo, wouldn't take long to do and would end up bankrupting Shasta, dispossessing its shareholders and getting this firm and its partners sued for more than our insurance and within an inch of our financial lives. And if that isn't enough to scare you," Franklin smiled, "picture George Santos in charge of *your* gas company."

"All that may be so but isn't it time we did the right thing and not bury the truth?"

"The right thing for whom?" Franklin sputtered. "For the plaintiffs who got two-thirds of $725 million and were made whole? For George Santos whose one-third of $725 million ought to keep him in jets, horses and women for a long time? For Wallendorf who never had a fair bone in his bloated body? For the State of California which commands you by statute to keep your mouth shut?"

David raised his voice. "For the right thing because it is the right thing. For the truth because it is the truth."

"Wait a second," Franklin fired back. "Let's not get too saintly about this. Don't forget that you're the courtroom magician who wrangled $725 million from the Brits and who deftly created the illusion that Shasta didn't know anything about corrosion in the trunk line."

David placed his palms flat on the desk and, as if in pain, pushed himself up to his feet. "You're right about my complicity. But I can't do this kind of thing anymore. A few months ago, I would've agreed with you. It would've been a no-brainer. But not anymore."

Trying to sound fatherly and change the subject at the same time, Franklin said, "Look, you're exhausted. Get away. Take that beautiful doctor friend of yours up to my place at Tahoe and do some skiing. Let's give this subject a rest and we'll kick it around after Christmas and after you've rested up."

The words "beautiful doctor friend" pumped even more emotional poison into David's bloodstream.

"Remember what I told you about seeing my dad in Utah last year."

"Yes, a tragic story." Franklin was relieved to be onto another subject.

"My father, the poor bastard, had it all wrong. For years, he thought that killing the Japanese soldier, shooting himself in the hand and getting court marshaled had done him in."

"I see."

"But the self-inflicted wound didn't bring him down. His lies about it did." David frowned. "If my father had admitted what *really* had happened on Peleliu, then we could have known him, accepted him and loved him as he was. At the same time, he could have known himself, come to terms with himself and not spent years in the agony of self-loathing and booze. Do you understand what

I'm saying?"

"Maybe, but it doesn't have anything to do with you or the Shasta case, David."

"It has everything to do with me and the Shasta case," David responded. "I've lied a thousand times more than my dad ever did and I didn't just destroy one marriage or one woman or one child."

"David, for God's sake, get a grip."

David ignored the directive. "You're right, I have been an illusionist but of the worst kind. I lied to our Governor. I squeezed money out of Industrial Risk on false pretenses. I created misleading impressions with technicalities, innuendo, suppression and empty promises. To make things even worse, I've dragged poor Warren into all of it and compromised him. Just like my father, I've lived with what wasn't, what isn't and what won't be. No wonder I'm depressed. No wonder I'm alone. No wonder I lost that beautiful doctor friend you just referred to."

"I didn't know about your losing Leah and I am truly sorry. But doesn't the California statute about confidentiality matter to you?"

"Of course it does. But I can't use the law anymore to hide my sins or perpetuate an injustice."

"Let Big George cleanup this injustice. He can call up the U.S. Attorney and tell her what he knows and, once that's done, we can all leave Fred's lies in the hands of the prosecutors where it belongs."

"Get real, John. You know that perjury is almost never prosecuted. To get the facts, the prosecutors would need information from Bonnie Cook who, even if she waives the marital privilege, only has a hearsay story to tell; from Danielson, who has already lied and who's got a Fifth Amendment right to invoke; or from us and we've got the attorney-client privilege that zips our lips."

David thought for a moment. "You may not know this but last year the U.S. Attorney came within inches of indicting Santos for tax fraud and she didn't but she told me that she thought he was a lying scumbag and, if he asked her to prosecute Danielson, she probably wouldn't listen to a word he said. Even if she were to listen, she might have a hard time seeing how Danielson undermined a trial where the plaintiffs got $725 million."

"Exactly my point, David. Now you're back on solid ground. This injustice is Danielson's dastardly perjury, lie or fib or whatever you want to call it but it didn't hurt anyone."

"John, listen to me. The injustice here isn't merely perjury."

"What do you mean?"

"I mean that, by ignoring what Cook told him and delaying the shutdown, Danielson killed and maimed hundreds of innocent human beings. Forget about the perjury, think about the poor bastards in Ridgemont that Danielson burned alive because he wanted some fucking money." Out of breath, David leaned against the wall of Franklin's office, pale and unsteady. In a weak voice, he said, "Jesus, I don't know right or wrong anymore. I just know that I can't live this way any more."

Hoping that his partner's crisis had passed, Franklin brightened up and said, "Well I know something and that is you *need* another drink. He swooped up David's glass, swiveled around, and, with the overture from *Lohengrin* playing in the background, clinked in a handful of ice cubes and drenched them with 28-year-old scotch. When he swung back around with the brimming glass, David was gone.

Chapter Thirty-Two

LAROUX

The Sunrise Village limo driver ignored the winter travel advisories from the Utah Highway Patrol, downshifted and eased the van into a sharp, snow-packed curve on State Route 51. "Mister, you're awful lucky that I'd drive into the Wasatch on a day like this," he said over the whine from low gear and the thudding of heavy-duty snow tires, "or else you woudda spent the night in Salt Lake while the highway department plowed and salted this road."

His lone passenger, David McQuade, said nothing. Instead, he stared out the window ahead of him, unable to tell the difference between the inside condensation and the outside fog.

Suddenly, the van fishtailed on an unseen patch of black ice and grazed the guardrail separating the highway from a steep, 200-foot drop-off that ran down into the frozen Nephi River. With a jerk, the full-bellied driver reacted to the van's sideways movement and to the rasp of metal against metal. He braked, spun the steering wheel, regained control and, after some wheezing, grumbled. "It's gotta be damned important for you to get to Sunrise Village today."

"It is." Those were the only words David spoke until after he had paid the driver, unloaded his garment bag at the main lodge and walked 20 yards down an enclosed, heated walkway to what the illuminated sign said was the "Sunrise Village Life Care and

Medical Center." It was dark, the temperature was near zero, and light snow was falling.

David pushed open the door, heard a bell chime and felt the warm, dry, inside air. Looking around the reception area, he saw a squat fir tree in the corner decorated with Christmas cards and strings of popcorn; linking chains of red, cut-out Santa Clauses hanging from an overhead light fixture; and a waiting area occupied by a sleeping black Labrador that wore a "Pet Me" sign. To his right was an alcove office where a young woman in white fussed with paperwork and hummed along with Nat King Cole as he sang "The Christmas Song" over a background sound system.

"Excuse me." David put down the garment bag and unbuttoned his overcoat. The young woman looked up at the visitor.

"My name is David McQuade and I'm here to see my father, Dr. Thomas McQuade, in the Alzheimer's ward. Yesterday afternoon, I spoke with your director, a Mr. Hunt I believe, of my request to spend the night with my dad."

"Let me see." Nat King Cole crooned on about "chestnuts roasting on an open fire" as she thumbed through some loose papers. "Yes, Mr. McQuade. We've put a cot in your father's room for you. I'll call Mr. Hunt and he'll take you back to the Alzheimer's ward."

Soon, a ruddy-cheeked man with a heavy Texas accent appeared and thrust out his right hand. "Glad to meetcha. I think we talked last year about getting Dr. McQuade out of his apartment and into assisted living quarters.

"That's right."

"And you were a friend of Stan Roberts, weren't you?"

"Yes, Stan and Lu were my surrogate parents."

"Such a shame how both of them went within two weeks of each other, wasn't it?"

"Yes, I miss them terribly."

"Your daddy must miss them too because they were always coming over here to see him and bringing him food and stuff."

The two men left the reception area and, as they approached a set of locked double doors, Hunt laughed. "I'll tell you something. That daddy of yours is one tough son-of-a-bitch. Last August, he damn near choked me to death." Hunt jerked his tie up into a simulated hangman's noose, stuck out his tongue and feigned a dying gasp.

"I learned that myself, first hand," David said.

Hunt punched a digital code into a wall panel and the double doors slowly opened. David accompanied the director through the double doors and down a wide, hospital-style corridor. As they walked, he peered into the different rooms they passed and saw pencil-thin, prune-faced residents lying asleep with their mouths open; machines laundering what Hunt called "soils," metal contraptions onto which the helpless were strapped and dunked into tubs of bath water; and a central toilet facility where orderlies hosed off residents and changed their diapers. From all directions, David overheard elevated baby talk as staff members tried to coax residents into taking pills, standing up, lying down, putting something on, taking something off or going to the bathroom.

"Your daddy, we call him 'Doc,' should be down here in our multi-purpose room." Hunt looked at his watch. "It's 6:40 p.m. and the more ambulatory residents will have just finished dinner." He led David to the end of the corridor and into a large, spare, pastel-colored room where white-coated young people were clearing away plastic dishes and utensils from unclothed tables and two nurses busied themselves at their work station.

Throughout the multi-purpose room, more than thirty men and women, mostly in their '70's and '80's but a few in their '60's and even late '50's, wore tennis shoes and wrinkled, unmatched clothes and wandered about or slumped in wheelchairs or clutched walkers or sat impassively against the far wall in a row of green, plastic-covered easy chairs and made low noises with the English language. Complexions pale and expressions bland, none of them looked demented, just off-centered, unwell.

David missed his father at first but then spotted him sitting in a green chair at the far side of the room, mumbling to no one in particular and hiding his left hand under a ragged *AMA Journal* that lay open on his lap. More than a hundred and fifty pounds gone, eyes leadened, skin charcoaled and shoulders hunched, Thomas McQuade looked like a voodoo doll of his former self.

"There he is." Hunt tugged David by the arm and led him over to the old man who looked up, expressionless and still mumbling. "Doc," Hunt said in one of those loud, sing-songy voices, "Your son, David, is here. He's come all the way from California just to visit you and we've even arranged for him to spend the night in your room. Isn't that nice?"

There were some blinks that might have meant recognition. Then a frail voice repeated the same name that Hunt had just mentioned. "David?"

"Hi, dad. My trial's over. And I'm back from San Francisco, just as I promised."

Tom fumbled for his cane, wobbled up to a lopsided stance and pushed his right hand out as far as it would go. Father and son shook hands. While looking suspiciously around the room at the other residents who had already lost interest in the visitor from California, Tom whispered out of the side of his mouth: "WevegottagetouttahereStan."

"Doc's always trying to run away," Hunt said, chuckling. "He'll stand by the locked double doors for hours at a time just to try to escape whenever anybody comes through." As an afterthought, Hunt added, "Funny, he always talks about running away to see someone named 'LaRoux?'"

"LaRoux?"

"Yeah, LaRoux. Strange name. Never heard it before."

Tom continued to hold a wary expression and scan the other residents as David explained who LaRoux was. "She was his mother. Her name was LaRoux and she died when he was ten in 1917, from an overdose of chloroform during ulcer surgery. He hasn't seen her in over 79 years."

"Well, that sure is interesting and he became a doctor himself?" Hunt took Tom's uncaned arm and guided him and his son out of the multi-purpose area, back up the corridor and into Tom's private room, where the presence of a rollaway cot humanized an otherwise sterile, slick-floored, twenty-by-thirty space that had nothing in it except a tightly made bed, a plastic-covered chair, one window with thin purple blinds that looked out on the Nephi River, a wash basin and a wall mirror where two Christmas cards had been stuck between the glass and the metal frame. David put his garment bag and overcoat down on the rollaway.

"It's almost Doc's bedtime," Hunt announced as a prelude to his own departure. "I'll get one of the staff in here to clean him up, change his diapers and give him something to sleep on. You guys'll have about an hour to talk until he gets his snack and then the medicine will knock him out. By the way, you'd better prepare yourself for some soiled pajamas and a wet bed in the morning. Breakfast is served at 7:15."

David fidgeted outside in the corridor while a young man, wearing a white uniform and a black back support belt, put fresh diapers on Tom and got him ready for bed. In ten minutes, father and son were seated a few feet across from each other on their parallel beds.

"Are they treating you all right?" To his surprise, David elevated his own voice and sounded patronizing.

"LetsgetouttahereSyd."

David looked around at the bare, cold room. "This place is clean and all that but, Jesus, it's not what I'd call cozy."

"LetsgogetouttahereandseeLaRoux."

"Dad, we're not going anywhere because I've come to spend the night with you here."

"Here?"

"Yeah, here."

"Thisplaceistheshits."

"The people seem nice but I tend to agree with you." He looked around again. "It doesn't seem to be a fun place to spend time."

Mustering some logic, Tom seized on his son's observation and started to stand up. "LetsgoSyd."

David leaned across the space between the beds, put a hand on his father's shoulder and gently pushed him back into a sitting position. "Dad, we can't do that."

Like a chastened child, Tom started to cry. "GottagogottagoseeLaRoux."

For several seconds, David didn't know what to say or do but then he remembered the photographs. "We can't leave, dad, but I'll tell you what." He reached into his coat pocket and withdrew a bulging envelope covered with advertising for Kodak film. "Before I left San Francisco, I went through some drawers and pulled out a bunch of family photographs to show you."

David moved from the cot to the bed and sat down next to his father. The tears stopped as David handed photographs, one-by-one, to the old man who took them in his right hand while keeping his misshapen left hand buried in the folds of his pale blue, hospital-style nightshirt.

The first photograph was of a young man playing a guitar. "That's Jim," David explained. "He's a musician and plays in rock bands and is in the process of finding himself." Tom riveted on the young man's image.

"Now here's your granddaughter." David handed his father a photograph of a smiling 23-year-old. "Her name's Julie. She went to Southern Cal for a semester and wants to be an artist but, at the moment, is studying crystal meth and inappropriate men." The old man gazed down at the other grandchild he had never seen.

For the next twenty minutes, Tom was rapt as he inspected dozens more photographs of his grandchildren. They were in baby clothes, Halloween costumes, soccer uniforms, Little League outfits, prom attire, graduation gowns, at beaches, under Christmas trees, on horses and in swimming pools.

"You know who this is?" David gave his father a series of crinkled, black and white shots taken of Virginia as an Illinois social worker in 1939, as Madame Fortuno at a Chicago USO show in 1945, and as a Utah housewife in the early 1950's.

Tom looked closely at each photograph and was stumped.

Next, David gave him a three-by-five, wire-framed, wedding photograph of Tom and Virginia standing in front of Henderson Chapel at Syracuse University. "Maybe this will give you a clue."

"Whosthatguy?" Tom put the photograph in his lap and pointed to himself.

"It's you, dad, next to mom at your wedding."

"Me?"

"Now here are some real oldies." David dug out a yellowed snapshot of Tom's father taken sometime shortly after he had emigrated from Scotland to become an open hearth furnace foreman for the Carnegie Steel Company. Wearing a pork-pie hat, Thomas McQuade was standing next to a sign that said "Welcome to Homestead, Pennsylvania. Home of The Carnegie Steel Company."

Without hesitation, Tom said, "Poppa."

The last photograph — a faded oval in a small, antique wooden frame — pictured a softly-featured, faintly smiling young woman who wore a white blouse with puffy sleeves and her hair done up in a soft Gibson Girl cushion. The old man knew exactly who it was.

"LaRoux," he said. "Thatsmymomma." Repeating her name with a long, slow "oo" sound, he pulled out his gnarled left hand from the folds of the nightshirt and held her photograph in both hands, staring. When David asked how he could recognize that face after almost 80 years, Tom responded with surprising articulation, "LaRoux, I'll remember."

Again and again, they pored over the same photographs and, each time, Tom reacted as if he were seeing them for the first time. An hour passed. An orderly delivered a custard snack and David helped his father brush his four remaining teeth.

By 8:15, Tom's eyes drooped. "Lemmeseeitagain."

David knew what "it" was and showed his father the face of that same young woman who smiled gently at her son from before 1917 and beyond his tomorrows. "LaRoux," the old man repeated, pronouncing her name with that same, evocative "oo" sound. "LaRoux, I'll remember."

Ten minutes later, Tom was asleep, wheezing and snoring. His son turned off the light and, with his street clothes on, lay down on the lumpy rollaway. He didn't sleep because he hadn't come to sleep. Repeating the Robert Frost poem to himself about "the woods are lovely, dark and deep, but I have promises to keep," David had come to Sunrise Village because of a loose promise he had made last year to his father and one that he hadn't intended to keep.

For the next five hours, David stared at the dark ceiling, wondering if he had the guts to keep that promise. When he was young, he would have done it out of hate. But this night, if he had the will, he would do it out of love.

By 1:15 a.m., he decided that he could, he must. Slowly, he sat up, swung his legs over the edge of the cot, took his pillow in both hands and addressed his sleeping father in low tones.

"Dad, when I saw you last year, you asked me to promise to do something that's illegal, that's probably manslaughter in this state. At the time, I casually said that I'd do it but I didn't really mean it. In fact, all my life I've promised things I didn't mean so I could be polite, placate, win, get something or avoid discomfort."

He felt his eyes moisten. "Since then, I've thought a lot about what we said to each other and what I learned from you about illusions, lies and false promises." After a pause, he went on speaking to the wheezing, snoring figure. "All that phoniness, all those false promises are over now."

David rose up into a crouch, took two steps toward the other bed and, after a deep breath, shoved the pillow down hard against his father's exposed face. Abruptly, the sounds of snoring and wheezing stopped. David continued to push on the pillow with as much force as possible and felt no struggle, no resistance, no wiggling, only the gradual relaxation of his father's body into the hard bed that was made even stiffer by a tightly-stretched, rubberized mattress cover.

After four, maybe five minutes, David's arms and shoulders started to ache and, gradually, he pulled the pillow away. There was no sound, no movement. David felt rivulets of sweat and tears run down his cheeks and, in the dim light that penetrated the blinds from the main lodge, he could see the lifeless form of Thomas Douglas McQuade.

David spoke one last time to his father. "You just busted out of this place, dad. Now you can escape those double doors and go to LaRoux if she's there for you."

After covering the old man's body with a sheet, David mopped his own brow and followed the light over to the window. He pulled back the blinds and gazed outside at the powerful arc lights that, from the roof of the main lodge, illuminated the Nephi River and the mouth of Uintah Canyon. It was still snowing and the flakes were heavy and slow.

As he stood at the window, David was bombarded by scenes from the past — magic, polio, murder — and by visions of the future — criminal prosecution, maybe prison, for what he had just done and malpractice, maybe disbarment, for what he had said in a letter to Judge Wallendorf.

For almost 15 minutes, he strained to block out the images by concentrating on single snowflakes and watching each one float to the ground. But, from before yesterday and beyond tomorrow, the flashbacks and flashforwards kept coming, commandeering every thought. David felt his legs weaken and he leaned against the windowsill for support.

Then, as if from a tape player inside his head, he heard a familiar female voice. "The disappearing boy trick is easy," Madame Fortuno was saying. "Just shut your eyes tight, Davey, and you'll be invisible. It's real magic."

In the early hours of a cold Utah morning, David McQuade stood at the window and closed his eyes. He disappeared into blackness.

About the Author

PETER BAIRD has written for *The New York Times Magazine, Newsweek, The Wall Street Journal, Men's Health, American Heritage, The Chicago Tribune Magazine, The Cleveland Plain Dealer Magazine, The Arizona Republic, Phoenix Magazine, Writer's Digest, Shark Tales* (Simon & Schuster), *Criminology* (Harcourt Brace Jovanovich), *My Brush With History* (Black Dog & Levnthal), and *Signs of Hope* (Pushcart Press).

Peter practices law with Lewis & Roca, LLP in Phoenix, Arizona and is a professional magician and musician. He holds a Bachelor of Arts, and Honorary Degrees from Carleton College and received his law degree from the Stanford University Law School.

Portrait by Susanne Baird

More Praise For Beyond Peleliu

"*Beyond Peleliu* is captivating, personally touching and thought provoking... The characters are alive with beating hearts and human desires. I could not put it down and suspect that every reader will do the same."
— Heather Froeschl, BOOKREVIEW.COM

"A must read book, not only for those who fought in World War II, but for all of us living in a time of many wars around the globe. This book can be a source of forgiveness and healing for those who inherited the demons of war."
— Sister Helen Prejean, Author of *Dead Man Walking* and *Death of Innocents*

"With the saga of the McQuades, Peter Baird has given us a picture of a complex family that is utterly compelling. This is a memorable, 'can't put it down' book."
— The Honorable, Janet Napolitano, GOVERNOR OF ARIZONA

"(Peter) writes a story about the McQuade family, their loss, disconnect, and discovery of truth after so many years. Once readers finish the last page, they feel as though they know the characters personally."
— Mona Lisa Safai, THE MIDWEST BOOK REVIEW

"'Post-traumatic stress disorder' wasn't part of the lexicon until Vietnam, but the trauma of war has always been with us. *Beyond Peleliu* brings into sharp focus the effect of the violence of World War II on our Greatest Generation and its progeny, the Silent Generation. As we learn in *Beyond Peleliu,* souls are mangled in courtrooms as well as in combat."
— Stephanie Shafer, Author of *Seeds of Doubt,*

Quiet Time, Extreme Indifference, and *Blind Spot*

"As Baird's marvelously entertaining but ultimately dark novel ends, this reviewer was once again reminded of the words of Thomas Wolf ~ words that could well serve as a coda for Baird's superb work."

> — The Honorable Farncis J. Larkin,
> AMERICAN BAR ASSOCIATION
> EXPERIENCE MAGAZINE

"Peter Baird...has created a novel filled with memorable characters and contemporary issues ~ the conflict between science and faith, the efffects of secrets and cover-up, the compromise of legal ethics, and in a controversial conclusion, how love lost can be regained."

> — Robert Aiken, California State Bar, LITIGATION
> MAGAZINE

"Baird's novel differs from the other lawyer stories by its depth and its characters. It is not characters in search of an author but characters who have found their author. When I put the book down, I knew I had spent time with real people."

> — Jacob Stein, Columnist, TRIAL LAWYER, and
> Author of *Legal Spectator & More*

"Peter Baird's stunning first novel is unquestionably the BEST first novel I've ever read... This is a story of three generations who hid from one another until they thought it was too late, only to find that it's never too late."

> — Gary L. Stuart, Trial Lawyer and Author of *Miranda: The Story of America's Right to Remain Silent*, and *The Gallup 14*

"*Beyond Peleliu* richly describes the ethical catastrophes of today's medical and legal professions. Peter Baird has created an epic of three generations that emlarges our grasp of these moral crises. From the World War II battle on the South Seas island of Peleliu, to a trial in San Francisco, to a prison cell in Utah, he splendidly comes to grips with the uncertainties of heroism and the consequence of choice."

> — The Honorable John L. Kane, Jr., UNITED
> STATES DISTRICT COURT JUDGE,
> DISTRICT OF COLORADO

Printed in the United States
88674LV00002B/159/A